LOUIS SIEGEL

The Doctor Will *Kill* You Now

THE DOCTOR WILL KILL YOU NOW

To my wife Ruth, OBM

ACKNOWLEDGMENTS

The idea for this book began in 2014 when I came across an article in *Wired* magazine by Kim Zetter titled, "It's Insanely Easy to Hack Hospital Equipment."

She reported on cybersecurity expert Scott Erven's findings of an investigation he made for his employer, Essentia Health, into the cybersecurity of over one hundred of their healthcare-related facilities.

Erven reported that by hacking the software that controlled most of the hospital's devices he was able to control them remotely, including turning them on and off, and these devices included lifesaving, life-supporting, and disease-detecting equipment.

I found the ease with which Erven was able to do this fascinating and downright scary.

It occurred to me that although Erven's hacking skills had much to do with his success, it was really the device's extraordinary built-in vulnerabilities to hacking that had allowed him to do it.

It was a small step from there to imagine the mayhem that a crazed and unethical hacker could cause should they want to take control of these medical devices, or the hospital itself, to satisfy evil desires.

Therein lies the story inside this book.

CONTENTS

I

Inconspicuous for the tips of the stethoscope peeking out from his left pant pocket, he strolls as nonchalantly as any doctor would through the dimly lit halls and corridors of Beaches End General Hospital to the nurses' station on the medical floor.

"Good evening, Doctor. Welcome to our hospital," the charge nurse says.

He acknowledges the greeting with a nod and a mischievous grin, then pulls up a chair to the vacant nurse's terminal, sits down, enters a pass code, and begins to access the networks for the hospital's power plant, chemotherapy-infusion center, dialysis center, imaging center, clinical labs, blood bank, patient databases, and more. Minutes later, he logs out of the hospital's master computer system, stands, exhales a sigh of satisfaction and relief, and strolls to the exit as calmly as he had entered.

Alas, he is neither a doctor nor a stranger to the hospital, having visited it, virtually, through his hacking many times in the weeks and months prior.

Being the courteous hacker he is, he leaves an anonymous—except for his signature avatar, — message to the system operator (SYSOP) that someone breached his server.

He is Harken Righteous, at ground zero of his eponymous Righteous Quest, as evil a mission as there ever was in all of hackerdom.

2

Who is Harken Righteous? His diary, a bound hodgepodge of handwritten and pasted-in computer-printed text, scattered doodles, QR codes, schematics, maps, and sketches tells us much about who he is. Found around the time the mayhem he caused was ending, it is a private manifesto and real-time account of his thoughts, plans, and actions, allowing insight into his very troubled mind.

Righteous had an odd, perverted, personal relationship with his diary. Among all his possessions and relationships, his diary was, perhaps, his best friend. His confidant. He turned to its pages in good times and bad or whenever he was in need. He dressed it in a variety of jacket covers, selecting now and then from its own diverse wardrobe. Sometimes he chose sweaters; other times he picked to suit his mood, the climate, or a local theme, much as a parent would for a child. Most days, if not every day, he talked to the diary and expressed his gratitude for its sympathetic responses.

His diary reveals that his homelife in Rochester, New

York, was not a happy one. That there was a difficult parental pathology that percolated throughout all his years at home. That his mother was subjugated by his father and was not well, and that his father, though alive, was rarely emotionally there for them. He experienced his life as a detached, accidental witness, much as a passenger through a window in a slow-moving car experiences the drama, chaos, and destruction of a horrible traffic accident just on the other side.

JANUARY. *Diary, it's late again, as I've had another horrible day. Ma's agoraphobia is getting worse. She still lives in mortal fear of leaving the house, which she can't do. This is an ironic curse for her, as the house, with my father in it, is her prison. To escape would be her fondest wish.*

Today, she thinks she might be able to walk from the front door to the end of the driveway. She says, "Harken, stand by the front door with me while I try to walk to the curb." To the friggin' curb, Diary! This would be a major feat. She spends a half hour staring out through the storm door gathering the courage to open it. "Go ahead, Ma, you can do it," I say. I watch her childlike fear and imagine what she sees on the other side of that door. It represents some kind of frontier for her. She sees normal people out there, some neighbors, some friends, children bundled up playing, a mom pushing a stroller, a man brushing the last remnants of snow off a car. A knowing neighbor shouts to Ma that she can do it. "C'mon out, Nora, you can do it!"

"I can't right now!" Ma yells back, making her voice sound strong, as if she could leave if she wanted.

Still inside the house, she hems and haws, starts to go, then stops. She grabs the doorknob but can't turn it. I'm standing there wondering how cruel this is, but there's nothing I can do. Half a turn of the knob, then a full turn, and she pushes the door open. An inch. I feel like I can actually hear her heart pounding. "Don't leave me, Harken," she pleads, looking at me to make sure I heard her. She has the doorknob in a death grip and twists it back and forth at a frenetic pace. Soon the whole door is rattling. Maybe the whole house. Now, one foot is out the cracked-open door, then the other, and she's still holding on to that lifeline of a doorknob. It's all just slow motion, with me as the helpless observer. She gives a glance that says she's sorry and has love for me. What am I supposed to do with that, Diary? Damn him. It's my father's fault. This is what his lack of loving her did to her—sapped the life right out, stole her will to even step outside. It makes me think, "Why live if you're not loved?" Then, without ever letting go of the doorknob, she makes a 180-degree turn back to the safety of the house. She can't do it. She'll never be able to do it! Diary, can you tell me why me or anyone should have to grow up like this? And why would I ever want to form a relationship if I could end up like this? And if Ma's suffering like this, why should anyone else be happy? And what's happiness anyway? Who even knows?

Interviews taken shortly after the mischief he caused tell of a mostly solitary youth. "He was never a child you could hold or hug. He'd squirm, stretch, grunt, and elbow his way out of any attempt to hold him," his parents later told those investigating who he was and the misdeeds he caused, along with anyone else who knew him when he was a child.

"He seems to be most at peace when he's alone, yet I believe he's very lonely. Like in another world. I don't think he liked people. No, that's not quite right. I think it's more that he doesn't know *how* to like people, how to be liked, or how to accept affection," Agnes Millhouse, his elementary school teacher, said of him.

"And there's the stealing," his father, Aarlen, volunteered. "He's obsessed with taking what isn't his. Taking joy and leaving misery was his favorite pastime. No doubt about it. The other strange thing about him is the amount of joy he gets from watching the misery of others. What were those fancy words the psychiatrist calls it? *Shad and Froid* is what they tell us it's called, I think?"

Early education told of pervasive failure. This, however, was not the record of what he learned and knew. He was always distracted in class beyond explanation and everyone's understanding at the time. "He seems to always be in another place at another time," one teacher had told his mother. On his report cards, all resplendent in red-inked Fs, his teachers wrote, "Harken could do much better if he would just pay attention." Typical report card advice. Righteous writes of his bitterness at his teachers and parents not knowing that his not paying attention wasn't his fault but the result of failed or miswired neuronal connections—attention deficit disorder, as we now know it. "He's sitting next to troublemakers and needs to change his seat," his exasperated mother had written back to teachers, desperate to explain. "It's a shame because he's a very, very smart kid," his mother and many teachers would say—and almost everyone agreed.

Though he barely graduated high school because of poor academic performance, he was learned beyond what one would predict from his grades alone. If anyone looked in the Righteous' basement, where Harken lived, they would have seen a warren of small Thomas Edison–like laboratory benches, each housing an experiment at the cutting edge of a different technology or field of science.

From online courses in electronics and communications, he learned and experimented with electronic circuit design, computer design, coding, and computer networking, including cybersecurity, with which he spent many late nights breaking into and entering public, private, and governmental websites and facilities.

He coded in everything from assembly language to Python to C++ to Java. Using a random number generator he wrote a program that continuously created random web addresses that crawled the entire web just to see which sites would come up. When crawling the web for hospitals to hack, he added modifiers, such as ER, pediatric intensive care, psychiatry, OB delivery, blood bank, dialysis, life support systems, infrastructure, and others in order to narrow his searches to services that interested him, perhaps for use at a later time for a not-yet-known agenda.

His basement home revealed that his interests also extended to biology and medicine, evidenced by rows of formaldehyde-filled jars holding a variety of parts of mortified small mammals and reptiles.

There is also evidence that he nourished his soul as well as his intellect with a considerable home library, which housed a collection on motorcycles, both the history of and the repair of, and a dozen volumes on Greek mythology. There were also two CDs. One CD, a work by American composer Virgil Thomson, bearing a title possibly befitting Righteous's personality: *Louisiana Story—Acadian Songs and Dances: Super Sadness*. The other CD contained a performance of the work of Italian composer Niccolò Paganini, his *Moto Perpetuo*. This frenetic piece of near-perfect perpetual motion also fit well with the features of Righteous's nature.

But what really fascinated Righteous and resonated with his core was breaking and entering computer

8

networks—the world at his fingertips. With only a few keystrokes, he discovered, he was able to invade the lives of others, take what wasn't his, and leave without meeting or talking to a single person. While his mother couldn't do something as pedestrian as leave her own home, he had access to the entire internet-connected world. These networks were, truly, his heaven on earth.

As a tinkerer, inventor, and fixer of everything mechanical, family and neighbors regularly called upon him to repair whatever needed fixing. He wrote in his diary about the satisfaction of putting things back together. One would wonder if he, indeed, was trying to put his life back together each time he restored a machine in disrepair. Here again, his relation to and affection for things, rather than people, seems quite telling.

He writes about how, as a teenager, he pedaled his Schwinn Roadster, with its whining, wheel-driven, electric headlight, *eeaw* horn, and chrome luggage rack holding his stuff—his diary, perhaps?—through the night, just he and his bike in paired solitude and comfort, the flickering headlight illuminating the path ahead through dark streets and alleys.

Later, engines fascinated him, and he graduated to motorcycles as the adult equivalent of his Schwinn. He tore them down and put them back together with ease, his Harley becoming his preferred mode of transportation. No one thought of him as a "Harley guy," and he wasn't in the ways folks usually think of the Harley type. It would seem the Harley gave him the *feeling* of belonging, without the social pain and discomfort true belonging might bring. He wrote often in his diary about how many times he had passed Harley riders who would give him that nod of solidarity and how he wouldn't ever know how to respond.

By the time Righteous graduated high school, it was clear he had major mental health issues. Allergists, nutritionists, endocrinologists, holistic practitioners, pediatricians, psychics, psychologists, psychiatrists, and others could not explain, or alter, the suite of pathologic and aberrant behaviors and moods Righteous presented to them.

"He didn't have a friend in the world, except them damn machines," his mother later said. Persistent isolation was always his social preference. At least from humans.

When not working on his machines, Righteous spent much of his free time collecting stray dogs–not to mention snakes, salamanders, and frogs. Maybe because they didn't talk back.

"Were we too hard on him?" his mother later wondered aloud in a tone of guilt and heartfelt regret.

"We certainly were. Well, at least I was," Aarlen had replied with a wad of latent remorse lodged in his throat. "You know, sometimes he would cry," his father later admitted. "I'd hear him late at night while standing at the top of the stairs to the basement. He'd be in the basement talking to some girl over the phone. It was always the same one. Susan, I think. Or was it Phyllis? Well, no matter. How and where he met her, I don't know. But anyway, she'd call him, and it sounded like she'd tell him she liked him and invite him somewhere. Then, as if he were in a major struggle between two parts of himself—the warm, feeling piece and the cold, indifferent piece—he'd blurt out, 'No,' in the coldest manner you ever heard. After hanging up, he'd cry and talk to himself about why he felt nothing when the girl called, knowing he should feel something. Then he'd just bawl real heavy like a baby. I wanted to go down and hug him and tell him it'd all be okay, but I knew he wouldn't let me touch him. Nobody could get close to him like that, especially not emotionally. I'd go to the bathroom, turn on the water real loud, and cry myself because there was nothing else I could do. I tell you it just broke my heart. Nora never knew." The question remains: Could young Righteous have been coaxed onto a different path had his father hugged him in those moments? In his most dire times of need?

Later, he enrolled in the Rochester Institute of Technology's night-course program on network cybersecurity and health-care informatics, which included human anatomy and biology, hospital infrastructure, and electronic medical-record systems. He graduated with a degree in health care informatics, something he would find very useful later on. Most of his further education he received online in the isolated comfort, solitude, and social safety of his parents' basement.

With the urging of his concerned parents, Righteous became a patient of Dr. Rob Norther, a Rochester, New York, psychiatrist who gave him the diagnosis of schizoid personality disorder (SPD)[1] because of his disinterest in social relationships, desire for a solitary and secretive lifestyle, emotional coldness, and severe apathy. Affected individuals sometimes also demonstrate a rich and elaborate internal fantasy world. Some authorities view SPD as a variant of normal. Paradoxically, sexual inadequacy, a feature commonly associated with SPD was, in Righteous, replaced by periodic sexual urges, on which he eventually sought to act. Harken Righteous was, in almost every way, the poster boy for SPD.

Righteous's frequent diary entries and reflections upon the sum of his past eventually told him it was time to leave his parents' basement, get out of Rochester, and hone and implement his hacking skills. He was finally ready to seek the only chance he believed he had at contentment, or what others had called "happiness"— that which would come from the misery he would inflict on others.

3

"Is that you, dear?" Heather says, hearing the front door open. She stands at the stove stirring a beef Bolognese sauce she knows her husband thinks is "to die for."

Charles Harper White, MD, internist par excellence, is not on call for the weekend and is looking forward to a break from the grind. He sets down an armful of charts on the hall bench just inside the front door, then puts down his briefcase bulging with even more charts. He hangs his jacket on the hat rack, already overflowing with his favorite ball caps, and makes a beeline to the kitchen.

"Your favorite drink's waiting for you on the counter, darling," Heather says without budging from the range. The eponymous Rum Charlie drink, so named by his wife, is a mix of fresh lemonade, coconut rum, and a hard-squeezed lime quarter.

"Damn, that's good," White says after a hearty and much-needed gulp.

Wasting no time, and now energized and emboldened

by the swig of his favorite potion, White walks up behind Heather, who has not missed a beat stirring the sauce.

Even looking at her from behind, White never ceases to be amazed by her beauty. Wearing six-inch shorts, her long legs lead his eyes to her narrow waist made even more so by the apron strings tied behind in a perfect bow at the center of her back.

"Nice," White says seductively, his pelvis now gently nudging her against the stove.

"What's ... nice?" Heather asks, becoming breathless and flustered, feeling the warmth of his body pressing against hers, now playing their little game of loving each other.

"You. You're nice," White says as he glides his hands into either side of her apron, then around her rib cage, until he cups her breasts. They swell over his hands as her breathing grows heavier.

"Hey there, Doctor. I can't make pasta Bolognese while you're feeling me up, now can I?" Heather struggles to say, starting to succumb.

"Guess it's decision time, Counselor. A good lawyer's trained to make snap decisions. What say ye?" White whispers in her ear, then kisses her, his arms now wrapped tightly around her, cocooning her, the two of them almost one.

"Tell me you turned off the stove," White whispers.

"I did," Heather murmurs as she recovers from their passionate sex and slowly regains her senses.

"Did I say, 'I love you'?" White asks.

"Yes, you did, and I never get tired of hearing that. Would you like the pasta now?"

"No, but thank you for making it. Do you realize how much pasta we've wasted over the years this way?"

"Oh, I do."

"Really? How much?"

"Hardly any."

"How's that?"

"Rusty."

"The dog? No way. Our cocker spaniel eats our pasta Bolognese?"

"Yep. I leave out of it things I know he can't eat and pour it over his dog food."

"No way! So, you've been feeding me dog food all these years?" White jokes, egging her on, squeezing her tighter.

"Well, it is our Friday night special," Heather says, wriggling deeper into the warm pocket of White's curled body.

"I wish we weren't so busy with work so there'd be more time for just loving each other and talking. I love lying here with you, feeling you so close, knowing sex is the closest our souls will ever be to touching," White says. "Oh, Christ. Where's my cell phone?" White remembers, panicked, groping around for it in the bed.

"Probably in your jacket, where you always leave it. You're not on call this weekend. It's okay to leave it there."

"Okay, but I feel so naked without it."

"Charlie."

"Yes?"

"You feel naked because you *are* naked," Heather says, trying to keep from giggling too hard and breaking the spell she's under. "So, tell me, my dear husband, what's going on in the office? Anything new?"

"Not much. Oh, we're thinking about hiring a PA."

4

FEBRUARY. *Diary, it's me, Harken, but you know that. I can't sleep. I awoke wondering what it would be like to take control of the lives of other people, as, in my way of thinking, my life has been taken over by my schizoid personality disorder, doctors, and parental forces. I think that to be able to control the life of another person would be a great technical accomplishment, heavenly, divine, and would provide me a personal joy beyond compare, greater than that gained from taking over a mere machine.*

That I can sit at my computer and with just a few keystrokes create such utter havoc this way that the whole world, perhaps even the Lord himself if he were watching, would stop and wonder what the hell is going on. I'm certain he wouldn't say the word hell.

The possibility of having this anonymous power is giving me an endorphic rush like no other and a euphoria that seems to be coming from everywhere within my marrow. It's from so deep it makes me shiver. For me to be able to turn the lives of others inside out and upside down I feel would create in me so much joy and satisfaction and would, in a sense, provide me the only counterpoint to the suffering I feel.

I learned from my all-night breaches, and googling around, that I am only clicks away from making someone who is actually well appear sick, at least in the digital hell of their electronic medical lab reports that I will hack and change. And, get this, with a few more keystrokes, I know I can turn a whole hospital dark.[2]

Suppose I hacked the computer system at a medical lab used by someone I know and then followed the results of my mischief. I would find out when they are going for a blood test and change their results in the lab's computer memory before being displayed or printed out. I would arrange to watch how the abnormal result affects them and, with some luck, makes their life miserable. Ideally, I'd want to be there and listen in when the doctor calls to tell the bad news and, depending on what I changed, be around as the doctor struggles to understand the reason for the abnormal results in such a well person. I will have created, my dear Diary, a treasure trove of angst, and would not their resulting turmoil become my personal joy and lift that cloud of dread always hanging over me?

Diary, I know there is a quirk in my development, that somewhere in my brain's mind there is a void, a vacancy of such malignant nature that not all of earth's evils can fill its cratered walls. No medicine can find its way down into those deep recesses where my evil thoughts simmer, bubble up, and burst to life, which is why they do not work. No psychiatrist or therapist can comprehend the boundless breadth and width of my depravity. Nor do I even have a good measure of them and my longings to do bad things.

Diary, I have crossed the lines that separate good from evil and right from wrong many times before, but I am now so far past those lane markers that there is no turning back. Diary, I am scared. Even I, possessing an overabundance of the DNA for apathy, do now experience an uncomfortable, disturbing fear and worry, new for me, that what I am about to do is very wrong. Very wrong, indeed.

Now, Diary, with the foulest of my thoughts adrift in the whorls and eddies of my already-tortured mind, my Righteous Quest mission is born. It is a big bang of sorts and, like the original one, something the world will experience the full effects of only later on.

5

LATER IN FEBRUARY. *Diary, something's been happening to me since my epiphany a week or so ago. I seem to be morphing into a deviant who is obsessed with the idea of becoming the best, and most creative—maybe the evilest, too—medical record hacker in the world. Why? Because I want to create misery for those folks who populate that joyful, loving, bowl-of-cherries world I see out there. Do you see that world, too, Diary? Of course, you do. You must. And clearly, you can see we are not members of that world. I see people only as encoded ones and zeros. They are nothing more than that to me, just digitized lives. And, as there is no room for empathy between ones and zeroes, all the better.*

If you are someone who is reading this diary and you shouldn't be, because it is my private diary, then I mean I'll hack your digital records, too. Your digital records form continuously, even while you read my diary, including the record of your reading my diary, and the aggregate of all of those records comprises the digital accounting of your whole life.

For example, if it happened to be the case, I'd find it a trivial hacking task to learn that last night you read a book from a Kindle download or that you bought the hard-copy book two days ago from Amazon. I could, using the video cameras around you, including the face-forward camera on the PC or TV monitor in front of you, watch you read it. Or, from your Amazon Echo or other Alexa devices, know that you yelled at your wife last night and then had sex with her, which is not nice of you after yelling at her. In my Righteous Quest vision, I could access these digital records and alter them, and then, I think, the madness and mayhem that would follow would be quite fulfilling and pleasing to me.

My Righteous Quest strategy is to access people's widely distributed digital records, then aggregate, collate, catalog, archive, and in every way curate them and remake them to my liking. The end result is that person's new, digital DNA that I can unspool, tinker with, then respool at will. Diary, does that make me a digital enzyme, ha, ha, ha? Not so funny because I believe it does. Call me harkenase, heh, heh. These records will include all digitized medical, legal, cell phone, credit card, financial, magnetic strip, computer keystroke, RFID devices, and—most recently and joyfully, I might add—the new Bluetooth thermostats, doorbells, and home-alarm systems. Oh, not to mention the wealth of digital info produced by new automobiles. All of these I will access in many ways, including from the clouds in cyberspace, the internet, routers, Wi-Fi, and cable boxes, even wireless printers that store the image of everything they ever printed—and in real time, too—and then analyze it all with my coding and then utilize it how I see fit.

For example, I can make the room you're in hotter or colder and watch you become miserable—or even undress—as I do it. From these data, I think I can construct, or reconstruct, an accurate "day in your life." But, more than that, oh so much more than that, I think I can alter those entries to suit my evil little heart's worst desires.

My belief, and one that has much merit, is that a part of my victim's digital records—the medical records part, the one that documents all the facets of a person's medical life—I can hack and strategically alter. This would allow me to control those unfortunate enough to become available to my digital laboratory universe and caught in my digital net. Specifically, by altering lab results, for example, I can make "well" people appear sick by their numbers, and, if I want, "sick" people appear better, or even cured, if only by their new numbers, of course. Yikes! Oh yes, you can, Harken!

In this way, I'm thinking, I will infuse joy into my otherwise drab, wretched, and victimized life, exact revenge against the world, and gain sweet pleasure doing it. Along the way, I'll vent my rage against anyone and everyone, but particularly my parents, who I view as responsible for my brain matter (which is true and inarguable) and my subsequent brain-matter-driven sins such as I am writing about doing here.

Oh, Diary, my only friend, I want to say for the record that I am not like ordinary hackers, from whom I fiercely distinguish myself because they seek only monetary gain from identity theft. No, for me, it is the satisfaction gained from the tantalizing and tasty assortment of morsels of power, control, and the bizarre endorphic high I get from taking from others what is not mine that drives my deviant behavior.

How, when, and where to do this? I wonder. I realize I not only want to execute these hacks but I want to—no, I must— witness the effects of my efforts close up or my joy will not be complete.

I realize my grand plan must include gaining the knowledge to understand enough medicine to know what medical records to change and the effects that will have on my victims, their families, and doctors. I need to know how doctors think. I'm not going to medical school because it takes too long, but I can become a physician assistant. Also, I'm not staying here, either, in the dark, cold, and dark—I know I wrote dark twice—of Rochester. I realize I must insinuate myself into the medical milieu of wherever I wind up and will commit myself to this with every bent and twisted fiber of my wretched soul. Before I go, I must try my skills here. Hmmm? Who shall be my first victim?

I've read about thyroid disease. Doctors check for it all the time, looking for low- or high-thyroid conditions. Any time a patient complains of being tired or feeling cold when they shouldn't be, the doc orders a thyroid blood test. Must be a moneymaker.

The blood tests they order almost always contain a test for

23

TSH, or thyroid stimulating hormone. It's a funny thing—the higher the numerical value of the TSH, the lower the amount of thyroid hormone in the blood. I guess that's why you need to be so smart to get into medical school. Here's my Righteous Quest Grand Plan:

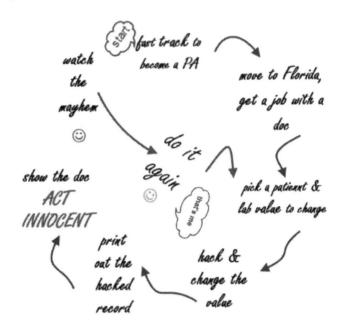

I learned that doctors are often overly eager to find and treat low-thyroid conditions, sometimes giving the diagnosis even when it doesn't exist. They stare at the TSH results as if some god of thyroid diseases is watching over their shoulders. Apparently, doctors even question patients with minimally elevated TSH results in such a way as to encourage the right answers to make the low-thyroid diagnosis.

So if the doc wants to know if you have any symptoms of

low thyroid, he can get the answer in several ways. One way, I read, is to inquire, simply, "Tell me how you're feeling lately." And if the patient's not sick, the answer's usually, "Fine." But this is risky, as it doesn't lead the patient to answer the way the doc wants to make the diagnosis. If the doc really, really wants to raise the likelihood of getting an answer that fits a high TSH or low-thyroid disease, the doc asks, "Have you been feeling tired or cold lately?" with an emphasis on have you that borders on haven't you. The answer is often, "Well, now that you mention it, I have been a little tired and cold lately." That's what they call a leading question.

Now, dear Diary, you can see how a person who's healthy, or at least has a normally functioning thyroid, could be made to sound otherwise and wind up being treated.

Oh, boy. If only my shrink, Dr. Norther, could hear me now. Maybe I'll hack his records, too. Why not, right?

Good night, Diary.

6

"Hello, Harken. Good to see you today," Dr. Rob Norther says, gaze fixed downward, feigning looking at his notes to avoid looking up at Righteous whom he despises.

"Bullshit, Doc. You never mean that."

"Have you been taking your meds, Harken?"

"No."

"Why are you here today, Harken? I don't care if you waste your time, but I'm not going to let you waste mine anymore."

"Hey, Doc, now don't get cranky on me. Remember: me patient, you doctor. Anyway, is it true, Doc?" Righteous asks, his eyes scanning the ceiling, fingers tapping the arms of the lushly upholstered, whiskey-colored leather chair and whistling nothing in particular to convey his cold indifference to the man.

"Is what true, Harken?" Norther says, sounding frustrated while pulling on a few eyebrow hairs he twisted together.

"That 'I think and, therefore, you are.' Is that true or just a line of bull?" Righteous struggles not to laugh as he

26

antagonizes Norther.

Norther grips the edge of his desk with both hands, blanching all ten fingertips. "You know, Harken, you're sounding giddy, maybe a bit manic. Tell me what's really on your mind today."

"Just more of the same, Doc. Same old shit, just different flies. Ha! Oh, there is one thing."

"Wonderful. Tell me about it, Harken."

"Okay, so you remember how I said I wanted to put my computer-coding skills to good use?"

"Of course, Harken. But as I recall, you weren't going to put them to anybody's 'good' use. I believe you said that you wanted to screw around with people's lives by rearranging their medical records the way *you'd* like them to be, or something like that."

"You got a great memory, Doc, or are you looking at your notes?"

"Can you actually do that, Harken?"

"Do what?" Righteous asks as he continues to rip and tear at Norther's psyche.

"You heard what I said, and you know what I mean. I'm asking you, can you … do you … have the means to actually alter people's medical records?"

Righteous looks around the room, intentionally ignoring the question to burn up Norther some more.

"Harken."

"Yes?"

"Can you do that?"

"I'm not sure what you're referring to."

"Damn it, Harken, can you just answer the question? Please?" Norther responds, red-faced, yanking out a few of his twisted eyebrow hairs.

"Yes, I can do that."

"Exactly what do you plan to do? And look, I don't like this cat-and-mouse conversation you're trying to pull, so talk to me straight."

"Wait, Doc, this is all confidential, right?"

"Well, yes and no. If I think you're a danger to yourself or others, I'm required to report that to authorities. Are you either one of those, Harken—a danger to yourself or others?"

"I'll tell you if you tell me, Doc."

"Always playing games, aren't you, Harken?"

"Aw, Doc, no. Really, I'm not. C'mon, I'm just jokin'. But, okay, if I *were* to do that, and I'm not saying I will, here's what my plan would be. Hey, and maybe you can let me know if it's a good plan, huh? I really need some feedback because no one else knows about this. You'll tell me, won't you?"

"Sure, Harken. Let's hear it. I have a feeling it's not something Mother Teresa would approve of, but go on."

"Well, Doc, here's how I think."

"I know how you think, Harken, and that's the problem."

"I'll ignore that one, Doc. Okay, look, a person is said to be 'well' until they become 'sick,' right? Some folks are sick but feel well while others are sick and feel sick. Isn't that right, Doc? Am I making sense?"

"Barely, Harken, but what's new?"

"Aw, Doc, that hurt. And it's not nice to berate your patient like this."

"Just get on with it, for crying out loud."

"Okay. Well, the case where someone 'becomes' sick but doesn't yet feel sick can happen when a routine lab result comes back abnormal and the doctor tells them that, according to the lab result, they're sick."

"All right. Where are you going with this?"

"Suppose you order a thyroid test on me. You remember from medical school the standard thyroid hormone blood test? You know, the one where if the TSH result is too high, then the patient has low thyroid? I realize you wouldn't order that because you're a psychiatrist, not a real doctor."

Norther tenses like he's doing all he can not to reach out and grab Righteous by the throat.

"Hey, now. Don't get all sensitive on me, Doc. Of course, you're a real doctor, in a sense. 'Hey, Doc.' 'What's up, Doc?' That was funny. Chill, I'm just pullin' your brain's chain here. You know if you keep this up you might need a shrink yourself."

Norther appears to be losing control. "Can you please

get to your point, Harken?"

"Sure, Doc. Okay. Let's say you did order the TSH blood test on me, and unbeknownst to you, I, with my magical, one-of-kind, Harken Righteous, badass coding skills, replaced my actual, normal TSH result in the lab's server with a very high TSH result telling you, the ordering doctor, that I'm very low on thyroid hormone in my blood. What would you do then?"

Norther moves to speak.

"You're right!" Righteous says, not giving Norther the time to answer. "You'd call me or bring me in and ask, 'Harken, have you been feeling a little tired lately?' Unfortunately, you asked me a leading question, which they should have taught you in medical school not to do, but I'll be gracious and say, 'Well, now that you mention it, Doc, yes. I have been a little tired.' I'd say this because I wouldn't want to ruin your questioning after you led me to the answer you wanted to hear. Also, everybody's a little tired, anyway, in this screwed-up world. Then you'd start me on thyroid-replacement pills, like Synthroid. And, ladies and gentlemen, it's Harken Righteous, one, patient, zero. *Boo!*" Righteous yells through hands cupped to his lips to form a megaphone.

"Jesus Christ, Harken, are you crazy? Can you really do that?" Norther blurts.

"Oh, Doc, now listen to you, poor fella. And you're sweating like a stuck pig. You're plucking your eyebrows to smithereens, and there's a pile of eyebrow hairs on your desk. I guess I got you all riled up. Do you know you just called your schizoid patient 'crazy'? That's reportable, you know. Reportable, indeed. To be honest, I found it very unlikable and offensive. Now I'm sad and hurt."

"Stop the 'sad and hurt' bullshit, Harken, and tell me whether you read this hacking crap somewhere in a medical fiction book or you can actually do this. More importantly, tell me if you *have* ever done it or have *plans* to actually do it. Have you actually ever done that, Harken, what you just said? And what's your endgame, Harken? Taking an entire town hostage?"

"Thank you for the compliment, Doc. What's my endgame, you ask? I don't know. But first I'd like to see whether I, Harken Righteous, could cause a doctor to prescribe a drug to a patient who doesn't need it without the doctor ever knowing that was the case. Strictly an intellectual exercise, of course. Oh, and to see if I can make a perfectly well person appear sick by the books I cook. You know, change his lab results. I wonder if he'd feel sick after that, don't you? Think about it; I can have you—yes, you, my dear Dr. Norther—started on a thyroid-replacement pill just by hacking into your lab's server and changing your TSH from normal to abnormal. Even my own mother, perhaps. Maybe that's a nice—"

"Okay, enough of this, Harken, damn it! Do you have any idea about the legality and morality of what you're saying? You'd better think about the answers to my next questions very, very carefully before you respond."

"There's more," Righteous continues. "What do you think a drug company would pay me to change large numbers of people's blood tests—nationally, I mean—in such a way that those people would need a product the company just happens to make? Huh, Doc? Like vitamin D, estrogen, or testosterone. You know, all the things you docs test for and then tell us patients we don't have enough of but need, but you know nobody really needs them. And, here's a better one—I can make a radiologist's bone density DEXA scanner report that every female patient tested has osteoporosis, and it so happens you can buy their special vitamin D and calcium supplements right there on the spot. And—"

"Enough! Jesus Christ, stop it!" Norther yells. "Your mood is clearly accelerating in front of my eyes, and I'm growing ever-more worried about you. Answer my question. Have you ever *actually* done any of this or *plan* to do any of this?"

Righteous hesitates. "I'm searching for the right answer. Well, let me see. Hmmm, of course it's illegal and immoral to do these things, Doc. Right? Make a note I said that, please. How am I doing so far?"

"Harken, I'm really very worried about you. It sounds like you're converting to either hypomania or full-blown mania. Your fantasies about hacking records are more consistent with schizophrenic features than SPD. You're not taking your meds. You're fantasizing. You're leaving reality. You're delusional. You see me only when you're in the mood and want to piss around. I would have discharged you as a patient a long time ago, and you know I do that for a lot less than this, except I've wanted to keep my eyes on you. Jesus Christ, you've become a danger to society, a real one-man weapon of digital mass destruction, a regular WDMD."

"Wow, Harken Righteous, WDMD. To think that little ole me, Harken Righteous, could be a danger to society, Doc. That's really something. Thank you," Righteous says, feigning humility while relishing the idea.

"Harken, please, be serious. You're not helping me here."

"Sorry, Doc."

"Just tell me, for the record, if you have any specific plans to carry out the hacking you just expressed to me. Yes or no, Harken? Yes or no?"

"Umm, no, Doc, I don't," Righteous says smugly.

"Fine. Our time's up. See you in three months. You never told me your reason for your appointment today."

"Oh, thanks for the reminder. I just wanted to tell you I'm leaving town for good in three days, that's all."

7

MARCH. *Diary, my friend. I've missed you. I don't tell you that enough. You know you are my friend. Perhaps my best friend. Maybe my only friend. That's a compliment, Diary. Every person needs someone to talk to and engage with. Even me. And if that someone is a something, like you, well, that's okay, too. A person also needs to be relevant, important, needed. I want that so badly. Maybe that's what's causing the void deep in my head. I cannot tolerate that void, that loneliness.*

I have schizoid personality disorder, or SPD. I'm sure I've told you about it. The wiring in my brain that controls forming normal relationships ain't there—or if there, it's goofy. Don't take this personally, Diary, but my thinking brain craves relationships with people—and, yes, women, too—though in SPD, it's not supposed to, but my action brain won't allow it. There's this gap—a great divide—between these two brains of mine for which I desperately need a bridge to cross. Are you, my dear Diary, that bridge?

Today, I saw that prick, sicker-than-I-am Norther. What a

tight asshole he is. If anybody needs to see a shrink, it's him. I've seen plenty of other shrinks, and they're all pretty much the same. All of them seeking answers for their own mental issues.

What's he like, you ask? I'll tell you. He's a balding, necktie-wearing, prim-and-proper-type guy. He tells me he's an "oenophile," and that's an example of what I mean about him. He pronounces it "weenie-file." Sometimes he'll even say he's an Italian wine oenophile, and then he says it in Italian, for Christ's sake, with his goofy little "I can speak Italian" shit smile.

He's got some tight-ass personal issues, too. If you're a no-show for an appointment, or you're even ten minutes late, it's new-asshole time for you, and then you're discharged. I've overheard him too many times when I'm on his office couch waiting for him to start with me and he's on the phone making sure I can hear him doing his classic patient ream job. Talk about venting anger. The last one he did was on some unfortunate female patient who apparently needed his help big-time. I guess she was gonna be ten minutes late, and he discharged her on the phone. He wanted to show me how big— actually tiny—his cojones are. Why did he discharge her? Because her two kids were sick and she was in the emergency room with them when, to his way of thinking, she should have been in his office receiving his Godlike help and paying him for it on her way out. "It's not my fault you're divorced and have sick kids!" he yelled into the phone. "I can't fill your

slot with another patient, so go find another psychiatrist!"
Ouch. That really made me angry. He got off the phone and
mumbled some justification for his inhumane behavior as he
plucked out a few right eyebrow hairs.

I went today to tell him goodbye, that I'm leaving this
place. You're the only one who knows where, Diary, and that's
Florida. Or have I not told you that yet? Anyhow, I purposely
didn't tell him I was going till the end of the visit. Boy, was he
really pissed.

I should be calling him Dr. Harper. Why, you ask, Diary?
Because he kept harping and harping on whether I'm going
to hack somebody's medical records. I know why he's doing it.
It's to protect his weenie-phile ass. If I do the hacking, the feds
will eventually come knocking on his door and ask how come
he didn't turn me in. I told him, no.

Anyway, Diary, hope you're okay. You know you're relevant
to me. We're moving to Florida, you and me, and I'm going
to buy you a new cover. I found one online—a guy, his
motorcycle, and a dog parked under a palm tree with a few
coconuts scattered around. I thought of us. Guess that means
we're gonna get a dog.

No offense.

I'm done for today. Sleep tight, my true friend.

Oops, one more thing to do before bed.

8

MARCH. *Diary, I wish you had ears and listened in with me to the call my ma got from her doctor. Here's how the whole thing went. So, imagine the phone's ringing.*

"Aarlen, get the phone, for Christ's sake! I'm in the bathroom!" my ma in the first-floor bathroom screams to my father, who is on the second floor somewhere when Ma hears the phone ring.

Then my father yells back, "The rule is, Ms. Nora, if you hear it, you get it!" He calls Ma Ms. Nora to be snide and nasty. My ma doesn't deserve that. So, there they were, off again, Diary, to "the war of the phones."

Kill each other off, please, I'm thinking, hearing the yelling from my basement living quarters for the third time that day. It would be a mercy killing, I'm thinking. I can't take too many more of these screaming phone wars my parents wage every day.

Here's how the doctor's call went. Make out you're listening in with me.

"Hello. Aarlen Righteous speaking. Who's calling?"

"Aarlen, Dr. Baker here. I'm calling to speak to Nora."

"Nora, pick up the other line! Dr. Baker wants to talk to you!" my father shouts.

"Yes, Dr. Baker, this is Nora."

"Nora, your blood test showed your thyroid hormone level is very low."

"Really? Low thyroid? How could that happen?"

At this point, Diary, it is all I can do not to laugh into the phone.

"Nora, have you been unusually tired lately?"

"Well, now that you mention it, Doctor, yes, I have been tired," my ma says.

Then, Diary, this is scary, my ma yells, "Aarlen, are you on the other line? It sounds like someone is on the other line!" It's me.

She screams that right into my ear, and I have to yank off the jerry-rigged headset I made for eavesdropping on my parents' upstairs phones.

Then, my father shouts back, "I'm not on the phone!"

Then Ma yells, "Harken, are you on the phone down there in your damn cave?" and she put a disdainful emphasis on cave. It's not a cave, you folks who live up there. It's my home! Right, Diary?

If this is not a house from hell, I don't know what would be.

Then the doctor continues on, "Nora, have you been feeling cold?"

"Now that you mention it, yes, I have, Dr. Baker."

And then Diary, and then ... Diary, the very moment I've been waiting for:

"Nora, I'm thinking, given your low thyroid level plus your complaints of being tired and cold, I'm going to start you on thyroid replacement now. Nora, I'm going to call in a prescription for a thyroid-replacement pill. Take it once a day in the morning, and in four weeks go to the same lab you always go to so I can check your thyroid level on the medication."

"Oh, yes, Dr. Baker. I certainly will, and good night and thanks for calling," my ma says.

9

EARLY APRIL. *Diary, it's me, Harken. Just kidding. I feel giddy tonight. Being bad does that to me. I hacked Ma's records and got her put on a medicine she didn't need. Does that make me a bad person? The medicine won't hurt her, I don't think.*

Breaching lab servers, then creatively altering them with a havoc-filled purpose in mind, is not a trivial thing, Diary. I'm more breaching people, not so much the servers associated with the people. I'm invading their very being.

The challenges are many. First, of course, is the technical one, but I'm mastering that. Another is having my breach cause a fundamental change, preferably for the worse, in the breached person's life. Eventually, I hope to be good at implanting a digital event into a person's life, like planting a digital seed, that changes that person's destiny. Diary, you can call me Dr. Destiny the Destiny Changer.

Take Ma, for example. A few keystrokes here, a few there, and whaddya know. Her new actual reality is the same as that of someone else who also has a hypothyroid condition. She'll take a pill every day, get a blood test every four to six months, and then the doctor will be so proud of his diagnosis when her results come back normal. Maybe she'll even feel so tired for a spell that bed rest is required.

My success, in this regard, should put an end to the common notions of fate and destiny, won't it, Diary? They're dumb ideas, anyway. Fate is the word people use to explain why an event, usually a bad one, happens to a person when there's no other apparent explanation for it. Somehow, when the name fate is given as the cause of an event, it becomes the reason in of itself for the event, seems sufficient to explain it, and thereby gives comfort. The word fate allows people to believe the event is predetermined, was unpreventable, and, most importantly, not the person's fault. Diary, some people think this is what God does for a living up there: he writes down people's fates. That's what I mean by a dumb idea.

When I wrote the code to change Ma's blood test result to abnormal on a certain date and time and put the software patch in the lab's server, did I not change her destiny? Diary, do you know what that makes me? What did you say, Diary? No way! Me? God?

I can control destiny because I can control the digital record—past, present, and future—of a person's life or their digital DNA, so to speak, which is the record of their historical destiny as it unfolds from past to present to future. Their cellular DNA tells the person's composition—you know, their attributes, eye color, and the like. Their digital DNA tells us what the person has done with their cellular DNA and, if up to me, predict what they will do with it in the future.

So, Ma's destiny changed when I caused her to appear to have low thyroid. Once her thyroid lab value changed, her destiny of going to the lab and taking thyroid pills wasn't any longer written in the stars. No way, José, it was written in the server—by me!

She does have low thyroid, right, Diary? Yes and no, you say? Well, just ask Ma or her doctor. Maybe query her medical records. Because they'll testify to the "fact" that she has low thyroid. Print out the lab result I changed, and you'll see she does. I mean, no one's going to yank her thyroid gland out of her neck and put it under a microscope.

Diary, I'll come back to more of this later, but for now, I need to make a record of all my misdeeds, for both now and in the future, for posterity's sake. It will be a running record of my breaches, hacks, and cracks. I can use you for this, Diary, can't I? Of course, I can.

The only thing is, I'm worried about somebody—the feds, maybe—finding this before I'm done all of my stuff and then my goose is cooked. Of course, someone finding this and the record of my hacks would be the only way to know about what I've accomplished or to reverse it. And to put my mark on the hack I left my signature 🐧 *avatar buried deep in the lab's server. There is no way they'll find it, and even if they do, there is no way to connect the avatar wearing a Russian Cossack hat to me. Why a Cossack hat? I've read a lot about Cossacks.[3] They are a people with a long history of bravery and military prowess. They have a strong ethic of family, education, caring for their children, and defending the rights of the oppressed. If I needed help, I know they would have defended me.*

I'm also typing you, Diary, into my PC and saving you on a memory stick that looks like Homer Simpson. I'll type the record of each of my hacking accomplishments there, too. I'll hide the memory device where only I know the location. And I'm also going to store what I did in a QR code, then print that QR code on a scrap of paper. That way, even if I lose the memory stick, I have the record in the QR code.

Here's an example of the description in a QR code of when I hacked Ma. This one can be read now by any QR reader without a password. Eventually, I'll use a password.

HACK 1 SUMMARY

Date of Hack: March 14

What/Who: Nora Righteous, my Ma.

What I Did: I changed her TSH from the normal result of 0.213 to an abnormally high TSH of 34.67 to make her look low thyroid.

Consequences: It made her doctor, Dr. Baker, start her on a thyroid supplement for low thyroid—something she doesn't need.

Terror-Creation Factor for Me: 3/10 = Poor. Meh

10

APRIL. *Diary, as you know, back in February I decided that to carry out my mission, I needed more medical knowledge and medical credentials. And because I want to savor the full effect of my hacking, I want to be where the action and reaction to my mischief will occur. I want to watch patients and families twist, turn, and suffer, and the closer I am to it all, the better it should feel.*

I've come to understand, and it is scary clear to me, that the depth of my social isolation and the insatiable hunger I have for committing dark deeds make me a socially dangerous animal. This would be alarming enough if I were just roaming the streets, but that I'm about to embark on my Righteous Quest makes these facts near apocalyptic. You're not scared of me, are you, Diary? I should really hope not.

To lighten my load, I'm going to view what I'm going to do as sport, a form of entertainment, maybe a reality show where I'm the producer, director, and audience, and the production is strictly for my pleasure and enjoyment.

For medical credentials, I looked for an offshore, online, low-residency physician assistant (PA) program. My goal was to obtain my diploma and PA license with the least human and institutional contact as possible. None would be best.

I googled these and found that many schools have very low (and flexible) entrance requirements. One school, Pegasus University, is on Cape Vernac, an island off the west coast of Africa. It has a GPA entrance requirement of 2.0. Most schools require at least 2.7 to 3.0. Pegasus requires as little as a high school transcript and proof of college graduation with a BS degree (or equivalent), all of which I have, can get, or will fabricate as need be. They even offer a BS program that leads to a PA degree that blends a small number of BS-degree course requirements with a concurrent, bare-bones PA curriculum, all online. They do require clinical experience, and graduates of the PA program, like all PA graduates, need to pass the Physician Assistant National Certifying Exam (PANCE) in order to obtain a state license before they can practice. All of these are no obstacle for me, given my oh-so-über cleverness, skills, and ability to deceive.

I, also, needed to get some inside stuff on becoming a PA and what it's like to work in Florida. So, I hacked my way onto the New York Association of Physician Assistants (NYAPA) website, logged on, and looked up their membership list. I found the list of all New York physician assistants, showing where they were educated, where they did their training, and where they've been and are currently employed. From the list, I found two PAs who worked in Florida and now work in Rochester.

I e-mailed the first one, Carlos Martín, telling him I found his name on a list of PAs and arranged to speak to him by phone.

Here's how the call went:

"Hi, Carlos. This is Harken Righteous calling. You may remember me from our brief e-mail correspondence."

"Yes, I do."

"Thanks for taking some time to chat."

"No problem, Harken. How can I help you?"

"Please, call me Harry."

"Okay, Harry, how can I help you?"

"I got your name from a list of physician assistants who worked in Florida and wonder if I could ask you a few questions about becoming a PA and working in the state. I plan to move to Florida and go to PA school."

"Sounds great. Where do you plan to do your schooling?"

"I don't know yet, but I'm looking for a low-residency program, maybe even one with an online offering."

"Oh, I looked into those, too. There are a number where you can finish pretty quickly. You need to make sure they're accredited, though."

"It's possible to go to an unaccredited school?"

"Well, they're either schools working to become accredited or ones that have lost their accreditation. You can't take your state licensing exam if you don't graduate from an accredited school. But here's what's weird. The ones that lost their accreditation won't tell you that when you apply. You have *to ask."*

"Wow! Thanks for that. What's the skinny on being a PA in Florida?"

"Well, I'll share some things with you, but forget where you heard them, okay? Doctors make a ton of money off their PAs. Not just in Florida but everywhere. They pay us a decent wage, maybe sixty to ninety grand a year, but that's less than half of what we bring in. They bill insurers for our work at their rate and pay us half. The bastards."

"No shit?"

"Yeah, I'm telling you true."

"What else can you tell me?"

"Well, patients think docs watch over our work. You know that we 'have to report to them' and that they review our charts and all that. But it's bullshit. You know what else the law says?[4] A doc who supervises PAs not only doesn't have to be in the same building as the PA but can be up to twenty-five miles away. I'm telling you that's the law in Florida and many other states."

"No way."

"Oh yes! The Florida law was changed around 2006 to make that happen. You know what else? They can supervise up to four offices. Christ, they make a fortune off us."

"But they have to tell you what you can and can't do and review your charts, right?"

"Wrong. The law says the doc not only doesn't have to have any written patient-care protocols for PAs to follow, but the

doc also doesn't even have to review or cosign PA patient notes. Docs don't even have to look at a patient's chart, ever. Nor do they even have to see the PA's patients, ever. Though they should, they never do. And get this. A PA can Baker Act anybody, even the doc you work for."

"What's that mean?"

"The Baker Act says that a licensed practitioner, meaning me as a PA, can refer a patient for an involuntary mental health evaluation—that is, commit someone to a mental institution—if the practitioner has experience regarding the diagnosis and treatment of mental and nervous disorders."

At this point, I wondered why he brought that up. Did he know something about me? I certainly had experience regarding the diagnosis and treatment of mental and nervous disorders, unfortunately all my own. Whatever.

The conversation kept going like this:

"So, where in Florida did you work?"

"On the west coast, outside Sarasota. A place called Beaches End."

"Can you tell me about it?"

"Sure. It's a great place, and I'd recommend it. It's a small town, maybe fifteen thousand people. There's one major hospital there—Beaches End General Hospital—three or four medical labs, and wealthy, nice people. There are about fifteen internists in town, and I worked for Charlie White, a real nice guy who has the biggest practice there. One to two PAs work for him at any time, and he leaves you alone.

I mean, he never bothers you, a real trusting guy. Oh, and smart as he is, he's too busy to hire people properly, all docs are. He hired me while he was leaning against the doorway of his office and I was standing in the hall. I remember him saying, 'I know my office manager checked your credentials,' except she never did, and then he said, 'When can you start?' That's just the way it was. Unbelievable!"

"That is unbelievable!"

"Indeed. And he's big into tech and knows a lot about it, too. Really computer savvy. He was a biomedical engineer in his prior life, designed computers, knows network stuff and all that, so he's heavy into electronic medical records and the like."

"Well, good to know."

"Oh, and his wife, Heather, is a real looker. She's a lawyer and smart, too. Make sure you get a good look at her. One nice perk of working there is their sample closet. He said that's where the drug reps leave their samples. We're supposed to use them only for patients, but the staff takes what they want, and no one seems to care. Another thing—treat White's patients with dignity. If you talk about them, use their name. Don't call Jack Schwartz 'the gallbladder.' Don't joke about them, criticize them, or make any mistakes with them. If you do any of those things, he'll grab you by your collar and toss your sorry ass out the door."

Diary, I made a list of things I needed to do.

1. Apply to Pegasus's PA program and send a forged college BS transcript and diploma. Make my GPA 2.3. Do all by un-traceable e-mail. Did that.

2. Note: Phish all e-mails—embed a software patch inside my e-mails so when they open my e-mail, it will automati-cally install a program to copy me with any e-mails or web search queries they send or receive regarding me. That way I can monitor, intercept, and manage any adverse inquires or responses. Did that.

3. Make sure I send my college reports to look like they come from the college, not from me. Include a forged doctor's note saying I have medical issues that would keep me from trave-ling there. Maybe do a Photoshop of me in a wheelchair. This is why I want to apply to their online, low-residency program. Better yet, try to make that a no-residency program, which they might allow if I pay them enough. Wonder if they ac-cept Bitcoin payments and donations? Did that, and paid in Bitcoin.

4. Pegasus likes their "distance learners" to pick an under-served specialty. I'll pick public health. Well, more like public death! Ha! That's really underserved. Did that.

5. Visit a Medicaid clinic near me, snatch their letterhead stationery, staff directory, and so on. Create my "clinical ex-perience" there for my Pegasus clinical experience require-ment. Oh, also phish the clinic so I can follow any e-mail communications between them and Pegasus. I'd better track any calls from Cape Vernac to them, which would only be about me, and download the conversation. Pegasus accepted my Medicaid Clinic "clinical experience" for theirs.

6. *Arrange for my diploma from Pegasus to be sent to me online.* Nah, I'll forge one.

7. *Arrange for credentials to take the PANCE.* Nah, I'll forge the results.

8. *Pass the PA certification test. Get a Florida PA license.* Nah, I'll just forge my license.

9. *Contact White's office and apply for a job.* Done.

10. *Rest.*

II

Eager to escape his too-long exposure to his parents, the dark and cold of Rochester, the pompous arrogance of Dr. Norther, and after talking with Carlos, Righteous decides to move to Florida and, as he writes in his diary, "invade Beaches End as a foreign species of reptile would invade an alien land." He is certain that, once there, the exposure to the almost constant sunshine and warmth will provide the perfect counterpoint to the darkness and cold of his misdoings.

He also hopes his exposure to the abundance of bikini-clad women will be just the prescription he needs to satisfy the nagging craving of his latent, possibly waning from lack of expression, hormones and obtain the sexual release he thinks he should have and that he feels his body needs.

In a matter of months, he had enrolled in Pegasus's PA program and completed the required online PA content courses. These came easily as they supplemented his own prior studies and home experiments. Not waiting to graduate, he then completed the tasks of creating, forging, hacking, and otherwise obtaining all the documents needed to appear a certified medical PA; and while he was at it, a computer engineer. Thinking ahead for all possible contingencies where he may need to present himself not as himself, he makes duplicates of these and other credentials under a number of aliases. With his PA certificate in hand, National PA Registry databases updated to include his name, and confidence that any inquiry about him to Pegasus or the National PA Registry would come to his attention before its intended destination, he contacts White's office. Using all the inside knowledge gained from Carlos, and stretching Carlos's permission to use his name as a reference, Righteous sets up an interview with Dr. White.

He is counting on several things to go right, and all of them going right around the same time.

One, his stay in Beaches End with White will be short. He plans to get hired, do his hacking, including a grand finale of some sort, experience the high of that, and then vamoose before anyone is the wiser. A few weeks, maybe a month or so.

Two, that the PA hiring procedure will be as Carlos told him—quick and superficial. It is an amazing fact, he learns, that most small, private doctors' offices are wildly unorganized, behind on everything, and run by whomever happens to be the office manager that day.

Doctors have neither the time nor the knowledge to do an investigation into whether the PA candidate in front of them is an actual, credentialed PA, up to date with continuing medical education (CME) credits, or is even the person they say they are. They accept the paperwork and the word of the candidate. The office manager du jour, or du heure, is even less interested or capable. Righteous is encouraged in his effort to get hired by his web searches that return a number of PA impersonators, including a teenager at a Central Florida Hospital.[5] Indeed, as if to confirm everything Carlos had told him, the spokesperson for the hospital who credentialed the teenager testified that "they never verified that he was a physician assistant because the office was very busy." And this was a major hospital.

Righteous packs his diary, PC, stethoscope, and whatever else he can stuff into the duffel strapped to the luggage rack of his Harley and winds his way south to Beaches End.

The trip is both an expedition and an opportunity to experience for days on end the peace of being in a world populated almost entirely by himself. He takes as much of the slower, old, two-lane Route 15 south from Rochester as he can. So much along the way gives him sensory pleasure; from the soothing *thump, thump, thump* the asphalt-filled seams of the road relay up to him from wheels, to shocks, to handlebars, to hands, to shoulders, and to the never-ending sight of church steeples lining the peaceful streets, each one punctuating a cloud as if it is an exclamation mark. Even an ancient, country-road, one-pump Esso Station he finds comforting for it being redolent of grease and oil, and having the "coldest Coke ever, the kind where ice sits suspended throughout the bottle."

Halfway to Beaches End, while stopped at a roadside gas station, a mutt pesters Righteous. The dog, unrelenting and undeterred in his belief he belongs to Righteous, follows him for miles, taking shortcuts to appear at each rest stop Righteous takes. Eventually he becomes a passenger in Righteous's lap, having awakened in Righteous his old habit of collecting and nurturing strays.

Using one of his aliases and ID documents he made for the purpose, Righteous rents a small, first-floor apartment in Beaches End not more than one hundred yards across the Hudson Bayou to the Beaches End General Hospital. He writes, "From the small, screened-in lanai off my bedroom, I can hear the occasional croaks of frogs and the whooshing sounds of the bayou's occasional waves that splash around the wooden piles placed there many years ago. In the other direction, I can see what looks like choreographed dances of ambulances, their whining sirens, and whirling lights a riot of color and sound as they come and go from the giant, welcoming maw of the Beaches End General Hospital's ER driveway."

Still gazing out across the lanai, his dog asleep at his feet, he ends the day's entry with the prophetic mention, "We're there, boy. Right under their noses."

And with that, Charlie White's life, and those of the gentle people of Beaches End, are about to dramatically change.

12

"Dr. White, Harken Righteous, the PA job candidate, is here for his interview," Sally, White's office manager, says, standing in the doorway of White's private office, his at his desk.

"I heard him coming on that damn motorcycle from a mile away and watched him park it outside my office. And tie his mutt up to it. That bike should make you feel right at home, Sal."

"It actually does, Dr. White. I've still got to get you on a bike one of these days. You'd love it."

"Don't think so—I like my bones the way they're arranged now, thank you."

"I like my bones, too, Dr. White, but I also like the freedom my bike gives me. When I'm on it and doing sixty, everything is left behind me—my cares, my woes, everything."

"Harken Righteous? What the hell kind of a name is Harken Righteous?" White snaps, almost loud enough for everyone in earshot, including possibly Righteous, to hear. "Tell Mr. Righteous I'm finishing up some charts and I'll be right with him."

"Sure will. You're right about the name, Dr. White, I googled the name *Harken Righteous*, and no one by that name came up. By the way, he says to call him *Harry*."

"Okay, Harry it is. Tell you what, give him a tour of the office."

Is it okay if I give his dog a bowl of water?"

"Be my guest. Use an emesis basin. Just don't invite him in."

"Harry, Dr. White is finishing up his last patient. He asked me to give you a tour of our office until he's done. Okay?"

"Sure, thanks, Sally."

"You can leave your helmet in my office. Your timing was perfect, Harry, calling us when you did. Our last PA just took a job at a local nursing home. I did call Carlos, and he did say he spoke with you. Do you have your PA credentials with you?"

"Yes, I do. I also have my National Practitioner Identifier number that you can look up. I did my clinicals at Rochester First Care, a Medicaid primary care clinic. Talk about seeing diseases late in their course. I saw all comers there. Boy, that was really something. I also took a CME course—you know, a continuing medical education course—called Recognizing Florida's Native Insects and

Snakes: Bites and Treatment. I have that certificate, too. Do you want to see that?"

"No, just show me your PA certificate and NPI registry, if you don't mind. I'm a little busy right now."

"I can bring up my NPI registration on my phone for you to see, if you'd like."

"I would, Harry; that will save me a bit of time. Ah, I see it. Thank God for these phones, huh, Harry? You have no prior employment as a PA, correct?"

"Yes, correct. Is that a problem?"

"No, not really. This way we can teach you what we want you to know."

"This is our front business, office, Harry. Waiting room is on the other side of the sliding windows. We still keep the old manila folder patient record files here, as you can see, but we have gone completely digital for the past three years. We think, by law, we have to keep the folders here for six years."

"So, have all the paper charts here been digitized?" Righteous asks, wanting to learn what is hackable.

"Yes, we had the company that set up our EMR system do that for us."

"EMR? That's the electronic medical record system, right?" Harken asks curiously and timidly, wanting to sound naive but knowing full well what *EMR* stands for.

"Yes, Harry, that's correct. Hello, ladies; Barb, Stacy, Maribeth, I want you to meet Harken Right—excuse me,

Harry Righteous. He's applying to work here as a PA."

"Actually, I go by *Harry Right.* It's quicker and easier to say. People have less trouble with that."

"Hi, Harry," the three women at the front desk practically sing in unison, clearly struck by his good looks and cool demeanor.

"Maribeth, can you briefly show Harry our EMR terminal?" Sally asks.

"My pleasure, Harry. Pull up a chair," Maribeth says sweetly, swiveling around in her chair toward him, then crossing her legs so they can be seen practically to the hilt without fail by Righteous.

Harry, trying to remember he is at White's office in part for reconnaissance as well as a job, rolls a chair toward Maribeth and struggles to keep his eyes on the keyboard and monitor and off her bare legs, as well as her lips, which she quickly buttered in a warm, pink gloss just for him.

Maribeth begins giving Righteous an overview of the system, first by entering him as a new patient, typing as slowly as possible to prolong her contact with him, making small talk as she types. Seemingly content to spend as much time as possible with Righteous, Maribeth gives no evidence she is ever going to stop the encounter, and to hell with the patients lining up at the window, forcing Sally to, eventually, interrupt.

"Okay, Harry, I had better get you out of here before

these girls attack you. Come with me," Sally says as she tugs his shirt.

"Bye, Maribeth, ladies. Hope to see you again soon," Righteous utters reflexively, being completely out of his comfort zone with the female attention he is getting.

"Bye, Harry," Maribeth sings, elongating each barely audible word, staring at him with droopy, moist eyes as he leaves the room with Sally.

Barely listening to Sally as they walk, Righteous is distracted and disturbed by the feelings Maribeth has unexpectedly aroused deep inside him. He remembers these feelings from the past, those then more from a distance, these now more up close and personal. These feelings dwell just beyond a certain line and across a certain divide in his mind that is too wide, too deep, and, he believes, too dangerous to cross or even approach.

He knows that on the other side of that divide, at times seemingly reachable, at other times not, is a place of normalcy. A place so rich in emotions where he is so wanting to be but cannot quite get. He recognizes these feelings as the same ones he felt when Susan would call him at home at night and ask him out.

Oh, how much he wanted to go out and be with Susan then, to touch her, to hold her. And perhaps more important to him, to be touched by her. She was a perfect porcelain doll, more than real, but even so, he just could not bring himself to say yes to her pleadings.

Why, oh, why, could I not just say yes to her? he wondered. *Careful, Righteous, you're just about to cry.*

Now weepy and mellow, Righteous starts to feel from Maribeth the same pull and tug on his heart that Susan created in him and recalls how that was answered then only by his uncontrollable crying after telling her no, that voice that spoke to him coming from somewhere on the other side of that dark divide.

He is now reliving those feelings of arousal he had from Susan, only now from Maribeth, and experiencing the same sense of an inner comfort and warmth that love and sex must bring other people and what he must have been feeling when he was talking to Susan. He feels now, at the sight of Maribeth, an urge to be with her. These feelings are confusing him and disturbing him. *Strange, very strange, but nice*, he thinks.

He begins to wonder if it is possible that a woman is the missing link in this puzzle that is his life. Could a woman hold the key to unlocking the dark within him and setting him free? Is it possible that someone, perhaps Maribeth, could awaken the primitive feelings of normal human emotion in him? What would it be like to live in the sunshine of life with her?

"Boy, is he cute," Maribeth says to her coworkers as she slowly swivels her chair back to resume her work, half watching Righteous disappear through the doorway and making sure her legs are the last to disappear from his view should he happen to turn around to say goodbye.

"Harry, are you okay? You seem to be off somewhere else," Sally says.

"Oh, I'm sorry. No, no, I'm fine."

"Are you sure, Harry? Are you crying? You look like you are crying. You are crying. What is it, Harry?"

"Oh, jeez. No, just having a bad moment. I'm fine. Let's continue."

"Do you want to sit a minute?"

"I guess I'd better."

"Let's sit in my office a few minutes. Do you want to share anything with me, Harry?"

"No, I'm fine, really, M—sorry, I mean, Sally." For a blistering millisecond, he caught himself almost saying *Ma* and was thinking Sally was about to hold him. "No, let's continue the tour."

"Uh, Sally, can I ask you a question? Uh, Maribeth, I'll bet she's married or has a boyfriend, right?" Righteous says so cautiously, not wanting to give away his interest in her and totally surprised, actually fearful, that he asked such a question.

"Oh, you have your eye on our Maribeth, now do ya? I think she's single last I heard, but you'd best ask her."

"No way," Harry retorts, blushing, now becoming embarrassed.

"These are our exam rooms, Harry. Dr. White uses exam rooms 1 and 2; Dr. Cohan uses exam rooms 3 and 4; Dr. Kawalczynski—or Dr. K, we call him—uses exam rooms 5 and 6; Dr. Travis uses rooms 7 and 8; and you would use exam rooms 9 and 10. Each doctor and PA has their own private office next to their two exam rooms. You would be the only PA in the office."

"Where would my private office be?" says Righteous, who can't believe he's asking and is half-afraid to find out.

"Right here," Sally says as they turn the hall into a spacious office.

"Wow, this office would be mine?"

"Yes, sir."

"What's in here?" Righteous asks, pointing to a closet with bifold, louvered doors right next to his office door.

"That's our samples closet, Harry."

"Oh, I see. How does the 'samples closet' work?" Righteous asks, not revealing he already knows, thanks to Carlos, exactly what it is and realizing he just saw, and might be located next to, the holy grail of the office.

"I will tell you, but first let me explain a few things you may not know and that the general patient population definitely does not know. There are four main reasons most doctors come to work. They are, one, the gorgeous drug reps with free drug samples; two, the gorgeous drug reps with free lunch; and three, the gorgeous drug reps with free trips. The do-gooders of the world hate drug reps. Doctors love them."

"You said there were four reasons. You said only three."

"Oh, four. Four. Yes, four. And, four is to see patients."

"I don't get it," Righteous replies.

"Well, look, doctors get beat up six ways from Sunday every day of the week. Insurance companies tell them what x-rays they can order and will pay for. HMOs—you know, health maintenance organizations—tell them what drugs they can prescribe and will pay for. Pharmacists tell the doctors' patients about side effects of drugs that don't even apply to them or their doctors don't want them to know. Every month, doctors get report cards from insurers telling them how poorly they are treating the insurer's patients and ding them a lot of money to punish them."

"What do you mean 'ding them a lot of money'?"

"Just what I said. HMOs will withhold hundreds or thousands of the doctors' already-earned dollars because the HMO hasn't seen a blood test ordered for diabetes in three months. And you know what? Most of the time, it's not even the doctor's fault. Almost all of those patients are dead, never returned for follow-up appointments, never went to get the tests the doctor told them to get, or left the practice and are seeing a different doctor."

"What's the drug rep have to do with all of that?"

"Ah, the answer is pleasure, a right not guaranteed by

the Constitution, by the way.[6] Among other things they do, the reps make lunch a feast for us. They understand what doctors go through and know they aren't treated that well, either. We get whatever we want to eat from whatever restaurant we choose. The reps like us and take good care of us. Silver chafing dishes brimming with lamb chops, prime rib, green beans, scalloped potatoes, you name it. Believe me, after a hard morning of problem solving and, sometimes, difficult patients, it's the perfect respite. And to break it up, in the summer, the reps themselves grill hot dogs and hamburgers for us. The do-gooders out there think doctors are influenced by the reps, you know, as if a doctor would prescribe a drug because the rep grilled them a hot dog. That is ludicrous. If you asked any doctor which drug company makes which drug, they most likely would not know the answer and don't care.

"And what do the reps ask in return? Five minutes, at the most. Five minutes for them to tell the doc about the latest, greatest drug their company is making or the most recent side effects reported for a drug. The doctors appreciate this and use this information a lot, and patients benefit greatly."

"What about the samples?" Righteous asks.

"Oh yes. The samples are invaluable to everyone. Doctors love them because it is more humane, downright decent, and good business for a drug company to have the doctor give a patient a sample of a $300 inhaler than have the patient spend that money only to find out in five days it doesn't help or the patient doesn't tolerate it. At the same time, those samples are in great demand by both the doctors and staff. Forget where you heard that, Harry."

Died and gone to heaven. An unlocked drug closet right outside the door of my office-to-be, Righteous thinks as he scans the closet for drugs of interest and any cameras focused there.

"Well, that's about it, Harry. I see Dr. White is ready to meet with you. It was really nice meeting you, and I hope to see you again soon."

"Same here, Sally, same here," Righteous manages to say, now off his normal evil-driven stride, mellower than usual, feeling somewhat at home and not knowing how to behave.

13

"Hello. It's Harry, right?"

"Yes, Dr. White. Sorry about that. My legal name is Harken Righteous, but that's a real eyebrow raiser, so I tell folks I go by Harry Right."

"I agree, that *is* a lot easier. Listen, I don't have a lot of time right now, Harry. Sorry about that. I know you spoke to Sally and am sure she'll check up on your credentials. Working here would be your first PA job, yes?"

"That's correct, sir. But I've had good clinical experience."

"All right. So, Harry, should you come to work here, there are a few things you need to know and never forget. We're a general, primary care practice. Folks see us first when they think they're sick. Remember, if they're here, they're here for a reason. That doesn't mean they're sick in our terms. They don't always have a disease as we know it, but they need to know, whatever the reason, it was good they came in. We're here to listen, figure out why they came, and have them feel better that they did. Never, and I mean *never*, cause a patient to think they wasted your time coming in. Every issue they have is an important one. Do you know what a 'ticket of admission' in a doctor's office is, Harry?"

"No, sir, I don't."

"Okay. Say you're a patient and having trouble getting an erection or you think your spouse is having an affair and you can't eat or sleep. You're constipated, have a hemorrhoid, any number of other embarrassing issues. Patients generally don't call for an appointment and say those things, because they're too embarrassed. They say they have a cold or a rash, anything other than the truth. That's their ticket of admission to the office. Do you know how to find that out when they're here, Harry?"

"How, sir?"

"You begin by recognizing the possibility that whatever the reason they claim to be seeing you for is the ticket of admission. It matters less if you're wrong. You listen carefully, read their mood, look them in the eyes and see if they're hurting, and then you'll know, but only if you care and ask. Here, we care and ask. You'll learn, if you want to, how to check Mary for the 'cold' she came in for but knows she doesn't have and tell her it was a good thing she came in for it and that it will be gone in a few days. Then you touch her, hold her hand, and say, 'Mary, tell me what *really* brought you here today,' and have a tissue in your other hand ready for her copious tears. That's what we do here, Harry. Anybody can learn to be a doctor or a PA, but not everybody can do what I just taught you."

"Whew … Dr. White. I never heard a doctor talk like that before. Thank you for that," Righteous says, taken aback by the unexpected humanity and caring. White's words seemed as a scalpel intended to carve from him every last shred of his malignant bitterness born of the lack of just that kind of caring and affection.

I wish you had been my doctor, Righteous thinks with genuine regret for what he is planning to do.

"Don't know if you know yet, Harry, but as soon as I'm done seeing patients each day, around five o'clock, I start making my phone calls to patients who called, starting with the ones who seem most urgent and then move on to those who called early in the morning. In all my years of practice, I've never left my office for the day without calling back everyone who called to speak to me."

"I see, Dr. White."

"Can you do that, Harry? Return all the calls, as I do?"

"Of course, Dr. White. Yes, I can and will."

"I wouldn't have a lot of time for supervising you, Harry. Do you need a lot of supervision?"

"Oh, that's no problem, Dr. White. I'm a self-starter and very comfortable seeing patients."

"Good. Well, I need a PA, and I hate this hiring business. Sally read your résumé and gave me a thumbs-up on you. Let us know if you want to join us, okay? Oh, and if so, when can you start?"

"I'm available anytime, Dr. White. I've moved here and settled in."

"Great! Just let Sally know."

"Will do, Dr. White. Will certainly do."

Why do I feel so badly? Whose voice is that I am I hearing, so faint, nearly muted? I hear it telling me, "No, Harken, don't do your evil stuff." But soon, it's gone again, whoever that was.

14

APRIL. *Diary, if you only had eyes and ears. You'd see me sitting on the lanai of my new home; the average temperature in Beaches End this time of year is eighty, compared to Rochester's forty-eight. Well, it's actually an apartment, not a "home" home. My flip-flopped feet are propped way up, my PC is on my lap, and the mutt, whom I've named Askim, is asleep by my side. There's a slice of moon overhead and a croak or two from a nearby frog. Now and then, I hear a wave splash over here and a wave whoosh over there. It's really quite nice. Then from across the bayou, its near-bank almost at my feet, come blazing lights and blaring sirens from the ambulances racing in and out of Beaches End General Hospital's gaping emergency entrance. The hospital lights just about reach me. This is as close to a slice of heaven that I can think of and as close to my next target as I want to be at the moment.*

My next hacking target is that beautiful hospital with those gorgeous lights, and this one's going to be a doozy. It's a real shame I can't get personal credit for it. Oh, I will make sure to leave a little message for the SYSOP that "someone" paid his network a little visit, and I'm hoping he'll discover it.

That's important because the world will know, eventually, that the hospital was hacked; I just can't tell them I did it. Well, not now, anyway, but maybe later. We'll know it was me, right, Diary? I have standards, so leaving the SYSOP a message is the right thing to do, and if they ever find me out, someone will say, "You know, that Harken Righteous was a nasty type, but at least he was a very courteous hacker." Gee, I hope they do.

Here's the deal, Diary. I need to test my hospital infrastructure network control knowledge, things like power plant switches, door lock controls, lighting control systems, those kinds of hacking skills. For that, I need the details of how the power plant of that hospital is organized. And for that, I need to pay the developer, Stargazer Systems, a little visit.

What got me started on hacking the hospital is the article Kim Zetter wrote[7] on hired security expert Scott Erven's[8] two-year investigation into over a hundred hospital facilities in Minnesota, North Dakota, Wisconsin, and Idaho. Erven found that virtually every device, medical and otherwise, in those facilities, including MRIs, surgical robots, defibrillators, lights, locks, even drug infusion devices, was hackable and their functions were controllable by him remotely. Medical records were equally vulnerable. I think Erven is my idol.

I'll need to know exactly how the hospital's networks, security systems, passwords, and the like are set up. I'm confident I've done everything to protect my IP addresses from anyone attempting to find me out. I've got all my hidden service codes in place, VPNs and encryption set, and created virtual rendezvous points, so I'm virtually untraceable. It's just a damn shame the hospital I'm going to hack hasn't taken the same interest in protecting itself from people like me as I have in figuring it out and protecting myself. If only they invested in setting up their records in blockchain, guys like me wouldn't stand a chance.

This hospital's server, I learned already from the internet, is the home of the central server for all the town's commercial labs, as well. Every commercial lab—like Sand Dollar Labs on Palm Avenue, Sunshine Labs on Siena Loop, even labs in the few smaller hospitals and urgent care clinics—saves their results to the bigger Beaches End General Hospital server. I need to remember this because if, and when, I change the value of a patient's results in the remote server, the main hospital server will change automatically. It's a real gift to me that all the remote servers dump into the central server, because by connecting to the central server, I can look up any doctor, any lab report, and any imaging report. You name it, it's all there. Is that dumb or what? I mean their system, not me.

Some of the details of the hospital's network, including its power system, were actually posted online when they dedicated the hospital some years ago—stupid them. It turns out that Stargazer Systems, located right here in Beaches End, posted on the internet that their system is "state of the art" and, I quote from their website, "this system is connected to the internet through the ethernet, giving us the most flexible, cost-efficient, and secure, password-protected system in the country." Yes, Stargazer dickheads, real secure and real vulnerable, too. Oh, and here's the stupidest thing they said: "Other hospitals have separate networks for communications, patient accounts, energy, power control, MRIs, infusion pumps, blood bank, and they cannot communicate with each other. Stargazer's system goes the next step and ties them all together." Well, this hacker-cracker boy thanks you very much, Stargazer and company, for making my life so simple. Because they're tied together, if I hack one network, then I've got an entrée, s'il vous plaît into all the others. All I need is the master password. Yeah!

I downloaded the schematic for their system. The entire hospital electronic system is set up as modules. I see that every module performs a function, and every function is programmable. For example, there's a module for the power system, and within that are modules for every subfunction, such as the HVAC system, every lighting system, every door, every alarm, everything. And it looks like every module has a digital address with a unique password. If I had the passwords, I could get to the server addresses for the lighting system and everything else. The digital storage registers at each server address contain the codes to turn individual lights on and off. All that is good and helpful but not good enough. Lots of things likely changed since the beginning. Things like upgraded software, new subroutines, maybe different passwords and the *like. I can't afford any mistakes. I think it best I pay Stargazer Systems a visit. Well, not me, exactly.*

So, here's my plan. Well, not my entire plan and not entirely mine. I just read a book called Ghost in the Wires *by Kevin Mitnick.*[9] *Diary, he was the ghost—do you believe it? He was the ghost in the wires. He's my idol, too, in many ways and not just because his childhood sucked like mine did or that he was on the FBI's top ten most-wanted list for his hacking. I'll never make it that far or be that good. He used what he called social engineering*[10] *and is the guru of the concept. Social engineering gets people to do what he wants without them knowing it. I read how he used it to hack his way into any bank or corporation, anywhere he wanted. I need to be clear, Diary, that he never changed anybody's medical records, and he wouldn't be a bit happy with me for doing it.*

He was an unhappy kid, too, and felt hacking was his way of getting back at the world. His father was also MIA much of the time, and his mom was his only real lifeline. Sort of like my case. She didn't have agoraphobia, though. Anyway, he found ways to get employee and private corporate information and use it to hack into companies. And that's what I'll do.

What I need *is Stargazer's personnel directory, work product printouts, and some e-mail addresses, content, and threads. Many companies today have their directories in the cloud online, and they contain everything imaginable. Stargazer does not. I know that personnel directories are often carelessly, and against the company's policy, left on employees' desks* or in an unlocked drawer. E-mail addresses are often in the company directory. Computer printouts are supposed to be put in slotted containers, then shredded, but too often they're carelessly thrown away by employees, usually in trash cans under their desks even when a shredder's nearby. Also, there are bills, invoices, and other statements containing account numbers and a host of other personal identifying information. I also need to not be seen by the video cameras they must have all over the place.

I want to say, Diary, here and now, that I know, and you know, what I'm about to do isn't all that nice. I really can't help myself, though, and you know that. My shrink, Norther, can't help me either.

But, just maybe, what I'm about to do is a good thing, you know? Teach these Florida folks a lesson for making all that information so readily available, maybe help bring them to their senses. At the same time, to tell the truth, doing this is very exciting and satisfying to me, like the digital equivalent of squashing bugs.

All I want to do is turn all the power off at the hospital for thirty minutes. That's all. Just thirty minutes, and maybe not all the power. We'll see. I know they have a backup generator system, so no one should get hurt, assuming the generator works, but I may disable that, too. Who knows? The reason this is a good way to start my hospital hacking work is that it's a big enough deal that I'll get feedback that it worked and hear about everything I did when I watch it on the news.

Stargazer, in a few hours, you will have the distinct privilege of saying good morning to the absolutely untraceable, never-was-before and, after tomorrow, never-will-be-again Mr. Quentin Wellcome … a.k.a. Harken Righteous.

Oh, Diary, I got the PA job!

15

"I'm Quentin Wellcome. I have a 9:00 appointment to see Ms. Eva Glanston," Righteous, now Wellcome, tells Don Brown, the security guard at the entrance to Stargazer Systems.

"Good morning, Mr. Wellcome. Should I say, 'Welcome, Mr. Wellcome'? Just kidding. Bet you hear that a lot. Would you please sign in, then open your backpack, sir? Also, please empty your pockets into the tray. Also, put your cell phone where I can see it, then turn it on, then off. Thank you," says Brown.

"Certainly," Righteous says, having fully prepared for this visit, including a bogus license plate doctored from Google Images for his motorcycle parked outside and a fake wallet ID showing he is Quentin Wellcome, all matching the résumé documents he'd sent to Stargazer as part of his job application.

"Somebody's birthday?" Brown asks upon seeing and quickly squeezing two gift-wrapped packages inside the backpack.

"Yeah, a couple of gifts for a girl I recently met. I didn't want to leave them on my motorcycle."

"Not a problem. You're good to go, sir. Take a seat. I'll let Ms. Glanston know you're here, Mr. Wellcome."

"Good morning, Quentin. I'm Eva. It's my pleasure to be with you this morning."

"Good morning to you, too, Eva."

"May I offer you some water? Coffee?"

"No, I'm fine. Thank you. I appreciate your coming in for me so early on a Saturday morning, Eva. Looks like no one's here but us," Righteous says, really asking the question to be reassured rather than making a statement—all part of his recon strategy.

"Well, that's okay. Yes, we're normally closed on Saturdays, but I wanted to accommodate you. No employees are scheduled to be here this morning, though some could wander in and usually do. Let's sit in my office for a bit, then I'll take you on a tour, okay?"

"Sounds good."

"I have your résumé here. Very impressive. I see you have education in health care and hospital automation, software, networking, and coding in multiple languages. You know our division here builds hospital infrastructures, data networks, and control systems that can control anything in a hospital from a single light or a door lock to the entire power plant or chemotherapy infusion center."

"Yes, that's what makes your company so interesting to me."

"We commonly hire electrical system engineers, computer software engineers, and coders, but anyone who has combined training in hospital and health-care technology is very special indeed. Oh, we're also starting a blockchain division and are looking for engineers and cryptographers. Do you have any skills along those lines?"

"No, no formal training in blockchain, but I am teaching myself how to write blockchain code in Python. And thank you for your kind words."

"You're welcome. We're glad you're interested in employment here. We have two divisions on the west coast of Florida—one here in Beaches End and one in Lakeland Ranch. Both are hospital systems divisions. We use Beaches End as one of our hospital beta sites. I can answer any questions you have, then give you a tour."

"No questions yet. May I have a copy of your company brochure I see on your desk? I like the title, 'Star*GAZING*.'"

"Thank you. Sure, here you go."

"Thanks! Now, I just need to use the men's room before our tour."

"Of course. It's out the door, turn right, down six desks, then turn right again."

With backpack in one hand, the brochure in the other, and his recon goals for the visit in mind, Righteous strolls toward the men's room, looking straight ahead with his eyes scanning for cameras along the way. He sees none. He's bothered by the odd sparkle each ceiling tile casts and wonders what that is and if the missing cameras and the sparkle may be related.

He spots a desk with what looks like the company directory sitting on the corner. *Eureka!* he thinks. Believing there still may be video cameras on him, he flops his backpack onto the desk so it completely covers the directory. Then, as a visual distraction, he sits on the desk next to the backpack, bends up his right leg, draws his shoe in closer to him, and unties and reties the sneaker as if the shoelace needs adjusting. He's counting on the sleight-of-hand distraction techniques magicians use. He knows that if there is a camera on him, the attention of the human attending the monitor will normally be drawn to his hands tying his shoelace, not his backpack sitting on the desk covering the directory.

Done with his shoes, Righteous stands, nonchalantly picks up the backpack and directory together in one swoop so the directory is hidden and leaves the brochure from Eva in the directory's place. He's hoping the brochure will visually replace the directory to any camera monitor operator who might be on duty and watching him as one of the few people in the building.

Righteous continues to the men's room. Once inside, he scans the stalls to make sure he's alone, then makes a beeline to the closest stall. There, he hangs the backpack on the hook on the back of the stall door, undoes his pants, lets them drop to the floor, pulls a toilet-seat cover he brought for this purpose out of his backpack, and sits down. He quickly scans the directory to make certain it's what he wants.

Eureka is right! It's the whole enchilada! All the company divisions are there. Every employee, department, department head, and so on. Every job description from coder to janitor. Every e-mail address, phone number, extension, everything. Even their birthdays. It's all there.

He now needs to know who works for whom and who's talking to whom and why. For that, he'll need computer work product and the threads and contents of company e-mails.

From his backpack, Righteous pulls out one of the gift-wrapped boxes he came in with. Having only partially wrapped it for this purpose and stuffing it with toilet paper to give it bulk, he opens the end flap he'd left unsealed, removes the toilet paper, and inserts the directory into the box, refolds the flap, and holds it together with a few Happy Birthday stickers. Then he puts the wrapped "gift" back in his backpack. The box will appear no different to the guard now from when he entered. He flushes the toilet paper from that box, and the second one he hopes to use next, down the toilet.

After pulling up his pants and looking under the stalls

again, he checks that no one else is in the bathroom, then takes the backpack off the hook, readies the other gift-wrapped box, and exits the stall. He barely opens the men's room door and scans the office. Righteous sees nobody and feels relatively secure, except for the worry that Eva will notice his absence and that there are certainly unseen surveillance cameras out there somewhere. He walks as normally as possible out of the bathroom.

Righteous returns to the desk where he'd gotten the directory and sees, beneath it, the trash can full of paper. This time, sitting in the chair behind the desk, he places his backpack on the floor. He keeps his back bent toward the ceiling to shield any camera lens that might be there, then pulls out the crumpled contents of the almost-filled trash can and flattens and squares up the sheets like a deck of cards. Then, using the desk and his body as a shield, slides the ream into the remaining gift-wrapped box still in the backpack, placing some more stickers on to keep it together. Worried even more that Eva will be looking for him, and needing a reason for being at the desk, he hurriedly puts one foot at a time on the desktop, then unties and reties his sneakers.

"Quentin, are you okay? I was getting worried about you," Eva says, startling him from the opposite side of the desk.

Oh, Christ. What did she see? he thinks.

"Oh, Eva, you startled me. Um, I'm fine. Just got a little

dizzy on the way out of the bathroom, so I sat down. Then I realized I needed to tie my shoes. These laces never stay tied."

"Okay, no problem. Are you sure you're up for a tour?"

"Sure am. Let's do it."

"Thank you for the tour, Eva. It was great. You have a fascinating company," Righteous says as he is escorted by Eva to security to leave, feeling secure that if she is letting him leave, then she didn't see him take anything.

"I'm glad you enjoyed the tour, and thanks for visiting us. I hope to see you again and that you will give Stargazer the opportunity to make you an offer. I ... Oh, Quentin, wait one minute, please. Don't leave yet. My security phone is ringing. Christ, now the building's security alarms are going off. I need to answer it *stat*."

Security guard Don Brown, now finished checking Righteous, done feeling his way around his backpack, and oblivious to Eva, gives Righteous the thumbs-up to leave, not yet dealing with the alarms.

"Happy birthday to your girlfriend," Brown says, seeing again on the way out the same wrapped packages with the labels inside the backpack that he'd seen on his way in.

Righteous, his exit pace now a fast walk that, upon hearing the alarms and Eva's security phone ringing, borders on a run, hoping the guard doesn't feel his heart pounding, ignores Eva's request to wait and inserts a skip or two as he heads out the exit door.

"Quentin, wait! Don't leave yet! Wait there a minute, Quentin. Don't leave!"

She snatches the ringing phone—"Hello, Larry, what's the matter?" Eva says, panicking, as she answers the now flashing and ringing red phone she must always carry for talking exclusively to Larry Demarseco, head of all security at Stargazer.

"How could that be? I was with him!" she says. "I was with him the whole time he was here."

16

The Saturday-morning sun sneaks its way through every crack and crevice of the louvered blinds behind the bed where Charlie and Heather White slept wrapped in each other's arms.

"Heather, where are you?" White shouts as he gropes for her in bed. Though his brain is craving more sleep, his heart is awakened by the absence of the warmth of her body against his.

"I'm in the kitchen, sweetheart. How does three blueberry pancakes with four strips of bacon and gen-u-wine maple syrup sound?" Heather calls back, knowing this will jump-start their morning.

"Be there in fifteen! Oh, that bac-own, oh, that bac-own. Oh, how that bac-own is callin' mah nayme," White sings, feeling happy, hot-coal-stepping his way to the shower.

Seated at the breakfast table, the feast Heather had prepared before them, White says, "This is the best! Damn!"

Heather smiles and bows her head. "Lord, we give thanks for all the good things we have and for the strength to deal with any adversity we may face."

"Amen," they both say, holding hands, in a spirit of genuine affection for each other and a strong belief in the Lord.

"Charlie, you need to let go of my hand if we're going to eat," Heather says half-heartedly as she, too, is reluctant to let go.

"If I said, 'I love you more than bacon,' you'd know that means I love you more than any other words could express, right?" White says, believing he has created the most profound expression of true love any man has ever uttered.

"Charlie, you're silly. I love bacon, too, but to be honest, I hope your love for me goes beyond yours for bacon. You know, we don't talk about this much, and guys don't often think this way, but women do. Anyway, I sometimes compare us to our friends. Girls talk, and they all talk about their husbands. I don't, ever. You wouldn't believe what they say about their husbands. Most of them are unhappy. Many are having affairs or don't even like their husbands."

"What? Our friends? You know, I do hear about affairs from patients, but only from women and only after they realize their husbands are having affairs. They always know, too—immediately. Then they stop eating, lose twenty-five pounds, and come to see me for anxiety and because they can't sleep. They don't mind the weight loss. Not one woman has ever volunteered to me that she was having an affair. And no man has ever boasted to me about it. So tell me, who's doing what to whom?"

"Boasted about it, Charlie? Boasted? Really?"

"I knew I said that wrong as soon as I said it."

"You sure did. And, no, I won't tell you who. But here's my point. I don't ever feel like that—like having an affair. And it never occurs to me that you would, either. To me, that makes us different."

"We are different, Heather. I've actually given this some thought, too. I think the fact that we're so happy and content with each other has a lot to do with the fact that we're content as people first, then as a couple. That's what gets us through problems. I also think our having been together since the seventh grade might have something to do with it. I mean, unlike a lot of couples, practically all the baggage we have we got together. Seriously, no surprises and no blasts from the past for either of us. No old girlfriends or boyfriends, no sleepless nights hungering for the touch of a long-lost love.

"I really think we have it all. We like what we do. Not to say we don't have issues or worries, but we deal with them. You know what it is? I think it's because we *like* each other, and that's different from saying we *love* each other. It's so easy to say, 'I love you,' but harder to say, 'I like you.' We all know what we mean when we say we like someone or something, but you know what, no one can say they know what they mean when they say they love someone. When we like something, we take care of it, don't we? We don't harm it, we preserve it, we make it better, not worse, we keep it safe, protect it. We don't diminish it; we uplift it. That's what we do for *things* we like. We should do the same for *people* we like, too. And isn't that just how we treat each other? That is us, Heather; we like each other, don't we? So what could be better?"

"Well said, Doctor. If you were a lawyer, I'd rest your case!"

"Well said, Counselor!"

"So, tell me, Charles, anything new and exciting you'd like to share with me? Having an affair, maybe? Just kidding, just kidding."

"Well, there is something. We finally hired a PA."

"You did? A him or a her?"

"A him."

"What's his name?"

"Harken Righteous."

"Harken who?"

"Right. I mean, yes. He actually goes by Harry Right."

"He has two names? That sounds fishy. Did you

interview him, or did Sally?"

"Both."

"Who saw his résumé?"

"Sally."

"She approved?"

"She did. She says he has all the right credentials."

"Did you do your usual due diligence?"

"I did more than my usual. I spent five minutes with him instead of the usual two. Truth is, and we've talked about this before, Heather, though it's sad, but this is how PAs and other staff get hired in many, if not most, doctors' offices. You know I have zero business training and even fewer business skills. In four years of college, four years of medical school, and three years of internship and residency, there wasn't a single hour devoted to running a practice, including hiring and firing. I'm busy seeing patients, and that's all I'm trained to do. Everything else is just an obstacle getting in my way of practicing medicine. This is one reason why docs like Steve and Gerry are selling their practices to hospitals and insurance companies; they can't hack the *business* of medicine, and the vultures who buy them out know that very, very well."

"I know, I know. I was just yanking your stethoscope. And don't feel bad, Charlie. You put your patients' care and welfare first, and that takes time. Your patients know and appreciate that, too. That's only one of the things that makes you so lovable and special.

"I'd like to meet your PA. I'll arrange to have him over for dinner as we do with all your new PA hires."

17

APRIL. *Dear Diary, it's me Harry—no, Quentin, or maybe it's both. Yes, of course, both. Here we are on our lanai, and I'm just about ready to breach Beaches End General Hospital's network. Thank you very much, Stargazer directory and trash. I'm going to shut down the hospital for thirty minutes. I visited Stargazer yesterday morning—well, Quentin did—and met Eva, the recruiter lady, a very nice person. She let me in, poor thing. She showed me around, and to say, "Thank you," I "borrowed" a few things from them—namely, their company directory and a bundle of discarded computer printouts that happened to include project work product printouts, password vault contents, phone system logins, and e-mail threads.*

Diary, there may be an issue. As I was leaving, Eva took a call from her security department, and then the building's security alarm went off. I got scared thinking they caught me. But, Diary, here's the thing—even if they did, there is no "me" to catch! At Stargazer, I was Quentin Wellcome, and I made sure he is untraceable. My bike had fake plates so any outside cameras will come up with a bogus plate. The name Quentin

Wellcome comes up zilch on Google. All my paperwork at Stargazer is bogus. So why worry? Right. No need, Diary. The only thing they have is an e-mail address to contact me, but this, too, I set up to be untraceable to me.[11]

Anyway, using what I learned from my Stargazer visit, I was able to locate and breach their password vault. That was easy because once I breached their server, I found that the master password to open the password vault is PasswordVault2019! Duh! See what I mean, Diary? They deserve what I'll be giving them. There I found the codes for the power grid and a host of medical devices at the hospital. And, Diary, you'll be so proud of me. Here is the over-the-top cleverness of my cleverness. From the SG trash, I learned the smart (really dumb) engineers over there programmed a "disable battery backup" switch for every device in their system. So, whereas the battery backup of every device I turn off would normally call for the automatic switchover to battery power, it can't when I disable it!

It's now 3:00 a.m., and I'm going to flip the doomsday switch on sleepy little BEGH.

Then, Diary, we'll turn on Where It's Happening *and watch the news to see the glory of my work.*

18

Diary, shhhhhhhhhhhh. Here it is!

"Ladies and gentlemen, this is Rodger Whitcomb with *Where It's Happening,* and we have some breaking news. About forty-five minutes ago, at exactly 3:00 this morning, in Beaches End, Florida, a small town near Lakewood Ranch just east of Sarasota, the Beaches End General Hospital lost almost complete power for a full thirty minutes. Our local CNN affiliate WBCD reporter, Joie Jergé, is right there, so let's hear from her."

"Rodger, this has to be seen to be believed, and even then, it is unbelievable. I've spoken to those who should know, and I'm told almost every light, door lock, infusion pump, the blood bank, and even the HVAC went out, was turned off, or became disabled. There was almost total darkness, and as I learned from several witnesses inside the hospital, sheer panic ensued. The backup generator was turned off."

Did you hear that, Diary? Sheer panic ensued! Yes! Righteous stands to fist-pump and shout that to his diary.

"But, Rodger, here's why I said 'almost,' and this is the part no one yet fully understands. The OR and maternity delivery rooms were spared. That's right—the entire hospital except those two services went dark and became disabled. Exactly thirty minutes after going dark, the siege was over. But there's more. The only service that did not get power back was the in-patient psychiatric service. The psychiatric ward remains dark as we speak. Does that have some insidious meaning we don't yet understand?

"Witnesses told me in heartbreaking detail about patients who had been lying on gurneys awaiting imaging or treatment. After the event, they were found desperately crawling the floors crying for help, some injured from falling out of their gurneys. Other patients, previously securely wedged or strapped into their infusion and dialysis chairs, had become partially or completely dislodged and were found dangling and clawing for something to grab on to. And one soul, who was alive and on life support prior to the event, was found dead when the lights came back on. Power went out in the emergency room, too, and the damage there has yet to be fully assessed. Elevators stopped mid-floor, trapping patients and staff members. Clinical blood analyzers printed out results bearing little resemblance to known normal values. One staff member said the hospital looked like a war zone that had been subjected to a weapon of mass destruction. Another staff member said that it felt like a 'medical hell' had descended upon their little hospital. She reported that several of her patients, who before the catastrophe had been breathing easily on oxygen, were found afterward gasping for air and groping to find their oxygen masks that had become displaced in the hysteria and confusion of the dark.

"There's more, Rodger. IV pumps stopped midstream and became reset to bizarre and dangerous settings when the power returned. Chemotherapy infusion pumps were found sputtering their lifesaving fluids onto the floor and ceiling. No one I asked can explain why the standard battery backup systems built into almost every device were not operational. As for the nurses and staff, they are bewildered, dazed, and stumbling into one another as if, one told me, awake inside a bad dream in a house of horrors. Currently, the hospital and grounds are a riot of police, federal agents, first responders of every kind, members of the press, worried relatives of hospitalized patients and staff members, and curious onlookers wondering what just happened and why.

"Rodger, right now, the hospital is convening a quickly called press conference. Felicity Spark, hospital spokesperson, and Eva Glanston, Stargazer Systems' director of human resources and corporate spokesperson for the hospital's infrastructure network provider, are just about to take our questions. Hang tight, viewers. There's much more to come."

19

MAY. *Oh, Diary. My hacking deed is done. What a special way to end a day and start a day! I created enough havoc and mayhem for one town, for one day, for one person, even for me. I'm going to save the summary of it in a QR code, which I will paste in you. I'll try to sleep now, but my adrenaline is flowing, and I may be too excited to sleep. Good night.*

Diary, it's me. I'm back. I can't sleep. I feel bad, but I feel good. Now I sound schizo, don't I? Maybe I have hacker's remorse. Is that something, hacker's remorse? I just made it up. Look, I understand what I did. Like I told you before, I may be crazy as hell, but I ain't stupid. I know what I did was bad, but, Diary, I have no good in my life to replace the bad. Yes, I start work with Dr. White soon, and I'll see Maribeth there. I'm thinking a lot more about her, but then I remember my plans aren't to stay there that long, anyway, so what's the use?

You know, if someone, anyone, showed me even a tiny bit of affection, even if they just said, "You're okay," or "I care about what happens to you," even that comforting little morsel could be just the thing to make me stop this hacking business and change my life.

I do have love to give. You know that, Diary.

And I have a place in me for love to live.

HACK 2 SUMMARY

Date of Hack: April 7

What/Who: Beaches End General Hospital power grid and stuff.

What I Did: Turned off most all services except the OR and maternity delivery rooms. I turned all back on in thirty minutes except psych.

Consequences: Plenty of damage.

Terror-Creation Factor for Me: 8/10 = Very good.

20

"Larry, this is crazy timing! I was just about to call you," Eva says, answering her phone. "Did you hear what just happened at Beaches End General Hospital?"

"I just heard it on the news. Where are you?"

"I'm at the hospital. Where are you?"

"Stargazer."

"They're holding a press conference here, and they want me to speak. What am I supposed to tell them?"

"Listen up, Eva, we have a major problem on our hands."

"No kidding! I know that."

"I don't think you do."

"What are you talking about?"

"Tell me everything you know about your visitor from yesterday morning."

"What does he have to do with this?"

"Who is he, Eva, and what was he doing here on a Saturday morning when we are supposed to be closed?"

"His name is Quentin Wellcome, and he was here for a

job interview. His résumé said he has training in hospital-related computer and network design."

"So, what the hell was he doing stealing a company directory and paper from one of the trash cans?"

"Stealing? He was with me the entire time. I didn't see him take anything."

"I have it on video, Eva. And no, he wasn't with you the entire time."

"You have him on video stealing a directory and trash?"

"Well, maybe. It's tricky. My overnight security video monitoring team called me. During the review of yesterday's surveillance imaging, they spotted suspicious behavior by your guest. They were alarmed enough to ask me to come in, and, well, it looks suspicious as hell."

"Larry, you know that Wellcome left the building through the security exit at the exact time you called me on the secure phone yelling about the alarms going off because the FedEx guy left the back door open."

"Yes, so."

"Well, security didn't find any stolen documents."

"Anyway, Eva, I have your man on video taking a company directory off a desk and taking it to the men's room. After he returned, I think he took some trash from a trash can, believe it or not. It was hard to see because his back concealed most of whatever he was doing under the desk."

"What the hell are you talking about? You're calling me at 4:30 in the morning because he took a directory into the men's room? This is the big emergency? Jesus Christ, Larry, the hospital's a mess!"

"Listen, Eva, I, also, asked Don Brown, and he said he didn't notice any stolen items. But I have the guy on video leaving the building with a backpack, which I presume contained the possibly stolen items."

"Larry, I think you mean you *assume*, not *presume*, because you're telling me you have no *actual* evidence of him leaving the building with anything proprietary to Stargazer. You have to be cautious with accusations like this! Did you look in the men's room to see if he left the directory in there?"

"Well, no. Probably too late now. Housekeeping would have taken it on their evening rounds and probably put it in a desk or pitched it in the mass dumpster."

"So, you can't really prove that he took it with him when he left. What are you going to do?"

"I don't know yet. They didn't catch it until the backup video review, which is why it took this long. I'm sure he did something bad; I just feel it, Eva. You'll understand better when you see the video. No one acts the way he did without having bad intentions. You'll see."

"Maybe, but I don't know. You'd have to be able to really *prove* it, and I'm still stuck on why anyone would want to steal a directory and some trash. Why would someone do that? What would they even do with it?"

"Why don't you just give that another millisecond's

thought, Eva? Come on, connect the dots!"

"Dots? What dots? Oh, mother of God. Don't tell me. You think Wellcome turned the hospital dark using information from the directory and the trash?"

"It kind of adds up, doesn't it?"

"I don't know, Larry; it seems like a reach to me. Do we tell corporate, the police, the FBI, all of them? Who?" Eva says on the verge of tears, now thinking this is all her fault. "They want me to speak at that news conference. I'm panicking! What do I say, Larry? Do I say anything about this?" Eva says, her voice lowered, cupping her hand over her mouth and phone to prevent anyone from hearing.

"No, don't say anything about this. I know nothing's certain. Just say it's too early to comment on the cause of the event, as we haven't even started, much less finished, an investigation yet. Make it up as you go. You're bright. You know a whole hell of a lot more about Stargazer's inner workings than most people."

"I don't know if I can do this. I can't lie."

"You're not lying. You're just postponing mentioning this until we fully know the truth, that's all. And if they ask if Stargazer has had any strange happenings that could be related to this, just punt. And please, Eva, calm down. Take an Ativan or something and relax. Immediately after you're done there, come back to Stargazer. Good luck. I gotta go."

"Wait! What if ...? Larry? Larry, are you there?"

2I

"Felicity, as the hospital's spokesperson, how do you explain the shutdown?" Joie, the CNN affiliate WBCD TV reporter, asked.

"First, I would like to extend my personal, and the hospital's, sincerest sympathies to the patients and families affected by this horrible event. I want to reassure everyone that everything is being done to find out what happened and who's responsible. Also, I want to say that Sarasota General Hospital and other health-care facilities are here tending to and transporting our patients to their facilities as needed. Also, all of the appropriate authorities have been notified and are on-site or on their way. That includes our local police, state troopers, the FBI, and the governor's office. Be assured we follow all the appropriate federal, state, and regional hospital crisis procedures as well.[12] Now, Joie, as for your question, I don't have that answer yet. I'm going to defer right now to Eva Glanston from Stargazer Systems, our infrastructure provider, to tell us what they know. Eva."

"Thank you, Felicity. I, too, want to extend my personal, as well as Stargazer's, sympathy to everyone harmed or affected by this terrible event and to assure everyone that we'll assist authorities in every way we can to find out exactly what happened and who's responsible. And although Stargazer is happy to be here to assist in the investigation, we're uncertain as of yet what central event caused this catastrophe. Let me say, too, that although I do have knowledge of the technical aspects of this hospital's infrastructure installation, I'm not our company's technical expert. However, I just finished talking to Mr. Larry Demarseco, head of security and networks at Stargazer, and he will provide more information as needed."

The crowd of reporters, panicked families of patients and staff, and onlookers stirs and shouts more questions. Eva raises a hand to silence them.

"I am able to say that, based on my understanding of the way this hospital's network is designed, wired, controlled, and protected, the selective decontrol of certain services and devices but not others as occurred here—making some service areas go dark or become inoperable, then sparing other service areas and leaving only one remaining dark—seems to eliminate ordinary equipment malfunction as a cause. The probability of all that happening from the ordinary and expected breakdown of one, or even two, component devices is extremely low. We've incorporated too much redundancy and too many fail-safe measures for that to happen."

"Eva, if the cause is not a simple equipment malfunction, how else could this happen?" Cindy Tasker, reporter for YourNetNews, a start-up, internet-based, real-time, streaming news service, asks.

"As I said, we don't yet know, but every person in my company having anything to do with the hospital's hardware- and software-infrastructure network has been notified and is already working on it."

"Eva, is it possible this could be an act of terrorism or a heinous aggression committed by a disgruntled patient or doctor? Maybe a hospital or Stargazer employee?" Joie asks.

"It's possible."

"Could this be in any way connected to a hostile nation entity—ISIS or Russia?" another reporter shouts.

"Anything's possible, but I don't see how they would have done it. The hospital network is an extremely sophisticated, fully integrated, and secure system using state-of-the-art software and hardware technology. It's fully encrypted with layers of multiple password-protected portals, threads of engineered-in redundancy, and plenty of error-checking methodology. Moreover, the details of these systems are proprietary to our company and closely guarded secrets. There are long chains of interwoven sequences of encrypted passwords and other safeguards guaranteeing a completely protected environment for proprietary company and client information. The entire system is installed, managed, and supported by us, Stargazer Systems, a totally US-owned and -operated company with an international reach specializing in secure hospital systems. There's no third-party involvement. I can say, for example, that the hospital's lighting systems are very complicated; they are not wired like a home, where they're simply connected to an electric service panel with a circuit breaker controlling each room. That's the best I can offer right now."

"Eva, it seems like you're saying your hospital network is so fail-safe that only someone with intimate knowledge of its design, or in charge of its operation, could make this terrible event happen. You make it sound like this could *only* have been an inside job. Is that what you're saying?" Tasker asks.

"No, I didn't mean that," Eva says, now worried she might say too much.

"But, Eva, you're telling us it couldn't have originated from within the equipment software or hardware itself, and you just can't walk into a room and accidentally flip some switches to make it happen. You'd have to understand the entire network to make this happen. So, doesn't that leave only some sort of intentional breach?" Joie says.

"Well, put that way, yes, that's one possible logical

conclusion, but here again, Joie, as I said, our system is very secure, so answering 'no' would be equally logically correct," Eva says, now broaching territory between truth and lie, where she does not want to be.

"Eva, has Stargazer Systems had any of their installations fail the way Beaches End's did this morning? Have any of your client installations, including this one or even your offices, been hacked, violated, or breached in any way?"

"I ... I, uh, can't answer that at this time as I might not be privy to that kind of information. I'm certain, as head of security, Mr. Demarseco can tell you more in the coming days. Be assured we'll be looking into every possible explanation, including what you just mentioned," Eva says, feeling guilty, complicit, dishonest.

"I'm sorry, but is it that you don't know or do know but can't say?" Joie asks.

"We'll share all relevant information with you as soon as it comes to our attention," Eva says.

"Eva, one more question, please. Where are Stargazer Systems' Beaches End General Hospital's engineering, development, and support teams located? You know, where all the relevant documentation might be?" Joie asks.

"Right here, in Beaches End," Eva says on her way out.

"Tony, Joie here," Joie says, calling Anthony D'Nochio, the retired chief detective at the Beaches End Police

Department, now WBCD TV network's lead criminal investigator. "You heard about what happened at the hospital this morning, right?"

"I did. My police radio has been buzzin' like a swarm of angry bees. Whaddya need?"

"Are you familiar with Stargazer Systems here in Beaches End?"

"Like the back of my hand, which you don't want to know if it's comin' at you, if you know what I mean?"

"I'll remember that, Tony. Look, I don't trust what their rep was saying at the press conference. I need you to obtain some urgent info for me in the way only you know how. I need to know if ..."

22

"Eva, please, shut the door," Larry Demarseco says. "I want to start by saying I listened to the press conference, and you were damn impressive and you held your own well. But with that said, I really don't understand what the hell happened here at Stargazer this weekend. You know our policy on visitors, and letting them roam around wherever the hell they feel like it isn't one of them."

"Larry, I didn't—"

"He left your sight and possibly breached our security. There are no excuses for that! Now we have to decide whether to notify corporate, the authorities, the public, or who knows who else and report that Stargazer likely suffered a physical breach and possibly an intellectual property breach. Keep in mind, it was only a lousy company directory and some discarded trash, if he took them at all, but still. And we don't have a clue what was in the trash. Could have been vital."

"Wait. Don't we *have* to report this to somebody?"

"I don't know, Eva. I've been trying to think this through since we last spoke. You know, my ass is on the line here if he really stole these things!"

"I feel badly for you, Larry, and I understand your situation. I can only imagine how you feel, you being head of security and all."

"Do you realize how poorly this will reflect on me if it's found out we were possibly breached? So much for my security systems and hard-built reputation.

"Look, if this gets out, I'm cooked. My reputation as security chief is shot. Remember, to our customers, we sell security. We *are* security."

"But isn't it true if we say nothing now, it will eventually become public knowledge anyway and come back on us demonstrating a lack of transparency and honesty? Whenever this becomes public, our reputation as a secure company may be damaged far more than if we were just honest up front."

"From my perspective, Eva, we must protect our company first, then our clients, then the public. Here are our choices as I see them. We could call the cops, the FBI, all the authorities, tell them to come over—and they will be here any minute, anyway—show them the video, and see what they think. Then what? It hits the papers with the headline STARGAZER SYSTEMS ROBBED OF VITAL HOSPITAL NETWORK INFORMATION – POSSIBLY LINKED TO HOSPITAL SHUTDOWN. Do you want that, Eva?"

"No, I guess not."

"Neither do I. So, maybe we just say nothing to the authorities just yet and do a little investigation of our own? Just me and you, you know? And think about this, too. How do we know what he did is even related to what happened at the hospital? I mean, he's here Saturday morning and, maybe at the worst, takes a company directory and some trash, and hours later, the hospital goes down? How does that prove a relationship, especially in such a short span of time? It's not like he stole our *Here's How to Take Down a Hospital* manual."

"I'm listening, Larry."

"Look, I've been searching my brain for hours to fully connect the dots. The only possibility, and this seems very remote, is that Wellcome was planning this for a long time, studied copious numbers of books, journals, and blogs to learn how to do it, and scouted our facilities. Then maybe all he needed was a few passwords buried deep in the bowels of the company. Could he have gotten that from some trash? Yes, possibly, but low probability. And then, after all that, he puts it together in a matter of hours? Now, Eva, tell me, who would really believe that?"

"I'm still listening, Larry."

"And one more thing, Eva. Let's assume the worst case—that there *is* a connection between what he took and the hospital hack. What we don't know is whether he's even the same person who used the information to shut down the hospital. Maybe it was someone else—an agent for a terrorist organization, perhaps. Or maybe Wellcome was hired to steal documents, then turn over what he got and disappear. Turning him in for petty theft wouldn't help solve that puzzle, now would it, Eva?"

"Look, Larry, what you're saying does make some sense, but not notifying the authorities … I don't know about that, either. It doesn't sit well with me."

"Eva, look, it was just some trash, for Christ's sake. Think about this. The alarms went off as he left and before you could say your goodbye and explain. He might have assumed the alarms were about him, but he wouldn't have known for sure. And since we haven't contacted him, nor have the authorities, nobody is banging down his door for answers. That being the case, and we never really saw him leave with anything, then it never happened, and who would be the wiser? Am I right? So, Eva, maybe he wasn't even ever here. I'll head over to security, check the guest login book, and pull Don Brown aside and make sure he understands Wellcome was never here. You deal with any reporters who call or come by."

"Well, I think you make a crucial point, Larry, that if he did take something, he must have counted on not being seen and getting away with it, particularly if he is going to show up here again. But if he didn't take anything, then it wouldn't matter to him at all if he were seen doing what you saw. And you're also right about what was potentially stolen—it wouldn't be missed by anyone. Who would know, or care, about a missing directory? And who pays attention to their trash?"

"Hang on a second, Eva, I need to get this call."

"What is it, Larry? You're pale as a sheet. You don't look so good."

"Eva, I had my investigators do a background check on our Mr. Wellcome. That was them calling. Quentin Wellcome is bogus! They queried every possible trail, and it leads to nowhere. I had them look at police records, speeding tickets, felonies, misdemeanors, sexual offenses, court documents, address information, phone numbers, civil judgments, properties owned, and much more. The license on his bike is a phony—it was a yet-to-be-issued plate number. How would anyone know the up-to-the-minute motorcycle plate number yet to be issued? Maybe he works there, I don't know. Unbelievable! His e-mail address is fictitious. It is now disabled and not associated with any e-mail client, and your e-mail threads were deleted from the cloud server. His entire web being is encrypted in blockchain methodology and untraceable to any person. As far as we can tell—and I can tell you they looked—he left no fingerprints, and unless he is a felon, it wouldn't matter. And nothing to swab for DNA. It's as if he never existed, was never here."

"So, Larry, I guess he isn't coming back to work."

23

"Joie, sweetheart, Tony D'Nochio here. I hope I didn't wake you. So, I did what you asked. I had an associate of mine talk to a Don Brown, the security guard who works weekends for Stargazer and let me tell you there are some funny shenanigans goin' on over there. After a complete and thorough investigation by my people, I can tell you they had a visit from someone who doesn't exist. That's what I said: *doesn't exist.* So, listen up, and I'll fill you in on everything."

Eva and Joie shake hands at Stargazer and have a seat in Eva's office.

"Eva, thanks so much for meeting me this morning. I know you were pretty hesitant about me stopping by, but there's a lot on my mind from the press conference earlier this morning. No matter how hard I look at what happened at the hospital, I always come back to the conclusion that something must have happened to the system your company manufactured and installed there.

I don't believe your company did anything intentional to cause the hospital to go dark, but I now have reason to believe your company has information that may be pertinent to the hack."

"Joie, we have nothing to hide. Anything I can do to help, I'll do."

"Okay, then. Has your company experienced any suspicious events, including possible breaching of your facilities, loss of documentation, software codes, or theft of any of your clients' systems documentation? And if so, what did you do about it? Did you report said breaches or theft? And if so, to whom?"

"Nothing for certain or definitively related to the hospital," Eva says, smart enough to gather from Joie's question that Joie knows something and that hedging isn't going to work.

"Okay, then. Tell me about the circumstances surrounding the visit you had with a Quentin Wellcome this weekend and the details surrounding his hurried exit from the building."

"I thought you came to chat about the hospital."

"I should add that when I signed in to the logbook today, I didn't see Mr. Wellcome's name there. More worrisome is that there was a sloppy Wite-Out job where his name should have been and a false name written in its place. That's not good, you know, Eva, removing potential evidence. I know for a fact he signed in when he was here yesterday. Have you notified the authorities yet? Look, I'm out of time and out of patience. My investigators tell me that Wellcome was here and that he left under seemingly suspicious circumstances."

"Joie, before we go any further, I really need to have Larry Demarseco, my security chief, here with me. Give me a minute, please," Eva says, then hurries over to Larry's office.

"Hello, Joie. Good morning to you. I'm Larry Demarseco. You have some questions?"

"Yes, Larry. I have reason to believe—cancel that—I *know* that, yesterday, Eva had a visit from a Quentin Wellcome, whose behavior here was felt by you to be suspicious. I'm told he left in a hurry with alarms going off."

"May I ask who told you that?"

"Of course, Larry, but as a reporter with good ethics, I can't reveal my sources."

"What happens if I don't answer?"

"I'll include in my report that Larry Demarseco refused to answer my questions and report what I already know anyway. It won't look good for you if I do that. And I'll get my answers in other ways. Either way, I know he was here, and you may suffer a major loss of credibility when the truth eventually comes out, especially if he was involved in the hospital hack. Also, Larry, having your security guard remove an entry from your company's visitor log is not only a bad idea—and I'm not a lawyer—but it might be a felony, as it is an act in support of a potential crime. Imagine explaining that to the swarm of feds who'll be flocking here soon and discover you are hiding facts."

"What about thinking of our answers and us as your sources and become confidential that way?" Larry says in a Hail Mary attempt to keep his name and the company's name out of the news.

"We're playing games here, Larry. I don't like games, but I am good at them. I don't reveal my sources if I'm asked not to. Period. However, if you *are* the story and not just the source of the story, then that's different. I report stories, just not always sources. Enough. Let's stop this nonsense. Now, I think there's something you need to tell me, possibly even show me. Isn't that so, Larry? Eva?"

"You're good, Joie. I read you loud and clear. Follow me."

"Nice video room. And I was wondering, why do you carry a strange-looking red phone and a regular phone?" Joie asks Larry as they enter the security surveillance room.

"The red phone's our hyper-secure, multipurpose, Stargazer-employee communication device. I'm glad you asked, because I hope it will serve as an example of just how technologically sophisticated we are here and how seriously we take security. It looks about like a regular cell phone in size and shape but is quite different. The case is integral with the phone, and each case and phone is unique to the assigned user."

"Oh? How so?" Joie asks.

"The case has a series of LED lights, each one a different color that signals different things. Green means power is on, all systems go. Orange indicates the phone's on signal standby. Red means a Stargazer-wide security alert, for example. On the case is a series of cameras with lenses oriented to capture the image of the user's face when the phone is held in talking mode. The phone will not function in talking mode unless it recognizes the face of the person assigned to it. That's our FacePrint technology. You'll also see on the case a set of five fingerprint-reading pads that reads the user's GripPrint, which is a unique pattern made up of the five fingerprints created by the user when the case is held in the phone talking position. Each case is custom molded to place the pads properly for each user's hand, and the phone is destroyed when the assigned user leaves the company for any reason, including if the phone is de-assigned or if we feel the user or the phone have been compromised in any way. For applications that I cannot go into with you because they involve foreign countries and high-level nation-state agencies, I can give you a tidbit more information to convey the degree of sophistication and expertise we have here at Stargazer. For example, the GripPrint fingerprint reader on the phone has a built-in pulse oximeter that tells us your instantaneous pulse wave form and resting blood oxygen saturation, baselines for both of which we have on file for comparison. This virtually eliminates someone putting the phone in the hand of a dead employee, agent, or spy.

"So, you ask why all the fuss about a phone, right? Well, it's not only a phone; it's also everything from a GPS receiver/sender recorder transmitter to a satellite telephone and communicator to a Wi-Fi hot spot to an LTE 5G relay, and so on. Most important, it can be used as a network interface into every in-house and client network."

"Can it connect to the hospital's network?" Joie asks.

"Well, yes, but it would take a lot of inside knowledge and authorization codes, not to mention passwords. Moving on, it can be dumbed down to be a highly secure phone and a hell of a lot more. Oh, and I forgot—another unique feature of the case, and why we discourage use of ordinary cell phones for secure communications, is that the phone has our proprietary VoiceEx voice-cancellation system built in that cancels, within a three-foot spherical volume all around the phone, the sound of the user's voice when speaking on the phone. That means I can stand next to you, within a three-foot radius, and not hear a word you say. Nice, huh?"

"Yes, it is!" Joie says.

"To use the phone in secure, voice-talk mode in a hostile environment, the calling party and the receiving party must also use our proprietary InstaFy two-piece security codes to enable the phone app. That code appears on a personal fob we call the UniFob. The InstaFy code is our proprietary security scheme that generates random four-digit security codes visible on every secure employee's UniFob digital readout window. The codes change randomly every millisecond. If you want to place a secure call to me, you enter my unique call code into the keypad, then press the Call button on your fob. The fob button will read your fingerprint and, if recognized, will let you bring up my name on your phone and your name on my phone. The phone will grab the last-generated fob code and send it to me and display it to you. You and I then have ten seconds to enter the unique code shown on our fobs. If our entered codes match what our fobs sent and our GripPrint fingerprints are verified, then we can talk on the red phone. I know that sounds elaborate, but it's quite easy and secure. And for secret agents, this becomes not only important but possibly a matter of life and death."

Joie nods, looking confused about the extensive detail.

"So, to answer your question, that's why two phones. I'll

finish by saying that the phone, its derivatives, support, and so on are a huge segment of our nonhospital intelligence business and, hopefully, should give you an even better idea about how sophisticated and secure Stargazer is."

"Well, that certainly is impressive and an elaborate scheme, which I suppose is necessary for secure communication," Joie says. "So, how breachable is it?"

"I never like to talk in absolutes, but on a real-world, relative, breachable scale, I'd say virtually impossible. Lord knows we've tried, even offering a $200,000 reward to anyone who finds a bug and breaches it. No winners so far."

Joie nods. "Very impressive indeed."

"Okay, let's look at the video, shall we? And before we start, I wanted to say that what we're showing you has not been turned over to any of the authorities, and it's our understanding that once you see the video and realize what we're potentially facing that you will *not* publicize it yet. Are we in agreement about this?" Larry says.

"As I said, I'm a reporter, and my job is to report the news. I don't make judgments about what news to hold back or not report because of some greater good. There have been cases where that has been an issue, but I don't know at this point if this is one of them. If I think reporting what you're about to show me would create a greater personal or public harm than not reporting it, then I may not make it public at this time, but I must say that is a very high bar. These are personal, ethical, and moral judgments and decisions, not legal ones. You don't look this up somewhere. So, show me what you've got."

24

"Okay, Joie, let's watch the video. See there, Wellcome is leaving Eva's office. At first glance, everything looks normal, right? Nothing suspicious. But look at his eyes scanning the ceiling, clearly looking for cameras. Fortunately for us, we're using our new ceiling tile–mounted, fiber-optic virtual-lens technology that we developed here. Nothing in the ceiling tiles looks like a camera or a lens. Our system's lenses are actually an array of optical fibers where each fiber terminates in a tiny crystal lens of our manufacture. The crystal lenses are integral with the ceiling tiles and distributed at irregular intervals, so no regular pattern is discernable. Groups of physical fibers with crystals at the ceiling tile end are virtually collated and aggregated by the software to form sets of distributed lenses. You'll notice the ceiling tiles have a little sparkle to them, and each sparkle is the reflection of the end of an optical glass fiber. We call our system StarrySkies. We're sure he was bothered and puzzled by the glitter and sparkle and frustrated at not seeing conventional cameras.

"Continuing with the video, here he is heading in the direction of the restroom, again scanning the ceiling. Now, look at the desk he's approaching on the right, just in front of him. See on the corner of the desk, there's something that looks like a magazine or brochure. Actually, when we finally zoomed in, it's a copy of our company directory. Leaving directories out on a desk, of course, is against company policy. Anyway, look at what he does next. Without missing a beat, he pulls a David Copperfield and places his backpack over the directory, then picks up the backpack *and* the directory, together, in one piece before he heads to the men's room. He leaves a company brochure, the one Eva gave him, in place of the directory in an attempt, I suppose, to fool our people watching the video monitors into thinking the directory's still there. That almost worked. It took him only a few seconds, which is why we missed it on the first look. Then we see him entering the men's room, where, alas, we don't have cameras, as it's illegal in most situations to put cameras where people have a reasonable expectation of privacy. I'm sure he knows this."

"Is that it, with the directory?" Joie asks.

"Well, yes," Larry says.

"So, he took a directory into the men's room."

"It seems that way."

"That doesn't sound like a crime to me."

"But it's *how* he took it, Joie. That sleight of hand, the grabbing the directory and backpack together in one piece that bothers me."

"I'd give him an Oscar for Best Carrying Efficiency in an Office Setting for being clever in minimizing what he has to carry. I mean, really, guys?" Joie says.

"Okay, then. Let's fast-forward a bit. Look here. He stops at this desk on his way back from the men's room. Then, in another matter of seconds, it looks like he grabs some trash from the trash can, and who knows what was in there? Could have been postal mail, company e-mails, work product printouts. Then there's some movement, like he's shuffling the pages before he stuffs them into his backpack. I say 'looks like' because whatever he's doing is hidden by his body bending over hiding it, and the lenses couldn't pick that up. Then, I'm thinking, when he leaves the building, the printouts and the directory are likely in his backpack, gift wrapped with birthday paper. I say this because Don Brown, the security guard, looked through his backpack when he was leaving and said he recalled seeing the same two gift-wrapped packages."

"So he came in with the two gift-wrapped packages?" Joie asks.

"Yes, he did," Larry says.

"And he left with two gift-wrapped packages. Wow. Scary stuff. Do you know what was in those packages when he came in? Did security check this?"

"No need to make light of this. No, we don't know what was in the packages upon entering or exiting."

"So, do you know for a fact that he left Stargazer with any proprietary company property?"

"Well, no, and that's the dilemma," Larry says.

"If you can't connect his putting the directory, and possibly the trash, into his backpack, then leaving your building with those items, how can you say, much less prove, he actually stole anything?"

A stunned and puzzled Eva and a deflated Larry look at each other, unsure of what to say.

"One more thing," Joie says. "You said earlier that you don't know specifically what kind of papers or documents were in the discarded trash, correct?"

"That's right," Larry says.

"Eva, do you?" Joie asks.

"I have no clue," Eva says.

"So, can either of you say with any degree of confidence that what he may have stolen could have been used to elaborately hack and turn a hospital dark?"

"No, I can't," Larry says.

"Neither can I," Eva says. "Not at all."

"Look, I want to get to the bottom of all of this as much as you do, but so far I've heard here no solid proof of any wrongdoing by Wellcome, much less anything potentially connected to the hospital breach as I had initially thought, and wrongly so on my part. It was a belief I needed to prove, or not, after the odd press conference. I hope you understand," Joie says. "So, what are your plans now?"

"Our engineers are working hard to figure out what went wrong over at Beaches End. We also need to talk to Dr. White in his capacity as medical-technical liaison between Stargazer and the hospital. We need to tell him about the video, show it to him if he wants to see it, and the little else we know," Larry says. "I think that's the best move at this point."

"That sounds fair, but you really don't have much to go on right now," Joie says.

"It's true, we don't, but the right next thing to do is to tell Dr. White. He's likely going to make this matter very personal. He's a great medical diagnostician and has an excellent way of looking at things. I'm betting if any of his patients are harmed—and even if not—he won't quit until whoever's messing with patients in his town is arrested. I'll call him as soon as we're done here," Larry says. "Joie, if you agree to hold off reporting what you saw here, I'll see to it that you're privy to all our investigative work and have the exclusive news rights to the entire story. Deal?"

"I'll discuss this with my producer first, but assume we have a deal."

"I'll be in touch as soon as I know something," Larry says.

"Oh, one more thing," Joie says. "Did you happen to do a background check on Mr. Wellcome?"

"Yes, that's the other thing. He doesn't exist."

"That's what my investigators tell me as well," Joie replies, reassured by Larry's honesty.

"Joie, excuse me a minute. That's my secure phone beeping me," Larry says, looking down at his phone. "I don't believe it. No way. This can't be happening!" he says, barely containing himself, his hand shaking as he shows Joie his phone screen bearing an avatar and two words: *was here.*

25

MAY. *Diary, can't stay long. I need to make note here of my Stargazer hack and get back enjoying the havoc and mayhem of my work. I think Larry Demarseco had to change his shorts when he saw my avatar after I broke into his phone and network. I know he saw it 'cause I got a call-answered message on my phone.*

The office is going to go crazy about the hospital, and I must say it is going to be very hard to act innocent while listening to all the speculation about the hacker. They will ask me who I think is doing it, and I'll just say it could be anyone.

Maribeth will likely say the person must be a real sicko and have no human feelings. I'll feel sick when she says that. I'll want so much to say to her, "No, Maribeth, that isn't necessarily so. It's me, I have feelings, and they are crying out to be heard."

HACK 3 SUMMARY

Date of Hack: May 10

What/Who: Stargazer's big shot Larry Demarseco's "secure phone"!

What I Did: Sent him my Cossack hat as my way of saying "Your secure phone sucks."

Consequences: Left him deeply worried about all this hacking. Got access to their network.

Terror-Creation Factor for Me: 9/10 = Excellent

26

"Charlie, your phone's making noise. You're not on call, are you?" Heather says, both of them in bed devouring the Sunday *New York Times*.

"Nope, not on call. Where is it?" White says, not looking up from the book review section and trying to avoid getting out of bed.

"Here's your phone, sweetheart," Heather says, tossing White's still-ringing phone as she flops back in bed. "It's Howie Kasoff," Heather says, having looked at the caller ID. Why is the hospital's Chief of Medicine calling you on a Sunday? "Are you playing with him today?"

"We have a one o'clock tee time on King's Dunes. He'd better not be bailing on me!"

He answers the phone. "Howie, you're not bailing for today, are you? We're still— . . . What? Say that again. . . . Holy Christ, you've got to be kidding. The power, lights, everything, stopped? . . . A patient died? Who? . . . What the hell happened?" White hears a beep for call waiting and checks the ID. "Howie, can you hold a second? I've got Larry Demarseco trying to reach me on the other line."

He switches over to the other call. "Larry, can you hold a second? I've got Howie Kasoff on the other line."

"What's going on, Charlie?" Heather asks.

"Hang on a second, Heather," White says before switching back over.

"Howie, I'm back. I'm betting Larry has something to tell me about all this. I asked him to wait. There's an emergency hospital board meeting now. I'll be there as soon as I can. See you soon."

He clicks back to Larry again. "Hey, Larry, sorry about that; I've got two calls going on here. Howie told me a little about what happened at the hospital, and Heather and I just turned on the news. What's that? You're coming over? All right, but make it quick; I have to get to the hospital pronto. I'll see you soon."

"What is it? What's going on, Charlie?" Heather asks.

"Heather, get decent. Larry Demarseco's coming over. I'll fill you in. Sit in with us, will you?"

"Hey, Larry, come on in. Can I get you something to drink? Iced tea, maybe?" Heather says.

"Iced tea sounds fine. Some sugar would be perfect."

"Are you up to date on what happened at the hospital this morning, and do you know what caused it?" White asks.

133

"Mainly just what I heard on the news and what Eva told me, but I've not been to the hospital yet. I'm actually on my way. No, I don't know yet what caused it. The hospital called Eva to be there representing Stargazer. Listen, Charlie, yesterday we had an unusual incident at Stargazer that may be related. It's a long shot, but I thought you should hear it from me first; that's why I'm here. We're committed to figuring this out, and complete transparency is key."

"Okay, let's hear it, but please make it quick; I've got to get to the hospital," White says, the three of them now sitting in the living room.

"So, I'm telling you this in your capacity as chair of the hospital's medical board and your capacity as medical-technical liaison between Stargazer's installation and the hospital. You know more about the medical and technical aspects of this installation than anybody. I don't know if what I'm about to tell you means much, but I'll let you decide. Early yesterday morning, an individual who called himself Quentin Wellcome had a meeting at Stargazer with Eva, ostensibly for a position in our company."

"What do you mean 'called himself' and 'ostensibly'?"

"I'll explain that in a minute. The issue is that he was seen during a review of our physical plant video surveillance displaying what I consider suspicious behavior. Eva and I, and maybe others, are at odds over whether it was suspicious or not and what it means."

"What was he doing?"

"It appears he took a copy of our company directory into the men's room."

"Are you joking? And?"

"He also took some trash from a trash can. I understand this sounds foolish, but I need to go with my gut, and if you saw him doing it, you might think differently. What I can't say is if he left the building with them."

"What am I missing here, Larry? Heather, did I miss something? You sure it wasn't a copy of *Playboy* or something?"

"Charlie, stop it. That's not nice," Heather says.

"Just kidding. But I see what you mean, Larry. *Playboy* would be far easier to understand than your company directory and more fun! Kidding again. Anyway, what's in your company directory that might be of interest to him and be related to the event at the hospital?"

"I know it sounds like a nothing burger; I get it. It was more the way he took it, hiding it under his backpack and all. The point is, I think he may have left the building with the directory and the trash. The trash could possibly have very sensitive and compromising computer printouts."

"Do you have video footage of him leaving your building with any of that?"

"No. As I said, not leaving with it. Taking it, yes. Leaving, no."

"What do you want me to say about that?"

"Do you want to see the video? I have it right here on a flash drive. If you see it, you'll know what I mean," Larry offers.

"Not now. I can't. I need to get going to the hospital. I believe you."

"Are you sure? At least you'll get a look at Mr. Quentin Wellcome. You might recognize him."

"Later, Larry, maybe. I need to pass at the moment, I really gotta go."

"Okay, later it is. I just needed to have you know this now, Charlie, so if it ever comes back that there was a relationship between this Quentin Wellcome and the events at the hospital, I want my bringing this up now on the record."

"Consider that done. Is that all?"

"Oh, there is one more thing. We have this hyper-secure phone system used throughout our company. It connects all employees who have the need to have one with one another and with the major systems within the company and through that to customer installations. It's a smartphone on steroids, with firewalls to match. At least, I'd thought so. With the correct passwords and authorization procedures, a user can access most internal systems and networks at Stargazer. It can behave the same as a terminal at the office but is even more protected. For someone having the special passwords, and a hell of lot of special knowledge and skill, they could waltz right through Stargazer networks."

"I'm listening."

"We even put a reward out for anyone who can breach the phone's security. Lots of folks tried; they all failed," Larry continues.

"Got it. Am I hearing a bit of 'The lady doth protest too much, methinks, Gertrude'? What happened that you haven't told me yet?"

"Take a look at this," Larry says, showing Charlie the image displayed on his hyper-secure phone. "This image appeared on my phone the day after Wellcome was there."

"Was your Mr. Wellcome wearing a Cossack hat?" Heather asks.

"That would be funny if not so sad," Larry says.

"Sorry. Didn't mean to make light of it."

"So, someone breached your phone, maybe your servers, and possibly even your networks, maybe the hospital. And you think it's Wellcome. Is that what you're saying, Larry? Is there more you need to tell me?" an insightful and now growing very worried White says.

"Yes, one more thing."

"Great. Before you tell me the 'one more thing,' let me make sure I know what you've told me so far," White says. "Saturday, a Mr. Quentin Wellcome, whoever the hell he is, visits Stargazer, ostensibly looking for a job. I am assuming you did a full background on him before he came, right? While at Stargazer, he maybe steals company information, and maybe he says thank you by sending a Cossack hat–wearing avatar to a Stargazer secure phone. By the next morning, Beaches End General Hospital, a customer of Stargazer, suffers a major network collapse resulting in a death and lots of pain and suffering. We're thinking this was a human-caused failure that could only have been orchestrated by someone with significant inside technical information, the right hacking skill set, and the means to do it. And, I might add, be a real sicko to cause this kind of harm. And of all the possible candidates for doing this, your pick is Quentin Wellcome. Correct?" White says.

"Yes," Larry says.

"So, some questions," White says. "First, could the information allegedly taken from Stargazer be used to do what was done at the hospital? Next, could he, whoever *he* is, have the ability and wherewithal to use that information presumably stolen to cause the havoc at the hospital? And further, if he did take information that could be used maliciously, was it even he that used it, as opposed to him giving it or selling it to others to use? Or are there other explanations here? We obviously can't answer these questions yet. Have you considered that Mr. Wellcome's behavior is a red herring and his presence at Stargazer is a mere coincidence? Have you considered the hacker might be a disgruntled employee? One of your coders, for example. And, if so, is he a lone wolf? Or is this the work of a nation-state? Russia, China, North Korea? Jesus. No, not Jesus. Also, shouldn't we prove there was not an explainable equipment malfunction that caused the hospital blackouts before we say there wasn't?"

"Exactly, Charlie. These are all excellent points. You're right. Maybe I am assuming too much here," Larry says.

"What kind of a name is Quentin Wellcome, anyway?" Heather asks.

"Am I missing something here? Why aren't we arresting this Mr. Wellcome? Bringing him in for questioning? And, Larry, you said there was one more thing. I can't wait to hear it," White says.

"No big deal. Quentin Wellcome. He doesn't exist."

27

"Oh, Charlie, you're home. I was getting worried. Oh, look, it's midnight already," Heather says, woken from where she was dozing, listening to the news about the hack, a wineglass emptied of its oaky chardonnay on the floor next to the couch where she lies.

"The hospital is a mess, Heather. They're shaking in their scrubs over there. Nurses, doctors, staff, patients. They're afraid it will happen again. Everyone's dreading the coming night. Patients are canceling their admissions and testing, and the few remaining hospitalized patients are self-discharging against medical advice. They all went over to Sarasota General or elsewhere. A few old folks with no family around just plain left. The staff is incredibly fearful for their patients on life support. We're getting them out of there, anyway. No one believes the authorities can do much to prevent this from happening again. Everyone's looking to me for answers, especially the board. But what can I really do?" White says.

"They know you, Charlie. They don't expect you to fix

it yourself. It's your guidance they want. Some comfort, you know. How you might handle it."

"Not that simple. All the authorities were at the meeting—state police, the FBI, local cops. Everyone and anyone concerned or in a possible helping role, including Larry, was there. The FBI believes this was most likely an intentional hack and not the result of equipment malfunction. The FBI will need to access all the computers and servers and scrub them for evidence, which will take a while. Oh, get this—the FBI said what happened there is the result of the new weapon of mass destruction. Forget the semi-automatic AR-15. It is now the fully automatic … *keyboard*! At one hundred clicks a minute, it's *tap, click, boom!* You're all dead. And all done from the comfort and convenience of your own home. Nice."

"Charlie, stop it. That sounds so frightening," Heather says.

"Trust me, it is," White says. "We had a long talk about what to do next, and the answer is that there's not much we can do right now. The sad story is that all we can do is regroup, be alert, and hope it never happens again. I'm sure Larry and the FBI will tell us if there's anything to do on the tech side—you know, firewalls, encryption, multilayer passwords, all that stuff. All I know is we're sitting ducks for whoever did this.

"What do you say, kid? It's late. Time to hit the sack. No

telling what tomorrow will bring," White says, helping Heather up and, with a firm hand, taking her to their bed.

"Doesn't your new PA start tomorrow?"

"Oh, right. I'd better bring him up to speed on what happened at the hospital. I wonder if he knows?"

28

MID-MAY. *Diary, I'm nervous, excited, and, as my buddy Dr. Norther would say, conflicted. He'd be happy to know that not only is my brain on fire but, finally, so is my dick. Did I talk dirty to you, Diary? Sorry.*

Here's the thing. As far as I can tell, I did a lot of damage over at the hospital, and among the billions and billions of neurons and synapses in my head telling me, "Good job, Harken," there are these rogue gang neurons banging around inside the walls of my skull saying, "Harken, you are a jerk." Ergo, the conflict. Also, being told I am a jerk, especially by myself, I do not need.

I'm still going to go through with my Righteous Quest plan, don't get me wrong, and I've got a few doozy ideas figured out, too. "Ooh, ooh, tell me one," I hear you say. Okay, here's what's next. I read about leukemia and how to make it look like someone has it. First, I need to make their white count really high.

I'll select one of White's well patients and change the white blood cell count result from the normal range of four thousand to eleven thousand to, say, a high thirty thousand or even a very high forty thousand—yippee!—to make it look like the patient has leukemia. I'll be around when he sees it, and when he shows me the result, I'll look sad. Here's the algorithm for my plan for leukemia:

This is very, very good if I say so myself, and thank you very much for your page-fanning applause.

So, Diary, guess what? I start work for Dr. White tomorrow, and I have a surprise for him. If I'm lucky, he'll never know about it. Here's what it is. I have an app[13] that will let me listen to every word spoken within listening distance of White's smartphone.

I noticed when I was there, White always keeps his phone in his lab coat's side pocket when he's walking around, then he puts it on the desk when in an exam room when he is with a patient, and on the lab counter when he stops there to dictate his notes or chat with the nurses. That means I can listen in whenever and wherever he's talking, no matter if he's on the office landline phone or his smartphone. It's like I'm always there at his side. And if he puts his phone on his end table at home when he's in bed, I'll hear every pillow-talk conversation with his wife, even during sex. Well, if he talks during sex, that is. Or if he even has sex. Hmm, this could be a good way of getting to know his wife.

So I'll use one of those apps I can buy—or better, one I can use for free—to remotely turn on his cell phone's microphone and listen in, without him having to turn on the phone or letting him know I'm listening in. I jotted down the link. One, mainly for a PC, not a phone, allows me to remotely record and listen to the microphone of anyone's computer.[14] It will also let me record every keystroke a person makes—that's called a keylogger—and let me turn their operating system on or off and even turn on their camera and control it. Another app[15] lets me listen in to everything in a phone's range. I downloaded one of these phone programs and changed it to do exactly what I want, including making the target phone not ring or vibrate.

Sally said I'll be shadowing Dr. White and seeing some of his patients with him the first week or so, but she said not to *expect too much of that. She said it's okay if I read some and talk to the staff to learn more about the office. All sounds good to me.*

Oh, Diary. Sally telling me to read journals made me think of a funny story I read about Frank W. Abagnale,[16] *another idol of mine. As a teenager, he was on the FBI's Ten Most Wanted list for impersonating an airline pilot, though he never piloted a plane, and a lawyer, though he never practiced law, among other professions. While on the run, he moved into a no-kids apartment building and told everyone he was a pediatrician, thinking with no kids around no one would bother him there or ask questions. Unfortunately, some retired pediatricians living there were asking him too many questions, and to put an end to it, he did something very cool. He went to the medical library and read abstracts of the most recent articles from current pediatric research. Then, instead of waiting to be asked questions, he asked them questions first based on whatever he'd just read. He'd say, "Hey, Doc, did you read that recent article in the American Journal of Pediatrics on childhood rectalitis? Or, "Hey, Doc, what's your take on pediatric lupus erythematosus?" Knowing docs never read journals to keep up to date, they started to avoid him, which solved his problem. "Can't talk right now. Catch me later," they'd say. He wrote a book about his life called* Catch Me If You Can.[17] *I may try that on Dr. White. "Hey, Dr. White, what's your thinking on acute frenzomatic hypercoagulable leukocytosis?" I'm betting he'll say, "Uh, can't talk right now,*

Harry. Get back to me on that, will ya?"

You know what, Diary? Abagnale came from a screwed-up family, too. Diary, seriously, why do all my idols come from screwed-up families?

Because all families are screwed up, you say?

Monday, I'll do some social engineering. I'm going to the medical library to register under Dr. White's name and take out a few journals. I'll put a few on my desk and a couple in my lab coat pocket where they can be seen.

Diary, here's the thing: I can't get Maribeth off my mind. I'll hopefully see her tomorrow. One day this week, I'm going to ask her to have some coffee with me after work. This is scary to me on many fronts. For one, I can't let her ask me too many questions I can't and don't want to answer. I think I've got that under control, though. More worrisome is, can I handle the tender spot inside me yearning for her touch?

29

"Good morning, Jack," White says to Jack Sloan, his old friend and new patient. Jack is sitting in White's private office fidgeting nervously, waiting for his complete physical exam.

"Good morning to you, Charlie. Say, what do you make of the hospital going dark yesterday? I hear it was a war zone there. They say the hospital was hacked."

"The feds are on it, Jack. A terrible thing, for sure. There's not a lot I have to say. They really don't know for certain what caused it; they're looking into that possible hacking you mentioned."

"Charlie, I gotta ask you a question of a different nature. I'm getting a complete physical today, right?"

"Right."

"Does that include a rectal exam?"

"Is that what you're worried about, my friend?"

"Not worried, just haven't figured how I'd ever be able to face you again on the golf course or when we're out to dinner with our wives with everyone knowing you had your Mr. Pointer Finger up my ass. I'm going to ask you to pass the salt, and all I'll see is your huge finger moving toward me. That's all. Oh, and Mr. Pointer Finger doesn't wear a little hat, does he?"

"Oh, no, Jack. But he does wear a boot with a spur at the end. I give it a little spin just before entry. Just kidding. We all have to have that done, and I'm pretty quick about it. But before we start, it's imperative that I say this, being that it's your first office visit with me. I want you to know that I have strict rules in this office, friend, or no friend. Outside the office, I'm regular Charlie. But here, I take my job, your life, and your well-being very seriously. In this office, I'm your doctor, not your friend. Confidant, maybe. Friend, no.

"First, what we discuss in this office stays in this office. For, example, if, when you leave today, you ask me to say hi to Heather for you, I won't. She won't know you were here unless *you* tell her. I don't discuss my patients with her, mutual friends or not. Next, if, because we're friends, you can't tell me what keeps you up at night, how you and Janice are getting along, if you're having an affair, if you can't get an erection, if you're constipated, then you're at the wrong doctor's office, my friend. To be honest, that's one reason I don't like having my friends as patients; it can deprive them of an open, honest doctor-patient relationship.

"Also, if I feel strongly about a health issue that concerns you, and you ignore my advice, I may discharge you as my patient. And by the same token, if you're unhappy with me as your physician, then you need to feel free to leave me and still show up for our tee times on the golf course. There's no reason, or need, to break up a doctor-patient relationship and a friendship at the same time. These are very delicate matters, Jack, and they do come up. One day, I might have to tell you that you have a serious disease, and that's when you'll depend on me for many things, trust and confidentiality among them. Tell me, Jack, can you agree to all that?"

"Sure, Charlie. Makes sense."

"Good, and lastly, favors. Don't ask me for any doctor favors. You don't know how many times a patient joins an exercise club or buys airline tickets, then decides he doesn't want to go and asks me to write a note that says he can't because he has leprosy, impetigo, botulism, or whatever. Come to think of it, they never have syphilis or gonorrhea. Either way, I won't write the note. Do you know why, Jack? Because if I lie for you, then you'll never trust me with the issues of your health, including those of life and death. If I act corrupt once, then I must be corrupt. So, whaddya say, Jack? Are we a go?"

"We're a go. But how come I didn't go through this when I started with Murray Cohen?"

"What's a lawyer know or care about ethics and morality?"

"Right there, Charlie."

"Okay. Now, tell me what's on your mind today. Why a physical, now?"

"Oh, do I call you Charlie, Doc, Dr. White, what?"

"Whatever you like."

"Okay, *Doc* it is. Well, I feel fine. Since I turned fifty, I just figured it was time for a complete physical."

"Sound thinking, I'd say. Let's get started."

"So, Jack, except for your blood pressure being a little high today, your exam went just fine, and you don't have any complaints. Go easy on the salt, and let me see you in a month to recheck your blood pressure. If it's high again, we'll proceed slowly before I put you on meds. We'll get some routine blood work done, and I'll call you with the results within a few days. Here's the requisition for your blood work. If you're fasting today—that is, haven't eaten since midnight—you can stop on the way out at Sand Dollar Labs right here in our building."

"Sure thing, Doc. I'll stop at the lab in the building on my way out and wait to hear from you. Say hi to Heather for me. Ha! Just kidding."

"Oh, Jack, before you leave, I want you to meet my new PA, Harry Right. He may be around to help you one day when I'm not here."

White pages, "Harry, can you stop in my office?" not realizing Righteous has heard every word using his phone app.

"Harry, this is my good friend, Jack Sloan."

"Hi, Harry. Lucky you to be working for such a great doctor."

"Thanks, Mr. Sloan. I feel that way, too. If I can ever help you out, please let me know."

"Talk soon, Jack," says White, then turns to Harry once they're alone. "Harry, hang on a minute. You probably heard about what happened at the hospital Saturday."

"Yes, I heard about it on CNN."

"The hospital was hit very hard. If there are any issues that come up related to the hospital, let me know. I've discharged all my patients, so no need for you to go over there."

"Yes, sir. Will do. Was wondering, Dr. White, what's being done to figure out what happened?"

30

EARLY JUNE. *Oh, Diary, my time has arrived. It's truly the coming of the Age of Harken Righteous. Or, better, the Age of the Rage of Harken Righteous. Today, Diary, Dr. White did a physical on his friend Jack Sloan, who got some blood work done at our lab. I'll tell you in a minute what I did, but first I need to talk to you about something else.*

You know, Diary, I just said the words what I did. But, Diary, I don't know who that I is anymore. I was named Harken Righteous when I was born, right? My mind, then, I guess, was normal. Who really knows? By the way, when I say mind, I mean how my brain works and makes me behave— act, talk, think. My brain does that. My "mind" has changed a lot over time, and maybe for the worse. It makes me so sad to think of that. I wonder if I was ever a nice person, someone who other people liked, maybe even loved. I want to be loved, Diary.[18] *You know that, don't you?*

My point is, at White's office, I told them my name was Harry Right. I told them it was to make it easier to say. I don't know why I changed my name then. It just came out of me.

It sounded so right, no pun intended, as if Harken Righteous died and Harry Right was born. Maybe my deep brain said, "Harken Righteous, it's time to start over. Harken Righteous as you know him is dead. He now lives as Harry, and as long as it will be Harry, it might as well be Harry Right."

Diary, can the brain do that without the owner—me—telling it what to do? Can Harken Righteous be born again and become Harry Right on its own? This is driving me loco!

Anyway, it's probably for the best—a new name for a new mind. Am I crazy, Diary, or am I making sense? Don't answer. Anyway, so far as I can tell, Harry Right may be eviler than Harken Righteous. Yikes, I didn't figure on that.

So, Diary, back to Jack Sloan. Here's what I did. I gave him a white count as if he has leukemia. You saw my plan. Leukemia's bad, I know, I know. What? Not nice, you say, Diary? Well, anyway, that's what I did. So, Sloan went to the lab today as White asked him to. I knew that because of the handy-dandy phone-spying app. I easily cracked the lab server and made his hacked white count show up as 32,570, instead of his perfectly normal 4,376.

Yikes!

I know the value I gave him was very high. It has to be if I want it to look like he has leukemia. I also wrote a little subroutine so that if and, likely, when White repeats the test, the value will come back 34,170. Oh, I left my signature 🗿 on the server, but you'd have to know where to look to find it.

Increasing the repeat value a bit is my little fake-lab-val

invention. I call it that because it's a fake lab value replacing a fake lab value. In a way, I could also call it "Fake Lab News." No repeat lab should ever be exactly the same as the first one. If I let that happen, that'd be really suspicious. So, I make it come back close, but not equal, to the original hacked value of 32,570, giving it the one, the only, the very special Harken Righteous, a.k.a. Harry Right, sign of fake a-u-t-h-e-n-t-i-c-i-t-y. Yeah!

I plan to catch White early in the morning before he brings up Jack's results on his desk monitor. I'll be at the office around 8:30, which is when he should get to the office after rounding at the hospital.

Oh, Diary, it's been a very long and emotional day, and my bed's calling my name. I gotta go.

Oops. Almost forgot.

HACK 4 SUMMARY

Date of Hack: June 12

What/Who: Jack Sloan's blood analyzer server.

What I Did: Changed his blood result to make it look like he has leukemia.

Consequences: His doc will be mucho upsetto.

Terror-Creation Factor for Me: 9/10 = Excellent.

155

31

"Good morning, Dr. White."

"Oh, good morning, Harry. You're here early. What's up?"

"Nothing much. Just wanted to come in. What are you looking at there?"

"Just checking up on these test re—Jesus Christ! His total white count is 32,570! That doesn't make any sense."

"Whose results, Dr. White?"

"Jack Sloan, my friend, my new patient. But his differential is normal. That's strange. You'd think with a white count that high he'd have a left-shift or some abnormal, early-form cells, like bands, in his blood. He had no signs of infection. No nodes. This doesn't make any sense, does it, Harry?"

"You're right, it doesn't, Dr. White," Righteous says, realizing White is smart and recognized the shortcut Righteous took by not changing cell types in the lab report.

"He's a healthy guy who just had a perfectly normal

exam with no complaints. I mean, it could be true, but it makes no sense. Also, his old records show he had a normal blood count three months ago when he saw his prior doc for a sinus infection with fever."

"Dr. White, your first patient is ready in room 1. Dr. White, your first patient is ready in room 1," a voice on the overhead paging system blares.

"Great. I have ten charts on my desk of calls that came in before I got here and lab reports I have to sort through to see what is urgent before I see the fifteen patients I have booked for this morning. As usual, I'm backed up before I start. And patients complain about doctors being behind.

"What to do, what to do? I need to call the lab and verify Jack's result to make sure it was his blood tube they ran and reported on. If so, I'll ask them to do a rerun of the test out of the same tube, stat, and call me here with the result. If there was a pretesting error, which can happen, then the rerun will most likely come back normal. On the other hand, if his count truly is that high, the rerun should come back close to the first result. Got that, Harry? You'd do the same thing, right, Harry?" White rattles off for Harry's benefit without waiting for a response.

"Would you like me to call them for you, Dr. White? I know you've got a lot on your plate this morning."

"Thanks, but I'll call myself." White pages Sally on her

direct page line. "Sally, after my next physical, please get the supervisor of Sand Dollar Labs on the line and interrupt me when you do. I want to speak to them about Jack Sloan's results. Ask him to have Jack Sloan's purple-top[19] and his CBC and diff report ready. I'm starting my physical now."

"Dr. White, you said 'if there was a pretesting error.' Whaddya mean by that?" Righteous asks.

"It's an error in the handling of specimens before testing, like the tech placing the wrong patient name labels on tubes,[20] that kind of thing. Do you know what the third leading cause of death in the United States is?"

I hope someday the answer to that question is Harken Righteous. They can put on my tombstone: Here Lies Harken Righteous—Third Leading Cause of Death in the USA. RIP, Righteous thinks.

"Uh, no, I don't, Dr. White."

"Medical errors.[21] First is cancer, then heart disease, then medical errors, to the tune of 250,000 deaths a year. Automobiles and flu kill about 30,000 each, I think. I don't want my friend to die of a medical error, especially one I committed or overlooked, or the lab committed and I didn't catch."

This is truly my day of days. Oyez, oyez. Harken Righteous has arrived, and the Righteous Quest has begun. The horns, the horns play the fanfare. Harken Righteous has successfully hacked a patient's lab value and created a sense of deep angst in the famous and overly caring Dr. Charles Harper White's heart. Three cheers, everybody!

"Harry, are you okay? Sally, get me Jack and Jan Sloan on the phone, pronto. I want to see them after hours today."

"Sorry, Dr. White, I was off in a daze. I'm concerned for Jack, too. Damn, leukemia, of all things!"

32

"What's so wrong with Jack's blood test that you couldn't tell him over the phone? Charlie, you've really got us worried," Janice Sloan says as she and Jack enter White's office.

"I'm sorry I made this mysterious and a worry. Jan, this is my new PA, Harry Right, who I asked to sit in with us. Is that okay? Jack met him when Jack was here for his physical."

This is exactly what I dreamed of, planned for, hoped for, and told Diary all about. A front-row-center seat for a major boohoo, life-altering event. Welcome, Beaches End, to HR Productions! Grief, anybody?

"Jack, I called you in because I have a concern about one of your lab results. It's your white blood count— the WBC, we call it. It's part of the routine blood work we did with your complete physical. The WBC is the number of white cells in your blood. It came back high. Very high, actually."

"How high? What was it?"

"It's a little complicated. When I saw the result, I didn't believe it. I called the lab to make sure your blood was drawn into the right kind of tube—a purple-top, they call it—and that your name and date of birth were put on the tube before it was filled. They were. I asked the lab to repeat the test using the same blood from the same tube, and the result came back almost the same. This tells me that the test made on the blood in that tube was done without what is called pretesting error."

"Charlie, how high?"

"I'll tell you in a moment."

"Charlie," Janice asks, "can you be certain that the blood in that tube was Jack's?"

"You are sharp, Jan; just because his name was on the label doesn't mean his blood was the blood in the tube. No, I can't. Truth is, there's a known window of opportunity for wrong-tube labeling to occur if the phlebotomist's habit is to label tubes *after* blood's taken from several patients. It happens more than we want to know or are willing to say. A recent study[22] I read looked at over four million tests over two years and found pretesting error rates, which included tube-labeling errors, from 1 percent to over 6 percent."

"That's astonishing, Charlie. Why don't we just redraw Jack's blood and label the tube under careful observation?" Janice says.

"Of course, but I needed you to know why we are doing

that," White says.

"So, why the fuss? Let's do it, Charlie. I'm curious, what were my results?" Jack asks.

"The first result was 32,570, and the repeat was 34,170. Normal is between 4,000 and 11,000."

"What could the high result mean?" Janice asks.

"Well, it could mean—and I stress *could* mean—that Jack acquired a blood disorder, possibly leukemia. He's not sick so I don't think he has an infection."

"Leukemia? You can die from that!" Jack asks, now looking even more worried.

"I don't think you have leukemia. Your blood work doesn't fit your clinical picture. Is it possible? Yes, but I don't think so. Let's redraw the blood under careful observation, or what is called *chain of custody*, making sure they label the tube correctly. All right?"

"Sounds good," Janice says.

"Charlie, should I go back to the same lab?" Jack asks.

"I see no reason to add another variable by changing labs."

"Dr. White, I'd be happy to go to the lab with Jack and watch them draw his blood, use the right tube, and label it correctly if that would help put everyone at ease," Righteous says.

"That's nice of you, Harry. Is that okay with you, Charlie?" Jack says.

"Sure."

"Harry, Jack and I want to speak to Dr. White privately for a few minutes. Some personal things. Would you give us a little time? After that, we can all go over to the lab, okay?"

"Sure thing, Mrs. Sloan. I'll just wait in my office."

Righteous now thinks, *Before I go, Jack, Jan, would you like to place your "blood test result wish" for the repeat blood count now? Let's see, you can choose from a) WBC back to normal. Nah. No fun. b) WBC similar to the last one. Nah. No fun. Or c) WBC even worse. Yeah! Take c! Take c!* The raucous crowd of nasty neurons rumbling around inside Righteous's head roars as he scurries back to his office to listen in on the conversation from which everyone in White's office thinks he's been excluded.

33

2 A.M., RIGHTEOUS AT HOME. His impulses still not completely satisfied from his only days-ago BEGH hospital-hacking foray, Righteous is awakened from a deep sleep by a compelling urge to hack again. Bleary-eyed and only somewhat in control of his still-asleep motor functions, he rises from bed and staggers to his computer.

He plops into the chair in front of his dimly lit desk and gropes for the mouse and keyboard. Without much thought, he hacks into Sarasota General Hospital's intranet via a link he discovered on the Stargazer platform. He scans the offerings, trying to keep his raging, marrow-deep impulses to hack in some sort of check.

The hackable offerings this early morning are ample but boring to him. Splicing into the video feed from the cameras there, he sees several IV pumps going, some delivering fluids, some antibiotics, some chemotherapy. There was one of particular interest that woke him a bit more, a machine squirting, the labels said, amylase, lipase, and some other essential enzymes directly into a sleeping patient's splenic artery through a subclavian port—an artificial pancreas. *Neat*, he thought. Then he saw several kidney dialysis chairs humming away pumping out poisonous fluids in a sort of a barter exchange for less poisonous fluids for people he thought were going to die soon anyway, so what was the point?

Feeling these options are giving him a Beaches End General Hospital déjà vu moment, he gives the mouse wheel another turn that takes him to radiology, where several MRIs and CTs are doing their things—a bit too much for him, as he just needs to breach something quickly and get back to sleep.

Then he does his "Harken Spin." He closes his eyes and gives the mouse wheel (that he weighted with lead for just this purpose) a mighty spin, and wherever the cursor lands is his target.

Ah, the blood bank. What can I do at the blood bank?

Righteous logs in and sees the blood bank's blood-request server has just one request in the queue—two units of type O blood for ninety-seven-year-old Avraham Kahanowitz. *Poor bastard.*

Righteous tries to remember the various blood-type transfusion rules that tell who can donate which type safely and who will suffer a life-threatening incompatibility reaction from which type. He then remembers from his PA course the phrase "O blood? *No* blood," reminding him that type O patients can only safely receive type O blood. With a couple of key taps, Righteous changes the "Request Blood Type Register" from O to A. Then, being the clever, perfectionist hacker he is, he changes the hospital's admission patient-demographic database to show Avraham's blood type is type A, so when the nurse reads his name on the wrist band bar code to confirm who he is, the bar code will look at the database and return type A. With those few keystrokes, he delivers a thrill-of-a-lifetime high to himself and an end-of-a-lifetime low to Avraham Kahanowitz. May he, soon, rest in peace.

Without much thought to risk or consequence, and yearning for more of the recognition he can't yet have, Righteous makes it so that printed on the corner of the label on each unit bag of blood will be his signature avatar , believing it will go unnoticed and, at least, not understood by anyone who sees it until it's too late. Perhaps he'll see these Cossack images one day and smile.

Righteous rides his orgasmic hacking juggernaut back to bed, plops down, curls up with his red worry rag in his right hand, knees to his chin, closes his eyes, and, with a smile of satisfaction that comes only from a job well done, he promptly reenters the place of sweet dreams he had just left behind.

34

"Charlie, the phone. They want you," Heather says, giving him a nudge just hard enough to wake him.

"Dr. White here," he says into the phone.

"Dr. White, this is Sarasota General ER. I have Dr. David Lesieg who wants to speak to you. Hang on, please."

"Okeydokey."

White rolls onto his back and waits for the transfer while thrumming his fingers on his chest to the tune of Tom Lehrer's "The Elements," trying to remain awake.

"Dr. White. Sorry to keep you waiting, sir. This is Dave Lesieg. I'm one of the ER residents on tonight."

"Whatcha got, Dave?"

"Well, first, let me say I'm sorry about what happened at your hospital."

"Thanks. Whatcha got, Dave?"

"Well, a ninety-seven-year-old patient of yours named Avie Kahanowitz was brought in by his daughter around ten last night complaining of feeling progressively weak over the past few days. His daughter, Lynne, said he's in good health for his age, but every few months, his red blood count gets low and he gets weak like this and gets a transfusion. She brought him here to be checked and get a transfusion, not wanting to take him to BEGH because of what happened over there. His workup was unremarkable, except he was moderately anemic with a hemoglobin of eight and hematocrit of twenty-four."

"I know him well. He runs a chronic anemia and does well with it and just needs to fill the tank from time to time when he gets to twenty-five or so. Go ahead and type and cross him and give him a couple of units of packed red cells."

"Thank you, Dr. White, but, unfortunately, there's more. After he came in, I brought up his records from BEGH and saw that everything the daughter said was true. He gets transfused every couple of months and last got blood three months ago. Because of that history, I treated him as a nonemergent, chronic, low-grade anemia, probably senile production issues, maybe low renal erythropoietin, so didn't think I needed to bother you and ordered blood just as he always gets."

"Better to call first, but that's fine, so why the phone call now?"

"He had an acute hemolytic transfusion reaction,[23] developed DIC, and died."

"*What?* What the hell happened?"

168

"He was typed and crossed just prior to transfusion according to our protocol, and he came back on the hospital's server as type A. The blood bank dispensed two units of type A blood."

"He's type O, not type A, Dave."

"Yes, sir, Dr. White, I know. On all prior admissions at BEGH, he has always been type O, but this time, when his blood type was checked just prior to transfusion, he came back type A. Also, when his wristband bar code was read, it returned type A, as well. As soon as the blood drip began, he started to crash, went into massive organ failure, developed fulminant disseminated intravascular coagulation, and died before we could deal with it."

"This is awful."

"I know. And here's the curious thing, Dr. White. I retyped his blood immediately after he died, and it came back type O, just like always. Somehow there was an error in the blood bank's computer so that for a very short time, it showed the wrong blood type. Another thing—when I look now on my monitor at his admissions information, his blood type shows type A, which is wrong, but the daughter showed me a printout of his admissions information that admissions gave her when he came in, and it says he's type O."

"This just doesn't add up, Dave."

"Dr. White, I can tell you we followed every protocol to the letter, and we transfuse all the time here. We're a busy Level I[24] trauma center. There was no mistake made by any staff. Somehow, someway, for a short window of time, the system for certifying and dispensing blood changed his blood type from O to A. That's the only explanation. It looks to me like our hospital and blood banking system may have been hacked. That's the only explanation I can think of."

"I need to think this over, Dave. Anything else funny going on there?"

"No."

"Well, it certainly could be what you said, but I need to think on this. Thanks for telling me, Dave. Is his daughter there?"

"Yes, she's right next to me wanting to know what happened."

"Tell her to stay there and that I'll be over there in twenty minutes."

"Will do. Oh, Dr. White, maybe there is one more thing. The printed labels on the bags of type A blood have a curious image about a half-inch high printed on them that shouldn't be there. It's right after the blood type labeling."

"What do you mean a 'curious image'?"

"It's a head wearing a Russian Cossack hat. Does that mean anything to you? And could this breach of our system be related in some way to what happened over at your hospital?"

"Hang on to those bags, Dave, and don't let them out of your sight, not for a second. There's someone I need to show them to."

35

"Christ, I don't believe it!" White says, looking at the monitor displaying Jack Sloan's repeat white count of almost forty thousand.

"Jack, Charlie, here. Your blood came back, and it's higher still. Do Jan and you want to come in to discuss the next step, or shall we do it over the phone?"

"I'm on the line, too, Charlie," Janice says. "Let's just talk here and now."

"Okay. As I told Jack, the WBC came back even higher. Again, his differential, the kinds of cells present, is normal, and that makes no sense. Any patient with leukemia or another issue that would raise the white count this high should also have a lot of abnormal-looking cells there, too, particularly what are called *early forms*, like bands, and Jack has zero of them."

"Tell me what that means in English, Charlie," Jack says.

"Sorry. It means your blood count and your cell types

don't go together. That usually doesn't happen. It's telling me something, but I don't know what yet. Here's what I think. Option one. We agree to accept the latest abnormal blood result, in which case I'd suggest you see a blood specialist. With your permission, I can call my hematologist friend Ed Swahl. He's the best. Of course, if there was someone else you'd like to see, that'd be fine, too. What they do next isn't simple. Most likely more blood tests to confirm what we found. Then, if indicated, a chest CT scan, a bone-marrow biopsy, imaging of the liver and spleen, more blood tests, and then more studies, depending on results."

"All right. Next option?" Jack says.

"Option two. If you remain feeling well, we wait a bit, say a couple of weeks, and just repeat the test. You do feel okay, right, Jack? No fever, chills, or sweats?"

"Absolutely. Feel fine. But here again, how do we trust the results then?"

"Right. That's the big question and the dilemma we're in. I guess the same holds true for the blood test Dr. Swahl would do. First, let's decide which path to take."

"What would you do, Charlie? I mean, if you were me—see Dr. Swahl or wait? Jan, your thoughts?" Jack asks, hoping to hear a dose of wisdom.

"It's really your call, Jack," Janice says. "I'm still processing it all. My first thought was I'd go straight to the Mayo Clinic in Rochester, Minnesota."

"I've been there," White says. "Most of it's a warren of underground tunnels, each one leading to a different service like medicine, orthopedics, surgery. Also, I remember a study I read about last year commissioned by the Mayo Clinic to look at the security of their network. They've been studied before,[25] and the outcomes show, unfortunately, they're as vulnerable to breaching as any other facility of that type. I recall they had about ten-thousand-plus Windows servers, eighty-thousand-plus workstations, and twenty-thousand-plus medical devices. And guess what? Most of these weren't secure."

"Well, that's just great. There's no safe medical harbor on earth," Jack says.

"Hang on a minute, Janice. Jack, do you want to respond to the Mayo Clinic idea?" White says.

"I don't know yet. Going to the Mayo is a big deal, trucking off to Rochester, smack-dab in the middle of nowhere. It could mean being there a week or more, not to mention the fortune Mayo would likely charge, and I'm sure my insurance won't cover that. No, I think, I'd like to 'hold the Mayo,' for now. 'Hold the Mayo.' That's a joke if anyone wants to laugh," Jack says.

"Funny, Jack. I'm going to call Ed Swahl for you and get you seen."

Good idea, Dr. White. That was my first choice, too, Righteous thinks, excitedly listening in through the app that turns on White's cell phone microphone.

36

"Oh, Harry, that was incredible," Maribeth says, panting, trying to catch her breath.

"Same for me, Maribeth."

"I must admit this was new for me, Harry."

"No different for me."

"I loved having my arms wrapped around you like that."

"It did feel good," Harry says, parking his motorcycle at the entrance of the restaurant he'd picked for their lunch, Maribeth still on the passenger seat of his Harley.

"I've been a passenger on a motorcycle before, and I've been through Old Florida before, but I never saw Old Florida from the back seat of a motorcycle before. Thank you. Those old-time, Florida cracker[26] houses on the palm-lined streets always give me a feeling of either having lived there before or wishing I lived there."

"Are those cracker houses expensive?"

"Very. Mainly because of the land they sit on. I've lived in Florida my whole life, and I see these houses are becoming scarce. They're being bought up a lot now; some are restored, but most are torn down, and the new Florida school of architecture–style houses are built in their place."

"My apartment near the hospital is in one of those old, cracker-style homes. I think so, anyway. It's an old house. What's the new Florida style?"

"Like those white, boxy houses we saw looking out of place between the cracker houses."

"Harry, how'd you know the Old Salty Dog is my favorite restaurant?" Maribeth asks shortly after sitting down at a table there on the deck overlooking Mullet Bay.

"Dunno, just found it riding around. I like off-the-beaten-track places. You find them all the time when you're on a bike. Maybe it's destiny."

"Oh, Harry, look at the flying fish!"

"I see. What are they?"

"Mullet. We're on Mullet Bay."

"Why do they jump?"

"Ah, that's a good question. Lots of theories. You mentioned destiny. Do you believe in destiny?"

"Hmm. I'd say yes, in a way."

"So, by destiny, I mean that a person's future is preprogrammed, you know, like everything we do has been decided before we do it and we can't change it. Do you believe that?"

"Do I believe our future is preprogrammed and can't be changed? No. I think it can be changed."

"Our meeting each other and winding up here today at the Old Salty Dog, would you say that was destiny?"

"Hmm. Yes," Harry says, feeling Maribeth's feet rubbing against his legs and moving toward his crotch. "You know, they have the best boiled, peel-and-eat shrimp here, Maribeth. Do you like that?"

"My favorite. Hmm, destiny again?"

"Might be," Righteous says with a sly smile.

Maribeth smiles back.

"Maribeth, do you think *your* destiny can be changed?"

"Maybe, if I work hard, set goals, that kind of thing."

"I meant … changed by someone other than you, someone else."

"I don't understand. How could anyone possibly do that?"

37

"How's the tea, Jan?" Heather asks.

"Good, just what I needed to calm my nerves a bit. And it's nice being out on the lanai."

"I'm glad to hear it. Now, please, tell me what's going on."

"I don't know where to start. Jack went to see Charlie for a complete physical. Jack's fifty, feels fine, and just thought it was time. He gets his physical, and the next thing we know, Charlie calls us and asks us to come to the office after hours. It scared the hell out of us. When we got there, Charlie tells us Jack's white count is very high—thirty-nine thousand or something like that— which could mean leukemia. Now he wants Jack to see a blood specialist."

"Oh, Jan, I'm so sorry. I didn't know Jack became Charlie's patient. Charlie has this hard-and-fast rule about patient privacy, so he never tells me anything about his patients, even if it involves our best friends. Unless, of course, the friend tells him it's okay. I think he takes it too far."

"Thank you. And there's something I didn't tell Charlie yet. When I was in his office, I asked his PA to leave so the three of us could talk privately about a personal matter. Shortly after, I needed to use the restroom. On the way back, I heard Charlie and Jack talking and laughing about golf, so I opened the door and walked in. Heather, it was the PA's office, not Charlie's. The PA was sitting at his desk listening to his phone. As soon as he saw me, he quickly shut off the phone. I said I was sorry, backed out, and closed the door."

"That's really strange. Are you sure you didn't just hear them down the hall?"

"I know what I heard, and it was coming from his phone. Should I tell Charlie?"

"Sure, and I'll mention it as well. Oh, I almost forgot, we're having Harry over for dinner Saturday."

38

"Charlie, where are you going? It's after midnight," Heather says, half-asleep, after being awakened by White getting out of bed.

"I just got an idea. I have to make a phone call, then a house call."

"Who are you calling this late? And a house call? Where?"

"Jack Sloan. His house."

"Charlie, they're going to think you're crazy."

"Heather, where are my old med school microscope and slides and stuff?"

"Somewhere in the garage, I think. If you are going to Jan's, I'm going with you."

"Jack, your phone's ringing. Who's calling at this time of night?" Janice says.

"Hello?" Jack says.

"Jack, sorry to wake you; it's Charlie."

"It's Charlie, Jan. Charlie, what's the matter now? Don't

tell me it's more bad news."

"No. I have an idea to solve your blood count issue."

"What idea?"

"Both of you get decent; I'll be over in ten minutes. Put on some coffee. Oh, close your blinds and turn off the driveway lights, too."

"Hi, Charlie. Oh, Heather, I didn't know you were coming, too. And what's with the suitcase, Charlie? You moving in? You guys have a fight?" Janice says.

"I want to look at Jack's white count myself. I haven't done this since med school, but I still know how."

The four of them go to the kitchen, and White has Jack sit at the counter.

"Heather, did you bring my cell phone?"

"No, I think we left it in your jacket in the rush to leave."

"No problem."

"Jack, I'm going to get a pinprick of blood, put it on a slide, give it a schmear with another slide, use a little blue stain, put on a little coverslip, put it under the microscope, and count, just the way I was taught in med school."

"Fine, but why all the mystery? Are we hiding from somebody?" Jack says.

"Don't know yet. Just maybe we are," White says. "Jack, give me your index finger."

"Well, I'll be hog-tied and hornswoggled."

"What is it, Charlie?" Janice says. "What's 'hogtied and hornswoggled' mean?"

"Don't know, it's something Gabby Hayes said a lot."

"Gabby who?"

"Hayes. Gabby Hayes. Roy Rogers. Trigger. Bullet. It doesn't matter; it's normal as apple pie. About four thousand and change, and all cells look normal. Jack, your white count's normal," White says, smiling and proud that he still has the stuff, as Jack and Janice stand bewildered, maybe worried about White's mental status, but damn happy and relieved.

"What does this mean, Charlie?" Jack asks.

"It means you don't have a blood count issue; no leukemia, and I can add you to the list."

"So, I don't need to see Dr. Swahl?"

"No. Well, I'm not sure. I'm still thinking about Swahl. Until I tell you otherwise, you are to act and talk as if nothing has changed."

"You've lost us all, Charlie. What list? What the hell is going on here?" Heather says.

"I don't know yet. Oh, the list. Add yourself to the list of strange happenings in sleepy ole Beaches End. Let's think about what's gone wrong here lately. A hospital's shut down for no apparent reason, Jack's blood count comes back ten times normal when it is actually normal, a ninety-seven-year-old patient of mine dies from an unexplained blood transfusion screwup, Russian Cossack hats are popping up everywhere I turn, and so on."

"You've still lost us, Charlie," Janice says.

"Sorry. Here's what I know I can tell you. After the hospital event, the hospital board and the investigative authorities met. The FBI informed us the hospital was hacked, no question about it. Question is, was Jack's blood work hacked, too? And is it the same hacker? I'm thinking anyone who can take down a hospital can do a little switcheroo of some numbers in a blood analyzer server.[27] I really need to talk with the authorities again, as well as some friends of mine. I've given this some thought. I know what I need to do; I just need to do it fast, before things get worse. The local authorities told me they have some skills and experience solving cybercrimes, but nothing at this level. The FBI's going to go too slow. They said, 'If you can catch him, be our guest.' It's time for me to roll up my sleeves and get to work."

"So, what are you going to do?" Heather asks.

"I'm going to meet with Larry Demarseco. He'll help answer some of these questions. Larry can also get into Jack's labs server to see if there's alien software sitting in there."

"You've really lost us, Charlie," Jack says.

"That's okay. Also, I have a friend, Abel Valentine, who has a cyber-tech company named SeeZAll Inc. headquartered not too far from here. I've talked a lot to him already about what's been happening and what to do about it. He wants to offer his services to help us figure this out and, if it is a hacker, catch him in action. He explained to me the only way to prove who is doing the hacking is to catch the person in the act. They've done this before and have elaborate schemes to do it. SeeZAll designs systems for industry, as well as nations, to monitor and measure all aspects of human and nonhuman activity—just consider their company name. They use drones for real-time surveillance and spying. He told me how they use drones to do flyover imaging of wind turbines. The drones follow an AI-designed surveillance route, updated in real time by the drone itself depending on what it 'sees.' It's a three-dimensional, Google Maps–like scanning route that runs all day, every day, with a stable of relay drones that exchange data with each other as their batteries wane—like human relay runners exchange batons. They have a control command center, too, at their HQs—it's right out of *Star Wars*. Abel thought his drones, some as small as a June bug, would be perfect to use in our case to spy on a suspected hacker and possibly catch him. To us, it seems outrageous to do this this way, but to Abel, it's just another day's work. We can use his control center as our headquarters, if we want.

"Well, that's all for me. Sorry for dumping all this on you. I know it's been a trying time. I just want to say that I take everything that's happened to our town and patients very personally. That's just who I am. I not only care *for* my patients, I care *about* them. I want to be involved in bringing justice to whoever's committing these acts and see that justice is served. I won't rest until I do that. I mean it from the bottom of my heart. So, lastly, I'm going to call a meeting of all those folks who have a nexus to this and those who I think can help us. By the way, we need a name for this venture. Any ideas?"

"How about Team Charlie?" Jack says.

"How about White's Crusaders?" suggested Jan.

"Thanks, Jack. I'll pass on that one. Thanks, Jan. I'll pass there, too."

"Team Nemesis," Heather says. "Nemesis was the Greek goddess of revenge."

"Team Nemesis. Sounds good to me. Any objections?" White asks.

Jack and Janice shake their heads.

"None? So, approved. Team Nemesis it is! Brilliant name, my dear. Brilliant. It's time to go, sweetheart," White says, giving Heather a soft peck on the cheek.

Jack and Janice stand on the porch, waving at White and Heather as they get into their car in the wee hours of the morning.

"Jan, do you think everybody's doctor's like that? I feel like I want to say, 'Who was that masked man?' I mean, he reminds me of the Lone Ranger," Jack says, not exactly serious, but not entirely joking, either.

"I have to say he sure does. Like the Lone Ranger," Janice says.

As the Whites' car slips away, leaving only a trail of swirling, red mist from the rear lights, the two of them embrace and watch their hero, Dr. Charles Harper White, disappear into the dark night's fog and chill.

39

LATER IN JUNE. *Diary. Me again. Just wanted to give a brief hello, as it's been a while. I'm still enjoying raising hell with Jack's blood results, so that's going well. But, I'm sad. "Why are you sad?" you ask. Okay. Couple of reasons. One is, I murdered somebody at 2:00 in the morning. You say, "Oh, just a 2:00 a.m. murder? That's all? Why should that make you sad? It sounds like something you would do." Oh, Diary, you say that so sarcastically and a bit mean-spiritedly, but rightfully so, as I am deserving of your sarcasm. The reason I'm sad is that my decent, normal brain I, the I racing around in my skull looking for a goddamned place to stop, didn't mean to do it. And why didn't I tell you about it until now? Maybe, because my decent brain is ashamed? Maybe, knowing that I—the decent I again—could be part of such a shameful thing scares the hell out of the decent me? Diary, I'm telling you, I was like an automaton that early morning. I was impulsive, without control. Robo-Righteous I was. Maybe I'm Victor Frankenstein and his monster all wrapped up in one, reincarnated?*

The other reason I'm sad? It's silly and selfish by comparison. It's because I read an online post that someone hacked[28] into healthcare.gov, the federal government's official website for the Patient Protection and Affordable Care Act, a.k.a. Obamacare. Why did that make me sad? You think it's because I feel sorry that millions of patients might have problems with their health insurance as a result? No, Dumbo. I'm sad because it wasn't me who broke into it! Sorry I yelled. Sorry I called you Dumbo. Sorry I murdered Avie. He was over ninety, you know, so that counts for something. No?

The Obamacare hacker implanted code to slow down the website at a later time. He didn't take anything and didn't change anything, just left malicious code. Where's the fun in that? I'm more advanced than that as far as creative hacking goes. Wonder why no one's doing what I'm doing yet?

Well, whatever.

It's all starting to feel a little lonely where my head is at, ole buddy. This head I got without asking for it.

Have nothing more to say to anyone, including you, right now.

Sorry I bothered you.

Good night.

Diary, it's me. Sorry to open you up again. I forgot to post the record of Avie's hack.

HACK 5 SUMMARY

Date of Hack: June 28

What/Who: Sarasota General Hospital's blood bank and patient Avraham Kahanowitz.

What I Did: Hacked the blood bank and changed his blood type from Type O to Type A.

Consequences: Caused a severe transfusion reaction. The operation was a success, but the patient died.

Terror-Creation Factor for Me: 9/10 = Excellent.

40

White begins, "Good morning, everyone, and welcome to the first meeting of Team Nemesis. Please take a minute to look over the list of names of those present on the name card, take a seat, and we'll begin.

"Thank you all for being here today. We're here to organize, strategize, and develop tactics to identify and catch a very evil person and put an end to the terror that has taken over our lives and, unfortunately, brought some lives to an end. I know of five instances where some part of Beaches End's medical network was breached, infected, and weaponized to create a kind of medical hell. What worries me also is what else he's done that we don't yet know about. In the first instance, Stargazer Systems, the company that provides our BEGH hospital's entire medical network, had their physical plant breached, and some possibly critical information may have been taken. This event was followed shortly after by the hospital being taken down. It is very hard to argue there was no association between the two events. Then, in what can only be taken as a clear effort by the hacker to make his presence known, there was a breach of Stargazer's secure phone system as evidenced by a signature avatar being left for all to see. In another instance, my patient's laboratory results were altered to make it look as if he had leukemia. And in another instance, a patient of mine died after he was transfused with the wrong blood type, the apparent result of the blood bank being hacked. In almost every instance, it appears, I am related to the targets of the malicious activity. That may or may not be important or could just be a coincidence, but it is something we need to keep in mind. The question is, of course, whether I am the center of just one hacking universe or if there are other hacking universes being affected the same way and I just don't know it. As of now, we don't know who is doing this to us. We have no idea where the perpetrator is located, whether right here under our noses in Beaches End or in Russia or China somewhere. Or he may be nomadic and ply his evil trade while on the run, a 'have keyboard, will travel and wreak havoc' sort of thing. We don't know if these actions are the work of one individual working alone or the work of a group. Is it a state actor for an unfriendly country? Or maybe the hacker is a lone wolf, or a disgruntled employee of Stargazer or the hospital, or a plain, out-and-out lunatic who is damn smart and evil as well. As of this moment, we not only do not know who he is, but worse, we have no idea what other malevolence he has already done.

"Because the hacker may very well be living here among us and may possibly know us, each of you agreed to a code of total and complete secrecy. You agreed also that you would either leave at home or, if that were not possible, leave in a locked cubicle outside of this room all of your personal items that could possibly become a hackable communication device. That included all electronics, including RFID fobs, smartphones, smart pads, smart notebooks, and all recording devices. We scanned you for hearing aids; those electronic marvels are capable of all kinds of spy mischief, as many today are Bluetooth enabled and smartphone-app connected. We had you not wear any jewelry, as many brooches and the like are actually sold as spyware. We even checked you for implanted acoustic bone stimulators used to treat a form of hearing impairment, many of which devices are Wi-Fi linked and programmable. We also scanned for pacemakers and implanted automatic defibrillators, all of which can be hacked and converted for malicious purposes, including being turned on and off by remote means.

"We also took your Fitbit, if you had one. It turns out that the Fitbit, and other dynamic step counters, possess potentially hackable GPS coordinate transmitters. There's also enough heat generated by Fitbit devices that they allowed our enemies in Iraq to use thermal detectors to track our military.[29] Wall surfaces here are lined with photic-, acoustic-, x-ray-, thermal-, and electromagnetic spectrum–insulating barriers, so transmission in or out of any photic, thermal, audio, or electromagnetic spectrum signal is not possible.

"Each of you is here because in some way you had a nexus with either the possible perpetrator or one of the recent tragic events, or you can possibly be of help to catch the hacker or hackers. We can't arrest anyone until we know exactly what was done and how those things can be undone, reversed, moderated, or in some way made right or otherwise managed. Just arresting a suspect could be a disaster if they're the wrong person or if he is part of a group and without knowing all that was done. If the arrest doesn't happen correctly, many people could suffer horrible consequences for the rest of their lives whether he is captured alive or, worse for us, dead.

"We have three goals and will seek to achieve all of them. The first, to identify the perpetrator. The second, to identify every breach made and develop strategies and tactics to reverse them when possible and to manage them when not. And third, to arrest the hacker or hackers and, as a result, stop this hacking devastation once and for all.

"I want to explain why I am so personally involved and determined more than most with putting an end to the hacking. It's because I am more than just an internist

here in Beaches End; I am also an attending at Beaches
End General Hospital, which means I have privileges to
admit patients there, and several of my patients were in-
patients at the time things went dark there. I am also
chairman of the hospital's medical board. And lastly, I am
the hospital's medical-technical liaison between Stargazer
Systems and BEGH, and that means, in many ways, my
name and stamp of approval are on the product Stargazer
installed at BEGH. But let me be clear, there is no conflict
of interest here. I receive no income from Stargazer or the
hospital for my services. My goal is to unravel the mystery
of what happened and bring it to a halt. For all of those
reasons, as well as others, you should easily understand
why I, along with Heather, formed Team Nemesis and
why I must lead it. The authorities are aware of our team
and are grateful for whatever we can do to help them.
They know that the hacking was a highly technical digital
assault on our community's health-care nervous system,
every fiber and synapse of it. It ranged from changing the
value of a single result in a single register in a single server
to fouling the very guts and sinew of a complex web of
hardware and software that comprise our state-of-the-art
area-wide hospital network systems. The person who
did this understood that system perfectly. To solve this
case will require criminal investigators with an equally
thorough understanding of the details of that system.
Success will require not just mastery of the art and science

of hacking but an understanding of medicine and health care technology and information delivery processes as well as expert criminal and forensic investigation tools and techniques. Team Nemesis possesses all of those skills and expertise, many components of which the authorities admit they lack.

"My reputation regarding my devotion to my patients is true, maybe even understated; I will stop at nothing in the defense of their safety, health, and welfare. That has always been paramount to me and is just who I am. Defending them in the face of this hacking assault is no different to me from dealing with a community-wide virus or plague. Indeed, that *is* what we are dealing with, nothing less than a digital virus borne of a keyboard and a computer and propagated by an evil human.

Finally, as an example of the fear he has instilled in my patients, one patient told me the other day that when he was in my waiting room and my nurse said to him, 'David, the doctor will see you now,' he said to her "You mean the doctor will kill you now." That's how much fear this hacker has put in the hearts and minds of the now fragile and fearful people who live in this town.

"Okay, enough about me and my motives. Let's go around and introduce ourselves. I think I've done my intro pretty well. Heather, you're next."

"My name's Heather White. I'm Dr. White's wife, of course. I'm an attorney with experience in criminal law and with a special interest and expertise in prosecuting cybercrimes. Cybercrime is a relatively new subspecialty of law and includes crimes in which a computer is the object of the crime or the means of conducting the crime. This includes hacking, phishing, spamming, and the like. I'll be providing general legal advice, deal with warrants and Fourth Amendment issues, give criminal investigatory guidance to our team, and be assisting in a variety of other ways as you will see."

"I'm Abel Joseph Valentine. I'm the founder of a number of technology-based corporations, including SeeZAll Inc., in whose headquarters we're all at today. It's my pleasure to welcome you here. I have a BS and MS in mathematics and computer engineering from the Johns Hopkins University, degrees I obtained by the time I was seventeen years old. I received a PhD in computer engineering from Cornell University at age twenty-three. Upon graduation, I formed Abel Enterprises to commercially develop my PhD thesis on artificial intelligence software that endows computer avatars with human immune-response characteristics.

"Anyway, again, it is my pleasure to welcome all of you here at my company headquarters today and have you experience our facilities, including our hyper-secure conference room and, as some of you will see in a bit, our state-of-the-art SeeZAll Surveillance Center that will become our Team Nemesis headquarters and that has no parallel anywhere in the world. As the name *SeeZAll* implies, there is virtually nothing on earth or in outer space that can escape the sensitivity, scope, and range of the sensors and instrumentation we developed and our equipment employs. I say 'outer space' because we placed there some of the most sophisticated spying and surveillance instrumentation ever devised. I hope you can now see that we can bring to bear a wide range of expertise to finding and stopping the hacker."

"Hello, all. I'm Joie Jergé, the boots-on-the-ground reporter for WBCD, the CNN local affiliate here in Beaches End. I covered the aftermath of the hospital going dark and have done some substantial subsequent investigation I will tell you about. I'm here to observe the process and report on it when appropriate."

"I'm next. My name's O. J. Sparks. I was invited here by Dr. and Mrs. White because of my Spycraft skills.

"I'm Deshaun Washington, and I work with O. J."

"Boris, you're next," White says.

"My name is Boris Natashnicov. Please excuse my Russian accent. I've been here in America for two years now and my accent is still with me. My job is the tech guy at BEGH for hospital network issues. I guess you could call me the System Administrator at BEGH. That's it for now."

"My turn. I'm Larry Demarseco. I'm head of security and network systems for Stargazer Systems, which you know by now developed, installed, and supports the software systems that run the infrastructure of Beaches End General Hospital. Having been a participant in the design and development of the BEGH's network, I am in a unique position to understand, with respect to the hacking, what was done, how it was done, and how to prevent it from happening again in the future."

"I'm Dr. David Lesieg. I'm an ER trauma doc at Sarasota General. I was in the ER when Dr. White's patient died after a transfusion reaction."

"I'm Ethyn Welch. I am an FBI special agent in their Cyber division. I have a law degree from George Washington and have, as does Mrs. White, a special interest in cybercrime, particularly cyberinvasion crimes. I'm here in a liaison capacity between your Team Nemesis and a task force that is a collaborative effort of local, state, and federal agencies. I will report back to all of them as we progress here and will keep us here up to date on their progress. We're working with you in a cooperative way, utilizing the best skills of each of us. The task force authorities understand who you are. They've already been briefed on your facility, they understand your technology, and they have been updated on your intel. They are all very impressed. They decided the shortest path to catching the hacker is through a cooperative venture with your team. Dr. White anticipated the Fourth Amendment question and asked me, along with Mrs.

White, to obtain all the necessary warrants. This we'll do once we've defined the exact parameters of our tactics."

White continues, "One big question we are all facing is whether what happened to Beaches End is an isolated event or has happened elsewhere in our country. To help answer that question, we looked into the US Department of Justice's Computer Crime and Intellectual Property Section, or CCIPS.[30] This section includes a database where cybercrimes can be reported and accessed. However, it is only as good as is the reporting to it. Furthermore, as they state on their website, 'internet-related crime, like any other crime, should be reported to appropriate law enforcement investigative authorities at the local, state, federal, or international levels, depending on the scope of the crime. Citizens who are aware of federal crimes should report them to local offices of federal law enforcement.' This, unfortunately, tells us there is no centralized national cybercrime reporting process or a central location. The best I can say is that although hacking of hospitals, insurance companies, even the Center for Medicare and Medicaid Services, or CMS, continues at a rapid pace—and I will tell you about them in a bit—there are as of now no other breaches reported that come close to the malicious, evil, and invasive nature as ours. I lose sleep every night wondering just why that is the case and which night will be the one that changes everything.

"For us to be successful, we all need to understand the big picture—like the famous NASA view of earth from outer space—of what is actually happening to us and exactly the psychopathic nature of who we are dealing with. There are two major forces at play here. One force is the continuous, unrelenting, ubiquitous journaling of our human history in digital form, and two, the utter susceptibility to invasion and rewriting of that history that that digital record allows. There is not much that can be done to stop the first force. There is much, theoretically, that can be done about the second force, if only there were the collective will to do it. Let me explain."

41

White continues, "As some of you may already know, I've had a long-standing scientific interest in the digital representation of our analog selves. Your analog self is everything about you that I experience when I use my analog senses to experience you, such as when I palpate your abdomen, listen to your heart and lungs, look at you, and the like. Ancient Greek physicians used all five senses to aid in diagnosis. Your digital life is all of those same things but converted to and stored in digital form. Let me tell you some things about our digital lives.

"A resident of a typical large American city walks into view of a recording camera an average of seventy-five times per day.[31] In addition to being visually recorded and stored that way, much of that person's behavior is recorded and stored in digital form in other ways. This includes, possibly, every keyboard keystroke, Kindle download, credit card swipe, hotel pass card swipe, stoplight, toll, and smart TV camera exposure, cell phone location, you name it, and it's likely electronically captured and digitized either with the person's knowledge or surreptitiously.

"The entire extent to which our cell phones surveil us is largely unknown, but if you have a cell phone on you or near you, its location is constantly examined and recorded as the phone automatically contacts, or pings, every cell phone tower it encounters, even if the phone isn't being used. Most modern cell phones come with GPS, enabling your exact location to be determined, even when your phone's off. Scarier yet, cell phones can be used as a listening device when the phone's microphone is remotely turned on and your conversations eavesdropped, even with the phone off.

"Now, all those captured events and images are stored somewhere, commonly in digital form on a variety of memory devices, some called *servers*, to be made available for access later. Collectively, these records form, in a sense, what I call a person's digital DNA and the basis for Project Digital DNA, my project with Abel. These seemingly disparate data exist in various repositories and with differing degrees of security, waiting for anyone, authorized or not, to enter and have their way with them, so to speak. I say 'seemingly disparate' because they can become a cohesive and organized record of someone's day, week, or life, as soon as that person chooses to aggregate, collate, catalog, and index the disparate records. If that person isn't just anyone but happens to be a deranged hacker who adds to, deletes, or alters the data in those records, then that hacker becomes a second owner of that data, and it could be said that the person's whole digital life was stolen. And I believe that's the type of individual we're dealing with now, and this is why we must stop him before he goes any further.

"Now, don't misunderstand me; it's not a trivial task to whole-life hack a person. It does take exceptional coding skill and also requires the perfect storm of that exceptional skill and a perverse will and nature that derives pleasure from stealing and causing havoc, mayhem, and misery to others. It seems to me that at no other time in our history do we have that perfect coincidence of user-friendly, easily available, high-technology devices and the base, cold, indifferent behavior of people working as individuals, corporations, and nations that make conditions ripe for the absconding of a person's digital life. I'm so very sorry to have to say that.

"Our modern digital well of human behavior data stored in memory devices is remarkable for its wealth of all-encompassing, critical, and sensitive personal information, including, as I've said, an individual's personal medical information. Collectively, for each person, these memory devices contain what's known and recorded of a person's biopsychosocial being, which defines the person biologically, psychologically, socially, medically, and in every other way possible. If the data are time-stamped, then all of that data becomes stored in real time. Now, depending on the circumstances, medical devices can also be breached in many ways. These include, but are by no means limited to, causing medical devices to turn on and off and change medical results to make it appear, incorrectly, that a well person is ill or an ill person is getting better.

"Let me tell you what got me started on this line of thinking. On April 25, 2014, Kim Zetter reported[32] on cybersecurity expert Scott Erven's two-year security investigation into over a hundred hospital facilities in Minnesota, North Dakota, Wisconsin, and Idaho. Erven, who was paid to do this by the owners of the hospital chain, found that virtually all devices, medical and otherwise, in those facilities, including MRIs, surgical robots, defibrillators, lights, door locks, even drug-infusion devices, were hackable, and their function was controllable by him—are you ready?—remotely from his office located off campus from the hospitals. Medical records were equally vulnerable."

"My God, this is scaring the hell out of me. So, what was done at BEGH hospital had been done before at other hospitals?" Joie asks.

"It was, but Erven didn't do it maliciously, and he just demonstrated that it could be done, that it's techni-cally possible and to demonstrate the security flaws in those health-care systems. No one was harmed. By now, it should be clear that our digital selves—our medical selves, at least—lay open and bare, exposed to the whims of those interested in, and capable of, doing us great digital harm. Is it too late to safeguard and secure our digital selves? Just how far can one talented, sociopathic hacker go? I don't know. But we who are here today may be early witnesses to the hell, havoc, and mayhem that just one disturbed hacker endowed with great skill and a corrupt mind unfettered by pathos or sensibilities can wreak upon an unprepared and defenseless society. If you're all stunned and frightened, that's good. I hope I've made the case that we carry a great burden of responsibility to not only help solve the issues before us now, quickly, and completely, but to make sure measures are put in place to prevent this from ever happening again. Okay, let's begin."

42

White continues, "The smorgasbord of hackable health-care digital delicacies waiting to be sampled has not gone unnoticed by the hacking community. *Healthcare IT News*[33] reported the years 2017 and 2018 provided hackers nothing less than a veritable feast. In the article, 'The Biggest Healthcare Data Breaches of 2018' they reported Healthcare continued to be a lucrative target for hackers in 2017 with weaponized ransomware, misconfigured cloud storage buckets and phishing e-mails dominating the year. They went on tell how in 2018 these threats will continue and cybercriminals will likely get more creative despite better awareness among healthcare organizations at the executive level for the funding needed to protect themselves.

"Our hacker, as malicious and evil as anyone could be, may be leading the way for those so far more timid but now emboldened. In many ways, hackers, until ours came along, have limited their hacking to the taking but not the altering of health-care data. Our hacker has taken his craft to a new level. However, this is not to say patients were not directly affected.

"Are we not one click away from a hacker giving someone famous a diagnosis of syphilis, a terminal disease, or a rap sheet showing pedophilia, and demanding a ransom to retract it? Or, are we there now?

"One more thing. I've described for you just how a keyboard can be weaponized. Given that, we need to understand whether the keyboard is a tool for mass murder as well as a weapon of mass destruction.

"Mass murder is the act of murdering a number of people, typically at the same time or over a relatively short period of time and in geographic proximity. The FBI defines mass murder[34] as murdering four or more persons during an event with no 'cooling-off period' between the murders. I'm thinking the AR-15 and the 'fully automatic keyboard' controlling malicious computer code would both qualify as weapons capable of mass murder. But what about as a weapon of mass destruction? To be a weapon of mass destruction (WMD)[35] the keyboard through the computer would have to kill and bring significant harm to a large number of humans. I think our experience here in Beaches End would teach the keyboard would qualify as a WMD.

"This makes sense. As a WMD, the malicious keyboard and the AR-15 differ only in the kind and scope of its destruction. An AR-15 in this comparison comes out as a dinosaur, a prehistoric tool that puts holes in individuals. But the malicious keyboard is a refined destructor that selectively puts holes in devices, networks, institutions, and civil activity. So, I'll leave you with the idea that as we debate the implementation of laws that control sales and distribution of guns according to age, mental health, and criminal record, should we not do the same for malicious code enabled by the keyboard and PC?

"I put in front of each of you a handout showing my 'Top Health-Care Hacks of 2018' based on the *Healthcare IT News*[36] report I just mentioned. This is to give you an idea of the scope and breadth of the hacking in our very recent past. I'll briefly run through some of them now and you can go over the details in the handout, later.

"In one case, a North Carolina-based medical center had to notify 20,000 patients that their personal data was breached after three successful phishing attacks. Phishing is the sending of bogus, but official-looking, emails that contain malicious code that runs when the email is opened. Once opened, the code obtains sensitive information from the recipient. In another example, the CMS responded to a data breach affecting 75,000 patients in a federal ACA portal. And, then, for the second time in one month, a researcher discovered another North Carolina-based health agency had been leaking protected, personal data through a misconfigured Amazon S3 storage bucket. These ten thousand files included patient names, email and postal addresses, phone numbers, dates of birth and Social Security numbers. Other files had recordings of patient evaluations and conversations with doctors, along with medications, allergies, and other detailed personal health data.

"I need to pause a minute so we can all grasp the enormity of this particular breach. Ten thousand patient files containing not only personal medical information but patient evaluations, doctors' comments, medications, allergies, to name a few. Now just imagine our hacker going into ten thousand records, editing them, then contacting the individuals and holding them ransom to return them to normal. It is nothing less than incomprehensible and downright scary! I'll continue," White says.

"Ready? Allscripts, a practice management and electronic health record technology company, was hit by ransomware, knocking some services offline. Users took to Twitter to complain about the cloud Electronic Health Record being down, with some unable to access patient information all day. Allscripts has 45,000 physician practices, 180,000 physicians, 19,000 post-acute agencies, 2,500 hospitals, 100,000 electronic prescribing physicians, 40,000 in-home clinicians, and 7.2 million patients."

"I think what is stunning is that a company of that size—I mean, they have over seven million patients and 180,000 docs—can still be vulnerable and exposed to ransomware. This tells me they are either not investing in protecting their data, or the problem has no easy solution.

"My accounting here should give us pause to consider the possible horrific consequences that technology can wreak upon our digital lives warehoused, as they are, unfettered by reasonable security safeguards. This is especially true if the technology is in the hands of someone ready, willing, and able to use it as a weapon of mass murder, or destruction."

"I understand that, Dr. White. I mean, *I* get that," Joie says. "But what bothers me is, do you think *our perp* gets that, too?"

43

"Okay, Boris, I'd like you to tell us what you know from your position at Stargazer about what the hacker did to the hospital system that fateful Sunday morning. Then I'll have Larry tell us what he knows about all this," White says.

"Yes, thank you, Dr. White. As I said, I am the main tech support person for the networks at BEGH. I knew nothing about the hacking until Larry told me about it and I was asked to be in this group. Then, Larry asked me go back in time a month or more and look at the complete code set installed for the network on the hospital local server and see if there is any evidence of hacking. He was to do the same at our company headquarters on the main server. I found one alien-code structure, an executable subroutine Stargazer did not write and it was code that did not belong there. The hacker saved the code in a server memory segment that code developers use for 'trash'—a place not for running code but for code development, like the side of notepad if you are writing something and you need a place to make notes. The code was a subroutine that let the hacker search the entire hospital system-wide code set. He executed a 'copy instruction' to copy only the code related to clinical labs, lab data, and log-on passwords for labs."

"Does any of this help explain the night the hospital went dark?" White asks.

"Yes. There he was very clever. He found deep in the system, all the passwords for the device-control subroutines section of the Stargazer control program. If he wanted, he could have caused us a living hell more than he did. He accessed subroutines for lights, pumps, everything you see that went wrong, then he wrote a control-timer-loop routine to turn them off for thirty minutes at 3:00 a.m., then back on a half hour later. That simple."

"Did he leave a signature?" White asks.

"None I saw."

"Don't most hackers leave a signature?"

"Some do."

"You found none. Certain of that?"

"Yes, I'm certain of that. I know what I didn't find."

"Thank you, Boris. I'd like to ask you a few more questions. You're Russian by birth, correct?"

"Yes, Dr. White."

"Where in Russia were you born?"

"The city of Tomsk in Siberia. Why?"

"That's a hub of internet and high-tech IT activities, including hacking, right?" White says, ignoring Boris's question.

"Yes, that's all true. I have a master's degree from Tomsk Polytechnic University. Very prestigious."

"Is the KGB there?"

"KGB gone now, Dr. White. KGB now the Federal Security Service of the Russian Federation or FSR, and the SVR or Foreign Intelligence Service. They are everywhere."

"Do you have family, friends, or colleagues there that you still communicate with?"

"This is like old KGB interrogation. Am I a suspect in this hacking business?"

"Sorry if it sounded like that. Let me ask you if you were able to tell if the copied lab codes were exported anywhere, ever left our system's memory, and if so, where they were sent. In other words, did the hacker copy the codes to any external hardware devices, personal, corporate, or otherwise?"

"Yes and no. When I look at the root code that monitors all of the system-management-level commands, there was a trail that showed a 'copy' request in a command queue. That is the 'yes' part of question."

"Did it say where the copy was sent?"

"That is the 'no' part of the question. There was a clever subroutine he wrote on the back end that erased the destination address as the last step in the exit loop. But he couldn't gain access to the root code, the deepest code layer, to erase his trail."

"I'm not surprised," White says. "So, we now know he has the lab client codes he shouldn't have. If the password codes were in the project-work-product and e-mail threads in the trash we suspect he took from Stargazer, then we've essentially closed the loop or the connection between the Stargazer directory and printout theft and the hospital-going-dark hack. What we still don't know is if he did the hacking himself. He could have passed off the codes to another bad actor, perhaps for money, or sent them to Russia or China. Who knows? Can I ask what happened to the integrity of the encryption and other security layers Stargazer was supposed to have to keep hacks like this from happening?"

"They were there. The hacker took a detour around it and breached all."

"Boris, is it common that a person in your position, and at your level, would have administrator access to a hospital's entire code set all the way down to the root layer?"

"I don't know if it is common."

"Do you have enough access to the network, and enough coding ability, to write executable code and insert it into the system the way we see here?" White asks.

"Yes, I have enough access and coding ability for this,

but it wasn't me, Dr. White."

"One more question, sorry. On what date was the alien patch you found deposited there?"

"The date it was deposited was deleted."

44

"Larry, as head of security and networks at Stargazer Systems, and Boris's boss, perhaps you could clarify this a bit and also tell us if there's anything you'd like to add to Boris's statement," White says.

"Yes, a few things. Boris, are you sure there isn't anything else you want to add?"

"No, nothing I can think of, boss. You, too, are making me nervous, boss."

"Don't mean to do that, Boris. Perhaps you didn't see it, or maybe you forgot to tell us that the hacker left a line of code for his signature."

"Uh, no, I didn't see that, boss. What did he leave? Where was it buried?"

"I found this as one line buried deep in a dummy file named MGTF1500."

Larry pulls out a small sheet of paper and shows Boris this image:

"You recognize that, Boris?"

"It's an image of a head wearing a hat."

Larry shows the group the symbol.

"Not any hat, Boris, a *Russian Cossack hat*."

"You think that is me, boss? You think I did the hack and put image of me there for all to see? I'm not the only Russian in town, you know, and, anyway, I wear Yankee's baseball cap."

"Does this symbol tell you anything, Larry, in terms of who the hacker might be? Are you saying Boris should be under suspicion because he is Russian?" White asks.

"I don't know for certain. But I do have reason to suspect Boris, but not because he's Boris, or Russian, but I have to suspect all my IT employees," Larry says.

"What are you talking about, Larry?" Joie asks.

"Yeah, boss, what are you talking about?" Boris says.

"I'm talking about malicious insider hacking which was discussed in an excellent article in *Tripwire*.[37] It's a growing problem and, as much as it pains me, it's critical that we eliminate it as a possibility here."

"What's 'insider hacking'?" Joie asks.

"I'll tell you. It's when an employee who has contact with criminals, or other threat actors, supplies them with the inside information needed to access company networks. Sometimes they're paid for this, sometimes they get favors in return, and in some cases blackmail is involved. Usually, the breach is done to exfiltrate data for resale. Russians, and many others, do this. In our case, the breach was used for malicious intent to cause personal harm, but that doesn't rule it out. If you think about it, the IT staff, as the article says, 'hold the keys to the kingdom.'

"And here's how bad it is. Sixty-two percent of respondents to Watchful Software's 2015 Insider Threat Spotlight Report[38] said insider threats have become more frequent, with evidence that data-rich vertical sectors, such as health care and telecommunications, are most targeted. Sixty-two percent! One more thing—often lower-wage, disgruntled employees are conscripted by promises of large sums of money, especially when they suspect their jobs will be eliminated, outsourced, or relocated. I cannot tell you if any of our employees fall into these categories, but the possibility's there."

"Do you think I am low wage and disgruntled, boss?"

"You're high wage, Boris, and hopefully not disgruntled."

"Okay, boss. Just checking."

"And, one last thing," Larry says. "Charlie and I have seen that Russian Cossack symbol before. It appeared on my *used-to-be-called* hyper-secure phone the day after the hospital was taken down. Joie saw it, too. We had just finished reviewing my company's security video that showed a visitor named Quentin Wellcome behaving in a way I felt was suspicious. On the video, it appeared he was stealing a company directory and some discarded trash. I'd say it is more than coincidental that on one day this stranger visits our company, behaves suspiciously, and then, shortly after, a hospital client of ours turns dark, and then the next day, I see the Russian Cossack hat avatar almost laughing at me and telling me without a doubt that my *hyper-secure* phone was just hacked. And there's more. After Charlie discovered one of his patient's lab results could very likely have been hacked and altered, he asked me to look at the blood lab's servers for any evidence of it. For the dates the patient was there, I ran a simple matching routine, searching register by register, to see if the code for that avatar was there. Guess what? The avatar was there every time the patient's labs were altered!"

"Larry, this has to be said, though unpleasant," White says. "It seems your systems are not as nearly secure as you once thought."

"Well, they are, but they're inadequate for the level of hacker we are currently dealing with," Larry says.

"I also saw that symbol printed on the labels of two bags of blood transfused in error that killed one of my patients," White says. That's why I invited Dr. David Lesieg from Sarasota General ER where it happened and where he noticed the symbols. Dave, can you raise up the blood bank bags and show us the symbols?"

"Sure, Dr. White."

The attendees mutter their disbelief and acknowledge it is the same avatar.

"Larry, is Sarasota General also a software infrastructure

client of Stargazer?" Joie asks.

"Yes, they are."

"Are there any algorithms, subroutines, passwords, and the like that Sarasota General's systems would share or have in common with BEGH?" Joie continues.

A pause, then a barely audible "Yes" stumbles slowly from Larry's lips.

"So, being in one hospital's network could get you into another hospital's network?" White asks.

"Yes. Possible. If you know how to do it," Larry says.

"Larry, we're not here to criticize. We're here first and foremost to find and stop this hacker, then learn from his handiwork what we can do better to prevent this in the future," White says.

"Larry, why would a hacker leave a symbol everywhere he goes? Seems stupid, if you ask me," Joie says.

"The symbol is a signature, and the reason it's left is mostly ego. Hackers, coders, they all do it, like a dog pissin' on a tree, excuse my English, marking its territory. Sometimes they leave a symbol as was done here, or a line of cryptic code. They play tricks, too, like a coder leaving errors in their code so if the program they wrote is stolen, it won't work in an unapproved environment. Mapmakers do that, too, leave intentional mistakes like an island that doesn't exist, then examine other maps to see if the island is there, and if it is, then that's proof their work was stolen. Nav-system software engineers also leave routes that don't exist and that show up only if the software's copied, then wait to hear about it," Larry says.

"And what do all these Cossack hats have in common? We do not have a connection between them and a person. Are you thinking this Quentin Wellcome is leaving all of these avatars and is our hacker?" Joie asks.

"Not yet, though Quentin Wellcome is the only shiny object we have so far."

"What am I missing here? Why not drag Quentin person's ass in and do interrogation? The Russians would have no problem with that and would have done already. Sorry for curse word," Boris says.

"Because as of this moment, he doesn't exist," Larry broadcasts in deep pain, embarrassment, and an element of shame.

"Excuse me, boss—what do you mean 'doesn't exist'? If he was there, then he exists. No? What am I missing?"

"I mean he left not one traceable molecule of himself. Believe me, Boris, we looked," Larry says.

"Doubt that, boss. He left trace."

"And, Larry, again, you are saying this nonexistent Quentin Wellcome is the closest person we have at the moment as the possible hacker?" Joie asks.

"'Fraid so, at the moment. We either need a major stroke of luck or, somehow, to figure out who he is."

45

Larry continues, "Okay, team, as I said, on the day after the hospital hack, my security folks, who review 24-7 Stargazer building-security video, noted some frames of this Quentin Wellcome engaging in subtle but possibly suspicious behavior during his visit to our facility. He was there on Saturday for a scheduled appointment with our human resources person, Eva Glanston, ostensibly for a job interview."

"What about his credentials, e-mails, contact info?" Joie asks.

"All bogus. We looked," Larry replies. "The staff brought the video imaging to my attention as soon as they saw what bothered them. I immediately showed it to Eva. We saw what for now I'll call *behavior* that could have been him taking company documents. We don't know for certain that he left the building with any of it, however. Moreover, if he did leave the building with the contents, we do not know if it would provide information needed to breach our network, except, possibly, for one thing;

we later determined that the desk he took the trash from was that of Dr. Johnathan Hanovver, our chief scientist for password development and management. He's working on two projects—one, the company-wide Password Unification Project, or PUP, and two, the ECH Password Control Center, or ECH PCC, for the new Everglades Children's Hospital, which opened a week ago and whose network we developed. On interview, Dr. Hanovver admitted to being less than faithful using the secure shredder a mere five steps away from his desk and instead stuffed his trash can with company documents, company work product memos, printouts, e-mails, personal bills, everything. Apparently, for Dr. Hanovver, being sedentary takes on a form of religious zeal. The contents of this trash can would be a hacker's gold mine if taken and could possibly provide access to our network."

"If the hacker goes to Everglades Children's, we will have a major catastrophe on our hands. This is very worrisome, very worrisome indeed," White says.

"The PUP's mission is to look at every password installed in all Stargazer-controlled devices at every installation, going all the way back. Our purpose is to analyze every password's uniqueness and degree of vulnerability, then recommend changes, if needed. The ECH PCC looks at every password each section project development engineer proposed for his ECH project and gives approval for use or not. So, there's a real possibility the papers in the trash could have some incredibly sensitive information," Larry says.

"Why would someone of Dr. Hanovver's importance be sitting out on an open floor and not in a private office with a locked door?" White asks.

"Welcome to the future," Larry says. "Stargazer, being the pioneering technology company it is, is also a leader in corporate organization and management—for example, open-office layouts. This means every employee has a desk in an open, interior, wall-less office floor, with no exceptions, starting with the CEO all the way down. There are partitions and lockable drawers and cabinets, but this open-plan policy, some think, creates a lax mind-set about security, and well, what happened here may be an expression of that. I'll finish by saying the potential theft presents many problems on different levels. If we were breached, Stargazer, their customers, and their projects are now highly vulnerable for either more hacking or being forced to pay a ransom to the hacker. For us here, there's a sense of urgency to arrest him before more damage is done."

White says, "I'm particularly worried about the reference to the Everglades Children's Hospital. It was just built to serve the pediatric needs of the populations on the edge of the Everglades, such as the upscale island communities of Marco Island and Naples and the indigenous Indian tribal communities that are scattered through the Everglades. This hospital is a crucial step in rebuilding the health-care services in that region. Some of you may remember Everglades Regional Medical Center[39] that was embroiled in a bitter fight that ended in abandonment of the hospital in 1998. Everglades Children's, and the community, could be devastated by a cyberattack. I've been wondering if we should notify Everglades Children's and put them on alert just in case. It is frightening, incomprehensible, to think anyone would interfere with the care of a sick child, but we're likely dealing with a very sick mind, and I wouldn't put anything past him. This means we need to be creative and thoughtful and do everything we can to stop him before his warped mind causes any more catastrophes. There have been prior cases of children's hospitals being hacked—for example, Boston Children's.[40] The hacker, under the name *Anonymous*, never harmed a child directly, as far as we know, but made a lot of trouble for the hospital. It had to do with a grievance about a custody matter.

"Anonymous employed a DDoS, or a distributed denial-of-service tactic. A denial-of-service attack is a cyberattack where the perpetrator makes the hospital's internet-based website unavailable to customers and patients by disrupting services of the hospital's internet provider. The hospital had to go to extreme measures to counter the attack. These included determining which hospital systems depended on a hosted internet and were, therefore, vulnerable, like e-prescribing, and those that didn't, like electronic medical records. This means the hacker could have prevented filling of prescriptions by delaying or denying internet access. The hospital had to figure out a way to replace their regular e-mail service, too, which was internet-based and vulnerable, and go to something else. Boston Children's used Voice over IP, which put their communications at great risk. It goes on and on and just reinforces how damn vulnerable we are."

"What about fingerprints, boss?" Boris says.

"We dusted everywhere. He left nothing."

"He left something, boss."

"What'd he leave?"

"He was there, wasn't he, boss?"

46

"Every instance of hacking we can find," White says, " —
beginning with when the hospital went dark, then Larry's
phone getting hacked, then the blood lab analyzer results changed, and finally the blood bank break-in—is
associated with the same Cossack hat symbol being left
in a server as a signature. And these are just the breaches
we know about. There could very likely be more local-
ly or even nationally. Leaving the same signature avatar
could mean it is one person or organization leaving it.
It's not proof, however, as multiple bad actors could col-
lude to leave the same symbol, or a variety of symbols or
signatures, as decoys to confuse us. What we haven't yet
done is associate or link the symbol with a real, living
person. The Stargazer–Quentin Wellcome association is
just a circumstantial possibility. The question is, what do
we know for certain to link the symbol and the person
who put it there? Answer: nothing yet. We know from
Larry that the Cossack hat avatar symbol was left on the
hospital's server, but we don't know who left it, or when.

Have we reviewed the hospital's video surveillance imaging for anything suspicious?"

"I'll check with the hospital security folks. What am I looking for?" Larry says.

"One thing, apart from anything suspicious, would be Quentin Wellcome. He was at Stargazer the day before the breach. If he was also at Beaches End hospital, then that tells me quite a lot. Only Eva, Don Brown, and Larry know from his visit to Stargazer what he looks like. Also, we don't know when he was at the hospital, if at all. One of you would have to watch hospital surveillance video 24-7 starting from the moment of takedown all the way back in time until who knows when. And that's every floor, every camera. I don't know if that is even doable, particularly when we don't know what we're looking for. Also, let's not forget that all the breaches—including the depositing of the avatar—can be and most likely were done remotely. Maybe that video review is not such a good idea," White says.

"Even if we spotted a stranger or suspicious behavior," White continues, "we would still need some way to connect the stranger or behavior to depositing the symbol that night and subsequent hacking behavior. I'm afraid the symbol being present is not directly associated with the malicious software being there—the symbol was in one place in memory, the malicious software in another. There is nothing to connect the two except that in every instance of hacking *we know about,* the symbol is there as well. A smart lawyer would say the symbol could be in countless servers that were not hacked, proving no connection between the symbol and the hack. He or she might ask, 'Do we know the hacker actually left the symbols with the malicious code, or is this all just unbelievable coincidence?'" White says. "The vicious hacking tells me the hacker is desperate, at the end of his line, and feels like he has nothing to lose. I'd say he's capable of anything. I'm thinking, talking clinically as a doctor, characters like this, in spite of their malicious behavior, are actually needy, want to be recognized, loved, and do not want to go down in infamy unknown, or, worse for them, unrecognized and forgotten altogether. Leaving the avatar is an expression of that need. It's a cry for recognition. He'd love to leave his name for full gratification, but the risk is too high. I'd bet he keeps a record of every hack he's ever made. If so, we need that record. He could be saving them on a memory chip, on a thumb drive, on a PC, or in the cloud. Maybe even in the very hospital server we're talking about now. And this is important; he may even be willing to give up what he did for a small reward like public recognition and forgiveness. Or for the least bit of love and affection."

47

"Dr. White, there is an RN from the hospital named Cassandra Cummings here at the reception counter. She says you know her and she needs to speak to you. She says it's important and you'll want to hear what she has to say. Your first two afternoon patients are in your exam rooms, and you have three overbooks already at 4:30. It's 1:00," Sally tells White over the private-line paging system as he is just returning to the office from lunch.

"Important, huh? As in 'now' important?" White replies.

"'Fraid so," Sally says.

"I know her. Show her to my office," White says.

Sally turns to Cassandra. "Dr. White said he'd be happy to see you. He's just about to start patients, so if you can, I'm sure he'd appreciate your being brief. It's down the hall; turn right at the narrow hallway where the file cabinet is sticking out. His is the last office on the right. Careful when you make the turn."

"Oops, excuse me. So sorry," Cassandra says after walking

smack into Harken Righteous as she turns into him in the narrow hallway on her way to White's office.

"No, my fault, ma'am," Righteous mutters reflexively, annoyed but not giving Cassandra even a glance as he continues reading a chart while walking away and not watching where he's going.

"Cassandra? Please come in. Are you okay? You look shaken? Please take a seat."

"Dr. White, this is so strange. You're not going to believe this; you'll probably think I'm crazy," Cassandra says, still pondering Righteous's face, certain he never saw hers.

"Cassandra, excuse me a second." White asks Sally over the private paging system, "Sally, I left my cell phone in my car; can you please get it and hold it for me till I'm done here? The car's unlocked."

"Dr. White," Cassandra starts after stealthily closing his office door. "I hope you remember me. You always see me on the medical floor, and we talk about patients a lot."

"Of course, Cassandra. What's going on?"

"I know everyone is looking for answers about who is responsible for the hacking business. I hear rumors, and I know it is a major problem," Cassandra says, leaning over White's desk, elbowing her way up just past her half of it, getting as close to White as possible, whispering her words.

"Do you know something about it? Are you here about the hacking? Why are you whispering?"

"Well, I've been racking my brain, and I keep coming up with this person, this stranger, well, until now a stranger, who waltzed into the hospital the evening before it went dark," Cassandra says.

"And you think this stranger had something to do with the incident at the hospital?"

"Well, here's the thing, Dr. White. He strolled in like he belonged there, and because he had a stethoscope—and a goofy one at that—hanging out of his pants pocket, I just assumed he was a doctor. I said, 'Good evening, Doctor,' or something like that, but I never saw him before. I mean, I didn't *know* he was a doctor. He looked straight at me and grinned. One of those grins you make when you know something that the person you are grinning at doesn't know you know."

"Why do you think he has something to do with the hospital hacking?"

"Okay, there's more. Two things more, actually. First, he acted like he had been there before, and more than once, too. But I'd never seen him there before."

"Acting how so?"

"He walked directly to a vacant nurse's terminal, didn't look left and didn't look right, just sat down and started typing on the keyboard as if he does it every day. I mean, really. You know how you can tell when someone knows what they are doing? I didn't see the screen, but he knew what he was doing. I mean, the rhythm and speed of the keystrokes, the pattern of typing, *tap, tap, wait, wait, tap, tap.* It has to do with the prompts or something. I hear similar patterns when we nurses log in. He came and he went. Five minutes at most. He didn't ask for help. He didn't ask about a patient, didn't pull a patient's chart, didn't enter a patient's room. He did nothing that a doctor would normally do. Dr. White, you know what I mean. It's what he *didn't* do as much as what he *did* do."

"You said 'until now a stranger.' You saw him again, I take it?"

"Yes, sir, I think I just walked into him as I made the turn down the hall to your office."

"What? Here? Just now? A patient?"

"If he was a patient, he was a patient wearing a white lab coat with a goofy stethoscope hanging out of his pocket, and his nose buried in a patient's chart."

"What kind of tie was he wearing?"

"A red bow tie."

"Shirt?"

"White."

"Shoes?"

"No idea. I kept staring at his face."

"Right answer. What was he wearing at the hospital the night you think you saw him?"

"I remember his face and the stethoscope because of

the same tape on the earpiece. Maybe a bow tie. Not sure."

"The person you are describing here sounds like my new PA. And you think because of how he acted that night makes him the hacker? You realize that is a major accusation you are making. How certain are you that the person you saw at the hospital is the same person you just saw here?"

"One hundred percent. Well, pretty certain."

"Once more, you believe this stranger was acting suspiciously enough, and in a certain way, to link him to the hacking?"

"Yes and no. All I can say is he didn't belong there and acted weird, and I thought someone should know, and I thought telling you was the right thing to do."

"Dr. White, I have your phone," Sally pages over the private line.

"Hold on to it a minute. Sally, where is Harry?" White says.

"He's been in Exam Room 10 with a patient since your visitor arrived."

"Hasn't come out?"

"No."

"Cassandra, if you recognized him, do you think he also recognized you just now?"

"It's possible, but he never lifted his face from the chart he was reading. Maybe his eyes glanced up at me for a second, but he didn't act as if he recognized me."

"Yes, that is a bad habit we noticed he has, reading while walking. His office is down that hall, and he made our turning that corner into a hazard. Okay, Cassandra. What to do? Would seem to me we should first confirm who it was you saw at the hospital that night."

"How would you do that, Dr. White?"

"That I know how to do. Cassandra, you have been very helpful, and I thank you for your coming forward like this. I need you do several things. Do you want to continue to help us out?"

"Yes, of course, Dr. White. That's why I'm here."

"Good. First, at this point, I cannot assume or say he is involved in any way. Neither can you. That would place an enormous burden of liability on us if we were to make that accusation, and it would be extremely unfair to him. I'm going to have to prove what you are saying is true, so I think it best that until I tell you otherwise, you are not to repeat to anyone what we discussed here today. You should forget for now that the events of that evening ever happened. If you did tell anyone of your suspicions or that you were coming to talk to me, then simply say, if asked, we did meet and I didn't make much of it. Best to avoid coming here again or talking to me about it, and to avoid or escape any situations where you may see him again. He has no patients in the hospital, and the hospital is not open for business anyway, so he has no business being over there. If he does confront you about that night or today, just convince him you never saw him before today. We'll agree you were here about a nursing issue you needed help with. I'm going to arrange to help you verify the events of the evening you say you saw him at the hospital. Leave me a personal cell number to reach you. I'm going to have you leave from my private entrance door, which is right out my office door to the left. I'll be in touch soon. And thanks."

After Cassandra leaves, White says over the private line, "Sally, please bring me my phone. I'm going into Room 1 to start seeing patients."

"No, you're not. I have Sarasota General ER on line 3; they need to speak to you stat about Helen Berger, who you sent up this morning."

"Okay."

"No, not okay; Harry wants you to look at Rebecca Fine in Room 10, whom he is seeing for you. He says she looks sick and may need to go to the ER."

48

"Abel, come in. I'm glad you could come to the house this evening."

White writes Abel a note telling Abel he is turning off his phone and putting it away in another room.

"What was that all about?"

"I'll explain later. Abel, I have what I believe is important information about the hacking. It's not something that rises to the level of involving the entire Team Nemesis yet, but it is something I thought you could help us figure out," White starts.

"This afternoon, a BEGH nurse by the name of Cassandra Cummings came to my office to say that she remembers that on the evening before the hospital went down a person she did not know walked onto her floor and behaved suspiciously enough to now make her wonder if he had something to do with the takedown."

"You agree with her on that?"

"I do. One other thing. While at my office, she literally collided with my PA, Harry Right. I mean, she said she physically walked into him, so she saw him up close and personal. I didn't see that happen, but that's what she said. She said he may have glanced at her."

"So?"

"She said my PA is the same person she saw at the hospital that night."

"Whoa! Let me get this straight. First, Cassandra came originally only to tell you about a stranger who acted suspiciously enough for her to bring him to your attention, wondering if he may have something to do with the hacking. Then, while in your office, by accident, she walks into your PA, and the PA happens to look exactly like the stranger? Did I get that right? And by logical extension, she's telling you that your PA could be the town hacker?"

"I told you what I know. The conclusions are yours, but it seems that way."

"That sounds so hard to believe. If all true, it is a major coincidence, and you know the odds are against major coincidences. But on the other hand, if I were a crazy, evil hacker, and I wanted to create some major misery and was crazy enough to want to see the results of my handiwork up close and personal, what would I do? Get a job near the scenes of my crimes, do my stuff, get some popcorn, and watch the fun I created," Abel says. "But let's think about this, Charlie. Are we saying Right was a normal PA first, then became crazy, then learned to code, then became an expert hacker terrorist who prefers patients and hospitals as his victims of choice, and you at the epicenter? Or, equally absurd, are we saying Right was a crazy hacker first who then found a way to become *a* PA, then became *your* PA after deciding to invade our town and take out his madness on your patients?"

"I'm not sure of the exact order of things, Abel, but it's really not that far-fetched. I'm sure the two scenarios you propose are not the only ones, but somewhere in the mix could be the answer. Also, and as you say, all the hacking events we know about have me at the epicenter. Look, I knew it was just a matter of time till someone found the courage to mention that subtle point. Don't know why it took so long. With each hacking event, it became clearer to me that, somehow, I was involved. I'd have to say making my PA the hacker goes a long way to explain that."

"It's kinda hard to ignore, Charlie."

"Do you think I'm his target, or is he just using me to ply his craft?"

"Unless you have a history with him, I think you are the accidental victim in the plot of a very disturbed mind. If he didn't get the job with you, he would have worked as a PA somewhere else and that doc would have been the victim."

"But wouldn't this very smart and crazy hacker know this would, in a short period of time, become obvious?"

"Yes, he would, but I'm thinking he's so smart that he

calculated that by the time that got figured out, he would be done and have vamoosed outta here."

"Wait a minute, Abel, hold on; we are getting way ahead of ourselves here. As far as I'm concerned, all of that is fantasy."

"What do we do now, Charlie?"

"How about this for a plan? I told Cassandra I have a way to confirm what she is saying. I'd like you to meet with her as discreetly as you can and review the hospital's surveillance video together. Go frame by frame backward starting at the blackout and scan for anyone looking out of place or acting suspiciously. And, of course, anyone she points out as being my PA or the stranger. If you agree, meet her at SeeZAll headquarters and breach the hospital's video surveillance servers."

"Sounds great. I'll l do it. Charlie, what are you going to do about your PA? I mean, can he still see patients?"

"I don't think I can ethically let him continue to see patients until we get this figured out. I think I'll ask him to do some chart reviews in the conference room. He probably shouldn't be looking at charts, either, but I need to keep my eye on him. I'll tell him it's part of a study and I could use the help."

"That's sounds good. I'll get with Cassandra right away."

"Thanks, Abel."

"Oh, Charlie, one more thought. Was he thoroughly vetted when you hired him?"

49

"Cassandra, thanks for coming with me to SeeZAll's headquarters to look at the video surveillance imaging," Abel says.

"Wow, this is weird—and scary, too. Dr. White told me you were going to set this up. Is Dr. White coming also?"

"No, we each have our things to do, and he, too, is doing something important tonight. This is Bobby Dawson. Bobby is a specialist who works with us at SeeZAll, not the hospital, and he is not affiliated with any of the authorities assigned to this case."

"Hi, Cassandra. Nice to meet you."

"And this is Ethyn Welch. He is an FBI special agent in their cybercrimes division."

"Hi, Cassandra. Nice to meet you. I have the clearance and authorization to do this."

"This is like the *Twilight Zone* or something."

"Yes, it is, Cassandra. Bobby is going to connect to the hospital's network and scroll down to their video files. He will then take us through the hospital's relevant surveillance video images, step by step. You are going to guide us, however, and tell us when you see something important. Then we'll pause and look. What we are doing and seeing here tonight can be told to no one, and I mean no one. Do you understand? Doing so could be under great penalty. Tell me if you agree."

"Oh, yes, sir, Mr. Valentine. I'm not telling anyone. Ever, never. But can I tell my husband?"

"*No one* includes your husband."

"Got it."

"Good. We're going to review the video starting with the period just before the event and look for any evidence of suspicious behavior and, in particular, the person you thought was acting suspiciously that evening. Bobby knows that. Ready?" Abel says.

"Let's do it," Cassandra says.

"Okay, Bobby, let her roll."

"*Stop.* There he is. Me, too. There, see? He's walking right to the terminal, gives me a nod and a shitty grin, sits down, and starts typing. He has no business being there."

"He doesn't belong there, you say?"

"No. And look, he's not even wearing a hospital staff ID or visitor's badge around his neck. And there's that bow tie and stethoscope with the tape around the earpiece," Cassandra says.

"Do you know him, Cassandra?" Abel says.

"I do now. Don't you know him, Mr. Valentine?"

"No, I've never seen him before."

"He's Dr. White's PA, for Christ's sake. *His PA!*" Cassandra says. "I hope this helps. Will you let Dr. White know? Dr. White doesn't want me communicating with him about this."

"I will show Dr. White the images we are looking at. He'll know if that person is his PA."

"You can tell him I was right."

"He'll know as soon as he sees the images."

"Oh, right."

"Bobby, please mark the images Cassandra notes to show the person of interest with the text *POI.* I'd like you to make me one copy of that entire sequence, beginning with where he strolls in and until he leaves the floor. Copy that to this special flash memory I'm giving you, and give it to me before we leave. The flash drive is specially NTFS formatted so large files can be transferred. It also contains our proprietary encryption at the front end so only I can read it. I want max pixel resolution and any shots of the screen he's typing into. Also, Bobby, please clear any read-sequence log files on the hospital's server controller so there is no trail that we were on their server. Cassandra, as soon as Bobby hands me the memory drive and we complete a chain of custody form, we are done here. Ethyn, what do you think?"

"Well, Abel, let me say this is excellent work. I wish

we at the DOJ had this expertise and so readily available and without the bureaucracy. What I've learned here is that Dr. White's PA visited the hospital the day before the takedown. Yes, his behavior was suspicious in some ways, but nothing overtly criminal or that can be linked to breaking and entering the hospital's network. You asked Bobby to capture images of him typing and the corresponding screenshots. Is there a way to reconstruct his keyboard strokes to learn what he was actually typing? That way, if we see he was entering network sites he shouldn't have been or was depositing malicious code, we nab him."

"That's a great idea; I just don't know if I have enough detail of his fingers on the keyboard and the associated screen prompts, but after we're done here, I will see what I can do to reconstruct his typing behavior," Bobby says.

"One more thing," Ethyn says. "I was thinking we can go to the PA and ask him directly what he was doing there that evening—though if we do and he is the perp, he will disappear in a heartbeat. Are we missing anything?"

"Mr. Valentine, don't forget to show it to Dr. White."

"I'll be seeing him at his house for dinner tonight. I'll show it to him then."

50

"Joie, thanks for joining me for an early dinner, particularly since you said you have an engagement a little later," said Larry. "I really enjoyed it, and it meant a lot to me. Since my wife passed away three years ago, I've learned that I am not good at being alone. Some guys are, but I am definitely not."

"I enjoyed it as well, Larry. Thank you. I've had my share of losses, so I understand. We'll do it again, okay?"

"Definitely okay. I am so alone I went to the movies by myself a few weeks ago and found myself holding my own hand!"

"No way, Larry. You're kidding me, right?"

"Right. Kidding. Yes, that was a joke. But I'm getting lonelier by the week."

"What do you mean?"

"Last week, I noticed my echo stopped talking back to me, and yesterday, I noticed my shadow stopped following me."

"Oh, Larry, you are so funny. I like men who are funny.

I think it says a lot about their personalities."

"Seriously, though, thanks for stopping with me at Stargazer's. You're going to be super impressed with what I'm about to show you."

"Can't wait. What is it? You've really got my curiosity going."

"I figured something out regarding the hacker. I'm going to reconvene the team in the morning to tell them, but until we meet, and since you're on the team, I thought I'd share this with you now. You okay with that?"

"I think so, but if it's about the hacking, don't you think you should tell everyone else on the team at the same time?"

"Yes, ideally, but it's important enough that I'll share it now. If after you see it and think I should tell Charlie now, I can do that. If not, I'll wait until tomorrow morning to tell him. Joie, I know you are a reporter, and you made your principles clear to me. I believe you will not publicize what I learned until I agree it is okay. I also want your help in deciding how to best go forward with what I've learned. Do I have your pledge of confidentiality as we've discussed before?"

"Of course, Larry. Same terms and conditions. What's this about?"

"I discovered who our Quentin Wellcome really is."

"No way. How did you do that? My people have been trying everything without success. Who is he?"

"Let me tell you what I did. First, I got our surveillance

video of when Quentin Wellcome was here at Stargazer. I then took the frame that had the best frontal image of his face and, using digital subtraction methods, deleted all the background, everything but the pixels that defined his face. See here, I've got his face up on the screen.

"Then I went to Amazon, of course."

"What does Amazon have to do with this?"

"Amazon has something to do with everything, Joie. They own an AI facial recognition software company called Amazon Rekognition.[41] I contacted them and explained our special situation, and they were excited to help us. I downloaded their facial recognition software, and using the special formatting instructions they gave me, I plugged in my facial image data string of Mr. Wellcome. I then ran the facial image data through a mash-up app we made that I'll call FaceFacts. That gave me a search-engine-format-compatible image of our Mr. Wellcome. I then used that to do a search of the National Motor Vehicle Title Information System (NMVTIS),[42] which is a searchable database of US driver's license plates and titles. Here is the best part—the database includes license photos. We obtained access to NMVTIS data at no cost through the Regional Information Sharing Systems (RISS) and Law Enforcement Online (LEO) hosted by the FBI using a new, national, searchable database.[43] This is composed of the digital facial image of every person who obtained a license for every kind and purpose, including motor vehicle, fishing, cosmetology, medicine, you name it. Think of it as a fingerprint search except it is a facialprint search. So, basically, what I figured out was a way to take the image of the face of our unknown person and do a search and compare to our national databases of license photographs."

"Brilliant, Larry. What happened?" Joie says.

"I got a match!"

"Who is he?"

"A person named Harken Righteous."

"What kind of a name is that?"

"Right, it's unusual, and one of a kind."

"Oh, it also picked up a photo of him on a different license application."

"What kind?"

"Physician assistant."

"Are you saying our suspect hacker is a licensed PA named Harken Righteous, a.k.a. Quentin Wellcome, and is also the person we saw on the Stargazer surveillance video? And who may be living, working, and hacking right here in Beaches End? Larry, are you thinking what I'm thinking?"

"Depends on what you're thinking."

"I'm thinking the epicenter to all these hacks is our dear Dr. Charlie White."

"So far, we're thinking the same things."

"Does Dr. White have a PA?" Joie asks.

"Don't rightly know. You realize, Joie, that all of this, even if it's true, is still circumstantial and does little, if anything, to connect Righteous to the hacking. A hacker must be caught in the act, or caught with the means and the intent to hack, to prove he is the hacker."

"How accurate is the matching?" Joie asks.

"Very. We obtained a match on the first pass with a facial-imaging-matching correlation of better than 99 percent. There's more. The only vehicle registered to Harken Righteous is a Harley Iron 833 Sportster. It is still registered and titled in Rochester, New York. From there, we got his official public documents, so we have his birth certificate, living addresses, and medical insurers— and from that, the docs he's seen, including a heap of psychiatric and other mental health professionals and everything else. All demographic information, however, still shows Rochester, New York, as his current address."

"This is all very circumstantial for him to be the perp, but as of now, that's all we've got. The only thing that rises to a real worry is that Harken Righteous masqueraded as another person. Why would he do that? To steal proprietary information from you? To hack his way through Beaches End? What am I missing?" Joie says.

"I got these results just minutes before we went out. I think we should tell Dr. White and set up a meeting."

"I'll be seeing Charlie and Heather at their home in just about an hour. I will tell them what you've found then."

249

5I

"Hello, Harry! Come on in. Glad you could join us for dinner," Heather says, standing in the doorway after hearing Harry's Harley announce his arrival in the home's front courtyard.

"Thank you, Mrs. White. Sorry about my loud bike, but I love it to pieces."

"I hear someone else here loves it as well." Heather winks and smiles, glancing over her shoulder to Maribeth.

"I do love it. Hi, Harry," Maribeth says in a soft, sweet tone as she stands in the doorway, anxious to see Harry again. Maribeth looks like a million bucks in a gold, almost-see-through-to-the-bra blouse over black pants and three-inch black heels sprinkled with glimmer, and perfume redolent of jasmine to match.

"Don't know if you know, Harry, but Maribeth is a longtime friend of ours. Her parents and my family go way, way back," Heather says.

Righteous smiles and nods and suddenly looks shy, embarrassed by the attention, not knowing what to make of it all and feeling a bit overwhelmed.

"Charlie, Harry's here!" Heather casts her voice across the great room into the open kitchen where White is busy at the range. "We're expecting two more guests; I can't wait for you to meet them," Heather says. "Charlie, can you come out for a minute to greet Harry?" she calls again, toward the kitchen. "Sorry about that, Harry. He's not being rude; he's just in there putting the finishing touches on his risotto Milanese. If you cook, you know risotto is temperamental and demanding. It's his specialty. So, what can I get you to drink?"

"Oh, some Coke will do, Mrs. White, thank you," Righteous says, taking in as much of Heather as he can while thinking Carlos had her good looks pegged just right.

"Miranda, would you get Mr. Right a Coke, please?" Heather asks one of the servers she's hired for the evening's soirée. "Oh, there's the doorbell. Excuse me, Harry," Heather says.

Opening the door, she says, "Joie, come on in. So glad you could join us for dinner. Oh, I love your outfit. That's from the Dream Weaver Collection on St. Armand's Circle. Am I right? Only ones of a kind there, kid. I'm so jealous. What would you like to drink?" Heather asks. "I've got a Rum Charlie. That's lemonade, coconut rum, and a squeeze of lime. It's Charlie's creation and namesake."

"Sounds great to me. You have a lovely home," Joie says as she pans the house.

"Camila, a Rum Charlie for Ms. Jergé, please," Heather instructs the other server. "Joie, come with me; I want you to meet Harry Right, Charlie's new PA. Harry, come over here! This is Joie Jergé, the local reporter for CNN. You may have seen her on TV reporting on the recent issue with the hospital. Ugh, what a mess!" Heather says, shaking her head in disgust over her mention of the hospital event.

"Hello, Har—I'm sorry, Heather, did you say, 'Harry Right'?"

"Yes, Joie. Why do you ask?"

"I didn't quite hear you." She turns to face Harry. "Harry, good to meet you." Joie is barely able to get the words out without hesitating as she looks at Harry, more inspecting him than just looking at him, squinting, confused and conflicted while breaking out with beads of perspiration along her brow. She is certain Heather just introduced him as Charlie's new PA, Harry Right, but she recognizes him as Quentin Wellcome, the suspected thief in the Stargazer video who Larry Demarseco showed her a short while ago—and identified him as Harken Righteous. She's baffled and confused, standing there in a state of limbo discussing with herself that Harry Right is actually Quentin Wellcome—the Harley-driving possible Stargazer thief and physician assistant, also known as Harken Righteous. *What's going on here?* she thinks. *Did I not just walk by a Harley in the Whites' driveway? And is Harry Right not Dr. White's physician assistant? How many aliases does this jerk have? Did I just meet the town hacker? Jesus Christ, does anyone else here know who he really is?*

"Joie, are you okay? You seem to have drifted off somewhere," Harry says.

"Oh, I'm fine. I was thinking how I forgot to turn over a steak I'm marinating at home. I don't know why some genius can't figure out a way to marinate the top and bottom of a steak without having to keep turning it over. Do you know, Harry? Harry, is that your beautiful Harley out there?" Joie asks.

"Yes, it is. Are you a hog lover?"

"No, not really. I do admire them, but honestly, I am afraid to get on one. Harry, can you please excuse me a second?"

She turns to Heather. "Can I speak to you, privately?" She gives Heather a hearty yank on her sleeve, pinches her arm, and looks daggers that emphasize the urgency of her request.

"Can it wait one minute? I need to get the door," Heather says. Opening the door, she says, "Abel Valentine! So glad you're here."

"Heather, good to see you. Thanks for inviting me. Here's a little something for you."

"How sweet of you. I'll open it in a bit. Would you like

something to drink?"

"No, I'm fine for now. Maybe in a while."

"Come here. I want you to meet some folks." Turning to Harry, she says, "Oh, Harry, can I interrupt you for just a minute?"

Turning back to Joie, she says, "I'll be right with you, I'm so sorry, darling."

To Abel, she says, "Abel, this is Harry Right, Charlie's new PA."

"Hi, Harry. Uh, *Harry*, did you say?"

"Yes, Harry Right."

"Hello, Harry," Abel says without a hitch, though realizing at once this person is the same person he'd just shown Cassandra as the stranger who appeared at BEGH the evening before the hack, and the one Cassandra believed she walked into in White's office. *Holy shit, he thinks, does anyone else here know who he really is? Do Charlie and Heather know? Can't be. They wouldn't have invited him here. Charlie would have told me. I've got to talk to Heather or Charlie pronto.*

"Harry, great to meet you. I think I'm going to take Heather up on that drink. Will you excuse me?"

Turning to Heather, he asks, "May I speak with you, privately, for a minute?"

"Oh, Joie, hi! Good to see you. Glad you are here," Abel says, comforted to see another Team Nemesis member there besides White and Heather.

"Oh, Abel, it's good to see you, too. You don't know how good. Did you meet *Harry*—or whoever he is—yet? He's Charlie's PA," Joie says, speaking softly and over Abel's shoulder, making sure Harry is at a distance that they cannot be overheard.

"I did, and I think I know why you ask," Abel says.

"Abel, I just learned some things from Larry Demarseco that says Harry may be our perp."

"I just learned that, too, but from someone else. I'll explain soon. Do Charlie or Heather know yet?"

"Don't know, but I don't think so. I was supposed to tell Charlie tonight and haven't been able to do it."

"Ditto here. I was to tell him what I learned, also."

"Right now, we need to get to Heather and Charlie—and pronto."

"Oh, Joie, Abel, there you are," Heather says. "You both said you need to speak to me privately. Is it something good, or is something wrong? What is it? Let's move out to the lanai. That should be private enough without being obvious. Are we making sure someone here doesn't hear us?"

"Yes." Joie nods while keeping Righteous in the corner of her vision where she can see him.

"Same here," Abel says, keeping Righteous where he can see him.

"May I say you both are acting kinda weird. What is it?"

"It's Team Nemesis related. It's Harry," they whisper in unison, looking at each other and Righteous with a sense of urgency.

"Heather, just trust us," Joie says. "We need to speak to Charlie, too, but, one, he's busy in the kitchen, and two, I don't want to draw attention to us. How about you and Abel wander over to the back of the lanai and I'll stay here with Harry and Maribeth."

"How's this?" Heather says.

"Great," Abel says. "Very, very briefly, Joie and I have good reason to believe Charlie's PA may be responsible for the hacking."

"What?! Where on earth did that come from? Are you certain?"

"As I said, although we need proof, we both have good reasons to believe it."

"Oh, my God, I'm thinking about Maribeth. Charlie's patients. Charlie."

"We need to get through this evening somehow, and we need to bring Charlie up to speed. And we need to convene Team Nemesis, stat. Best we go back."

"Dinner is served. Please take your places at the dining room table," White announces, ringing his obligatory dinner bell, oblivious to the current state of affairs unfolding in his house, his only worry at the moment that his risotto remains a perfect al dente when served.

"So, Harry, where you hail from?" Abel asks. They are now seated around the dinner table finishing off the risotto sided by a salad of braised fennel, leeks, and Meyer lemon.

"I came here from Rochester, New York," Righteous answers, scanning the table, hoping no one at the table is from there and might know him somehow. He is just starting to wonder if his coming to dinner was such a good idea.

"Never been there," Abel lies, giving Righteous a false sense of comfort.

"You're lucky. It's cold and dark. Did I say cold?" Righteous says, grinning and scanning the table.

"That's funny. It's really cold, I guess, huh?" Joie says, sensing the need.

"The risotto is perfect and delicious, Dr. White," Righteous says, his comfort level not permitting even a minute's worth of silence to linger around the dinner table.

"Yes, it is, Dr. White," Maribeth says, sensing Harry's discomfort and wanting something to say. "Did you all know Harry is not only a PA, he fixes things? Anything, actually. Or is it everything?" Maribeth adds with a giggle, wanting to keep the conversation going.

"Really? What do you fix, Harry?" Joie asks.

"You name it. I always liked to see how things worked.

As a kid, I'd take my mom's appliances apart—like her vacuum cleaner and washing machine. I put most of them back together again."

"That's funny—'put *most* of them back together.' You can fix my vacuum cleaner right now," Heather says as the table laughs at all the banter.

"Make room for dessert, guys. Grand Marnier soufflé," Heather says.

"Harry, I hate to ask you this, but Maribeth brought it up first. Just kidding, Maribeth," Abel says.

"What is it, Mr. Valentine?" Harry says, letting go of his defenses as he is feeling more and more comfortable, perhaps consuming too much Grand Marnier from the soufflé.

"Maribeth says you fix things. I'm desperate. On the way over, my phone went on the fritz. It's frozen in time. I think it might be the battery. I'm pretty tech savvy, but these new phones have me stumped. You don't happen to know anything about these complicated gadgets, do you? I'm lost without it," Abel says, having just moments earlier slipped away to the bathroom to wipe clean his phone's memory, e-mails, and contacts, leaving a few of no significance, intentionally corrupting it in such a way that only an expert could understand the problem he'd created and be able to fix.

"Maybe. Can I see it?" Harry says, all his guards down now, not at all seeing that all at the table, except Maribeth, have dropped their jaws, knowing this must be a ploy, as there is not a thing electronic Abel doesn't understand and cannot fix.

"Hmm. Is there any data in the phone you can't lose?" Harry says.

"Not that I know of. Well, maybe my contacts. Don't use it that much except to talk."

"Did you restart the phone?"

"I did. That I know how to do." Abel laughs, encouraging the others to do the same.

"I'll do what's called a *soft reset*. That won't delete anything." Harry, now the center of attention, is happily immersed up to his eyeballs in the adulation and amazement of Maribeth and everyone else there, including the hired staff, who are now gathered around him.

"Hmm, that didn't work. May I try something else?" Harry asks.

"Please, be my guest," Abel says, watching Harry dig his deserving grave.

"More of anything to eat, anybody? Coffee?" Heather asks, but all are oblivious to everything but Harry's continuing performance.

"There we go," Harry says five minutes and a hundred key punches in rapid succession later.

"What?" Abel says.

"Your phone got corrupted. It's working now," Harry

says.

"Oh, Harry, that was incredible," Maribeth says, squeezing Harry's arm with both hands as the house erupts in applause and Harry never felt so good in all his life.

"Wow! Thanks so much. Boy, did I luck out," Abel says, now realizing he has his work cut out for him if he wants to outsmart this very intelligent but very evil person.

"Mrs. White, would it be okay if Harry and I took a walk around the grounds?" Maribeth asks.

"Of course. Have fun. We'll be here."

52

"Harry, you were so terrific in there. I'm so proud of you," Maribeth says.

"Thank you, Maribeth. This sure is a beautiful home," Harry says as they wander hand in hand around the grounds. In spite of having been out with her a few times, he still struggles with those unfamiliar feelings of attraction to a woman and not knowing exactly how to deal with them. But after his performance at dinner, he felt comfort, and now he feels emboldened.

"I wonder," he begins.

"You wonder what?"

"You caught me, Maribeth. No, I was wondering if I would ever have a home like this, but it wouldn't work."

"Would you like a home like this?"

"Sure. Who wouldn't?"

"If you want something badly enough, you can have it. Do you believe that?"

"Wow, Maribeth, look at that over there!" Harry says, pulling her with him and changing the subject. "Is that a pool or a lake? What's another pool doing way back here? It looks like a cave opening in the water." Harry marvels at the beauty of the entrance to the Whites' grotto. It is dimly lit and surrounded by palms of every type, orchids dangling and swaying over its entrance, their lips and columns like snooping cameras spying on who goes in and what goes on inside, while ferns of every type disguise and conceal its entrance so conveniently located far from the main house.

"Do you swim, Harry?"

"I do, but haven't in a while. Do you?"

"I do," Maribeth says, now rubbing her breast against Harry's elbow and drawing him tightly against it as they stroll the garden's path toward the grotto.

"Does that feel good, Harry?" Maribeth says.

"Sure does," Harry says, drawing ever closer to Maribeth and both of them losing control by the second.

"Does this feel good, Harry?" Maribeth asks as she rubs Harry's ever-growing penis with her other hand. "Time for a swim, you think?" she says softly through lips nibbling his neck.

"Guess so," Harry says. They both manage to peel off their clothes even as they remain stuck to each other, he refusing to succumb to those too familiar urgent warning calls of restraint blaring within his head and struggling to make themselves heard.

53

Now crouched over the dining room table, Abel begins, "Well, let's make this quick while the two of them are still outside. What about the folks you hired here tonight? Can they hear us?"

"No, we're okay; they're in the kitchen," Heather says.

"What's the big secret, guys?" White says, now realizing something is going on.

"Charlie, Heather," Abel continues, "this is going to be hard to believe, but earlier today, using cutting-edge technology, Cassandra and I, at SeeZAll headquarters, reviewed the hospital video, and she confirmed your PA is the stranger she saw at the hospital that evening."

"That is really worrisome on so many levels," White says.

"Wait, Charlie, there's more," Abel says. "Then, also earlier today, Larry, with Joie there, reviewed Stargazer surveillance video and confirmed that the suspicious person who likely took documents from Stargazer is your PA."

"What! What the hell is going on here?" White says.

"Hang on, Charlie," Abel says. "What we're saying is that your PA, Harken Righteous, who right now is meandering around your property with Maribeth and doing God knows what with her, is Quentin Wellcome. I will fill you in on the details, but we need a plan to catch this guy in the act and put an end to his malfeasance once and for all. He is very clever and will be hard to catch," Abel says.

"This is so hard to believe," White says. "Do I have it right that you, Joie, and you, Abel, each came to dinner tonight not knowing what the other knew *and* also didn't know Righteous was here?"

"You got that correct, Charlie," Heather says.

"Holy shit. Sounds a little like that game Clue to me. That's a movie right there. Was it Professor Plum in the dining room with the candlestick?" White, still absorbing the magnitude of all of this, was trying to find some humor in it all. "I was wondering what you were doing with the phone, Abel, but now I get it. Don't we have enough to tell the authorities and just get him arrested?"

"Charlie, look. What we know for a fact is that he was at the hospital the night before the attack, but so were a lot of other people, so it proves nothing. What, at worst, can we say? That he was impersonating a doctor with a pocketed stethoscope? C'mon. He didn't treat anybody. He never said he was a doctor. And as far as Stargazer is concerned, it is a big nothing burger. Yes, Larry has more to do in terms of what he did there, but I don't think there is a direct link to hacking. Let's face it—we have nothing but suspicion and speculation," Abel says.

"I was afraid you'd say that. We have plans for going forward. I'll let the authorities know what we just learned, and we will hold a Team Nemesis meeting as soon as possible. Now, let's—"

"Oh, hello there! Hi, guys. Welcome back," Heather says, catching Harry and Maribeth just walking into the house from the lanai. "Did you have a nice walk?" she asks as the two return from the grotto, now dried off and back into their clothes, having enjoyed all the benefits of the grotto and the amenities of the nearby guesthouse.

"We took a dip. Nice grotto. If it's okay, Harry wants to take me for a ride. Would it be rude to leave, Mrs. White?" Maribeth asks.

"I suppose not," Heather says.

"Thanks for dinner, Dr. and Mrs. White," they both say, Maribeth pulling Righteous's hand and racing out the door. "Good night, Mr. Valentine, Ms. Jergé," they both say as they race out the door, their last words before the roar of the Harley's engine fills the house.

54

White begins, "Thanks to all of you for being here at Team Nemesis headquarters today. We have briefed everyone here that our suspect is my PA, Harken Righteous, a.k.a. Harry Right, a.k.a. Quentin Wellcome. I emphasize *suspect*. We are here to develop strategies and tactics to catch him in the act of hacking and then arrest him. I asked Harry to do a project at the library today and told him I'll be out of the office.

"For the purpose of making sure everyone here is equally informed and starting at the same point, I'm going to go over the important facts as we know them that led us to our conclusion. Because it's crucial for us to understand the psychopathology of the hacker, when I learned of Righteous's frequent health provider visits, I arranged for his psychiatrist, Dr. Rob Norther, to talk to us from Rochester, New York, Righteous's hometown. He is here with us via a SeeZAll A/V link."

"Thank you, Dr. White."

"Special Agent Welch, is there anything you want to say

at this point?"

"Just that I, and the collaborative group of agencies I represent here, are up to date with everything. They agree with our plans. For now, I am in listening mode."

"Okay, then. I asked Abel to take us all back in time to BEGH and that one evening shortly before the hospital was taken down. He'll do that using his company's special imaging technology that will project the 3-D holographic image of Righteous when he impersonated a doctor on the floor that evening, and to whom nurse Cassandra Cummings greeted with 'Good evening, Doctor.' I asked Cassandra to join us to confirm to all that who you are looking at in the hologram is the image of the same person she saw on the medical floor," White says.

"Oh, my God, that's him!" Cassandra says, staring at the life-sized, three-dimensional image seemingly suspended somehow in midair in front of her in the middle of the circular conference table around which all of the attendees are sitting. "It looks like he's right here in the room," she says in some degree of shock and wonderment while half-standing up to reach over and swoosh her hands through the life-like image. "Did he just move, Dr. White?" Cassandra asks.

"I think he may have. No, maybe not. I want to say that, using SeeZAll technology, we are working on capturing his keystrokes in order to reproduce what he was typing when he was at the nurse's computer terminal. That would be a cutting-edge feat. Abel came up with the idea that the mirror image of his keystrokes was very likely reflected onto the computer screen. He thinks by subtracting out spurious reflections like the fluorescent lights, the user himself, and other techniques, he'll be left with just the keystrokes. Is that nifty or what? We'll keep you posted on that," White says. "I'm going to go around the room and ask each of you to tell us what you know or think we need to know about any facet of this from your experience. By the time we leave here, we should have a plan to monitor the hacker, know his every move and location, have a plan for the hacker's arrest, and have a plan for dealing with the post-hacker environment. Okay, Cassandra, anything you want to add?" White says.

"I don't have much more to say. As I said, I was the RN on duty the night he came into the hospital. I was on the medical floor with a patient and greeted him with the usual 'Good evening, Doctor,' just like you said. He just nodded back with a funny, devilish grin. He was there no more than five minutes. I just assumed he was a doctor because he had that stupid stethoscope sticking out of his stupid pocket, and he looked like he knew where he was going and what he was doing. He really fooled me. I see a lot of doctors who I don't know come in. They say they're doctors, anyway. I guess a stethoscope in your pocket doesn't make you a doctor. Oh, one more thing. After he left, I was in a patient's room making a bed, and

I looked out the window toward the parking area. I saw him there. He put on a helmet, got on a motorcycle, and roared off."

"Thank you, Cassandra. We have that episode on surveillances video. He was likely there scouting the place, testing password access to the network, maybe dropping some code into the servers, maybe his signature, and getting a look at the place before the destruction. Pretty sick. That may be his modus operandi—to come in before a destructive hack, test access codes, plug in software patches, and look at his innocent victims before he crushes the place like so many bugs. For that reason alone, to predict his behavior, and prevent that from happening again, we need 24-7 video and GPS location surveillance of him. Wait till you hear our plans for that. You will find it nothing short of unbelievable."

55

White continues, "Because it's crucial for us to understand the psychopathology of the hacker, when I learned of Righteous's frequent mental health provider visits, I arranged for his psychiatrist, Dr. Rob Norther, to talk to us from Rochester, New York, Righteous's hometown. He is here with us via a SeeZAll A/V link. Dr. Norther made sure, as he will explain, all necessary issues of confidentiality have been satisfied," White says."

Dr. Norther begins, "Thank you, Dr. White. After much thought, I now think that my role in this Righteous matter falls into two categories. One category is where my responsibilities to my community take precedence over those to my patient and exceed the customary and usual interpretation and application of HIPAA[44] and other codes and regulations that govern privacy and ethical physician behavior. There is another category. That is when there is a possible greater danger to my patient if I do not share my knowledge about him with you than if I do.

"We have in Righteous a person who thrives on experiencing the misery of others, preferably when he causes it, and who is driven by stealing, plain and simple. It is not stealing in the conventional sense, like the taking of an object; no, it is more the taking from others the good he believes they have in excess compared to the good he has, so as to even those out. The classic meaning of *getting even*. This includes taking away their sense of well-being by taking away their belief they are in good health. A good measure of his personality—though not all of it, mind you—enjoys this taking what isn't his and also hurting others. All of you may see him just hacking medical records, but what you don't see is that it makes him smile on the inside; it really brings him pleasure. He told me when I last saw him that he was thinking of doing exactly these things, but when I pressed him on it, and he knew I would have to notify the authorities if he said he would actually do this, he flatly denied he would. So, what was I to do?

"The problem is how to get him to tell us everything he's done and to whom and when he did it. During one session, he told me he kept a diary. Given his nature, it seems he would keep a detailed account of what he's done. I don't know any more about that. Getting him to share that could be difficult, except for the fact that he's extremely lonely. He's desperate for a relationship, and as hard as he's tried, he was never successful at forming one. This desire is a major conflict for him given his diagnosis, which would suggest otherwise. I believe he has intense repressed sexual urges and a deep desire to be loved. If he were ever able to form a relationship, then he might relent, lessen his malbehaviors, and possibly share that diary."

"Thank you, Dr. Norther," White says. "There's another issue. I've become aware that Harry, and one of my office assistants, Maribeth, have been seeing quite a bit of each other. He's taken her on his motorcycle. I'm certain they've been intimate. Should we tell her what we know about Harry and maybe—and I know this is a stretch— even ask her to help us? Maybe we need to warn her to keep her distance, as he might be dangerous, and if so, how do I explain why he is still working for us, or for anybody for that matter? I need to explain why he isn't being arrested right now. We have a difficult conundrum here—needing to wait to arrest him in order to get sufficient proof, and not waiting to arrest him in order to protect society. In either case, we might have a lot of explaining to do. With that in mind, I have to ask you, Dr. Norther, how depraved and dangerous is he? We know he's a psychopath, at least when behind a computer screen tapping at a keyboard—and violent with it, to say the least—but what I'm asking about is how dangerous at the one-on-one level, like when he is with Maribeth. Would he harm her?" White asks.

"Let me explain about Mr. Righteous," Norther begins. "This complex individual desperately seeks human tenderness and affection, so harming anyone from whom he might get these would be anathema to him. Quite to the contrary, he would protect that person in the hope of getting the affection he wants. That's one side of his mental coin, so to speak. The other side is where he believes these human emotions were stolen from him, hence his belief he has the right to steal from others. Yet the absence of fulfillment of his all-consuming desire to be loved makes him bitter and resentful, and so he lashes out in anger to society for denying him these things. He has issues, don't get me wrong, but it is my considered opinion that person-to-person violence isn't one of them. He isn't the kind to set fires or blow up rabbits. To the contrary, he would collect stray and orphaned animals of all kinds, some left on his doorstep, and secure their care.

"You should also know about the measure of his depravity and the luck of coincidence," Norther says. "I play squash at Midtown Athletic Club; I've done so with the same partner for ten years or more. Squash, if anything, is a violent game. Unlike a racquetball ball, which bounces when dropped, a squash ball doesn't bounce at all, or about as much as would a rock. The game, therefore, is one of swatting a rock-like ball as hard as you can to cause it to bounce off a wall in such a way as to have your partner miss the return. That said, one day, my squash partner, Bob Baker an internist in Rochester, said, 'Rob, can I get a curbside psych consult? What do you call, psychiatrically speaking, a person who changes his mother's lab result to make her look sick, which then causes me, her doctor, upon reading the report, to prescribe a medication for her she didn't need?' I said, 'I'd call him crazy, and also Harken Righteous.' Stunned, Baker said to me, 'You know him?' I said it was a wild guess, but that yes, I knew him. I asked Bob how he knew Righteous did that. He said that Righteous came to him one day to say he was Nora's son and knew he was her doctor. He said he was leaving Rochester for good and that he was screwing around on his computer and while experimenting managed to change her thyroid test for the fun of it. He said he didn't mean to hurt her. And, Baker said, the son was on the phone listening in when Baker called to tell his mom about it. He told Bob he was sorry and would never do it again. I didn't report it because I couldn't prove he did it. Bob had no way to connect me to the son. Righteous *told* Dr. Baker to call his mom and tell her to stop the medicine and he'll recheck her thyroid in a few weeks and it would likely be normal. Can you imagine? He's telling the doctor what to do. This, my friends, is one example of his twisted personality. And that, ladies and gentlemen, is our boy. Oh, as for your question, no, I don't think he would harm Maribeth."

"So," White says, "Maribeth, acting as a mole, so to speak, could work. If they are already going out, then the relationship wouldn't be new or seem out of the ordinary for him or make him suspicious. When she learns what we have to say about him, it'll be a major shock to her, I'm sure. Heather, what about liability issues?"

"If we explain everything to her—the risks and the rewards—I think we're okay," Heather says. "But, you know, you guys, did you stop to think Maribeth may have true affection for Harry? You just don't go up to her and say, 'Well, I know you may love Harry, but would you mind spying on him for us?' You guys are something else. Men!"

"You're right, Heather. Who will recruit Maribeth?" White asks, as all turn and look at Heather.

"Hey, wait a minute, this wasn't my idea," Heather says as the group falls silent and continues staring.

"Heather, I really think that of everyone here you are the one Maribeth would listen to the most. Don't you agree?" White says.

"I suppose you're right. I'll invite her over as soon as possible and ask if she'll do it."

56

"Maribeth, thank you for coming over on such short notice."

"What is it, Mrs. White? Did I do something wrong? We shouldn't have left after dinner as we did. I'm sorry."

"No, it's not that. I need to tell you something you may find hard to believe and possibly hurtful."

"What is it?"

"Maribeth, I'll need you to swear that what I'm about to tell you will be held in strict confidence. If you share this with anyone, particularly Harry, the consequences could be disastrous for you, Harry, all of us. Do you understand and agree?"

"Yes, Mrs. White, I do."

"We have reason to believe Harry is the Beaches End hacker."

"What are you saying? No way. How can that be? I'm with him so much and I've seen nothing to suggest that."

"I'll tell you what we know."

"Charlie, I spoke to Maribeth about Harry as you had asked me to do. She was heartbroken at the idea that Harry could have done all those horrible things. She finds it hard to believe and sees him as a kind, gentle, affectionate man. I think she might even be in love with him. She'll help us any way she can, but she said she hopes to prove Harry isn't the person we think he might be. He's been nothing but nice to her."

"Maybe so, but a man can wear many masks. We'll see who the real Harken Righteous is soon enough."

57

White addresses Team Nemesis: "Here's our plan. We will need to know where Righteous is at all times. We will wire both Righteous and his motorcycle, placing a GPS-location receiver and transmitter on him and on his bike and feeding that location data into our Team Nemesis HQ computers. With him and his bike on GPS, we'll know where he is and how far away he is from his apartment at all times and how much time we would have there. Deshaun, O. J., you are here because of your expertise in these matters. Tell us what you know and can do."

"Yes, Dr. White," Deshaun says. "As part of my work in the Division of Forensic Services, which is a part of the Illinois Police Department, I've had some experience with buggin' bikes. We used some thin-film, nanotechnology, Bluetooth-enabled, GPS-location senders, or transmitters. We modified a nano-GPS-locator device that was about the size of a penny and made it thinner than a playing card. It was flexible, too, and when we were done it was smaller than a dime. Now there are even smaller ones, like the Israelis have.[45] I spoke with the Israelis and they shipped us ones weighing just 2.5 grams. It's called the Micro Hornet GPS chip and is the world's smallest. The Micro Hornet has the added benefit of including an integrated antenna, along with all the filters, radio frequency shields, and processing capabilities of full-sized chips, making it ideal for devices that require low-profile components, like ours."

Deshaun continues. "We watched bikers at bike stops and made a few observations. One, Harley owners love everything Harley Davidson, including jewelry. We got one of the Harley bar-and-shield logo necklaces and had one of our jeweler operatives mill out a pocket on the back for the GPS-locator device, then glue on a matching back cover. You couldn't tell a thing had been done. The back cover was also a one-way mirror, so random light would charge the thing, and it didn't take much light to charge it. Then, we put the bugged necklace in a Harley gift box and left it on the guy's bike with a note. The note was in biker lingo and said something like, 'Dude, nice hog. Here's a little gift from your local Harley owners' group. Stop by our church any day.' He wore it, and our inside Harley guy told us he never showed up at their church, which is slang for their clubhouse. And you know, you can now buy jewelry[46] with GPS senders and cameras right off the internet. We were first."

"Very nice, Deshaun," White says. "I think I'd like you to work with O. J. and do the necklace thing to our guy. By the way, he has a dog, too, who goes just about everywhere with him. He keeps wanting to bring it to work. I told him no. I want to wire the dog."

"No problem, Dr. White," O. J. says. "We actually did this before. Once we had one of our officers dress up as an old lady—cane, shawl, and everything—and hobble up to the perp and ask what the dog's name was while bending down to pet the dog a few times. Unbeknownst to the perp, our officer stuck a nano-GPS device with adhesive on one side underneath the dog's collar. We can work up something like that, too, if you want."

"Excellent. Very good, Let's do it," White says.

"What's Righteous's dog's name?" O. J. asks.

"Oh, you won't believe this, either," White says. "He has this nasty game he plays. I watched him do it outside our office once. A patient of mine was there and asked him the dog's name, and Righteous said, 'Askim.' This sounds like he's telling the person to ask the dog his name—you know, like, 'Ask him, don't ask me.' This is guaranteed to upset the person asking, so the patient kept asking Righteous for the dog's name, and Righteous kept saying, 'Askim,' while my patient kept getting angrier and angrier. Finally, Righteous spelled the name out, and the patient just wanted to kill him. Funny and pitiful at the same time. So we have a lunatic hacker with a sick sense of humor. Before I forget, can you put an audio channel on each of those senders, as well?"

"Can do," Deshaun says.

"Okay, Deshaun, you work with O. J. to get the GPS devices installed on the perp and the dog and coordinate the transmission to headquarters with Abel. Is that okay, Abel?" White says.

"Sure thing, Charlie. All sounds so good."

"Oh, I also want to have a GPS-locater receiver-transmitter with a video camera and audio channel on his bike. Is that possible Deshaun? O.J.?" White asks.

"No problem there either, Dr. White," Deshaun says. "Right O. J.? Putting a GPS and imaging device on a bike is a little problematic because these biker folks go over their bikes with a fine-toothed comb. Whenever they park their bikes, they're always left in their line of sight. We've done it before, but we need ten to fifteen minutes of unseen access to the bike, which means distracting the guy for that long. We'd need to first ID the make and model of the perp's bike and the headlamp. We take a photo of the headlamp to get the make and model and the mounting brackets and the front bezel."

"That's something Sally might be able to do for us when Righteous is in the office and not watching. He does park the bike outside of the rooms he uses, and they have windows. We're going to keep him in the library room where he can be seen. I'll ask Sally to work it out," White says.

"Sometimes these bikers replace original equipment with fancy upgrades, so we need to know what he did in order to know what we need to do. Then we buy either the OEM—sorry, that stands for *original equipment manufacturer*—replacement headlamp, or whatever's actually on the bike, and install our audio-video system inside the housing, with the camera right behind the clear part of the lens of the headlamp, all before we mount it on the bike. Our stuff's solar powered, so power's no problem. Our replacement process is usually to remove a few screws holding on the headlight's bezel, that's the rim, pop out the old lamp, plug in our modified lamp, put back the bezel, and we're out of there. Right, O. J.?" Deshaun says.

"Check," O. J. says with a wink to Deshaun.

"Excellent again," White says. "Okay, Deshaun, you, O. J., and Abel are in charge of getting the bike, the dog, and the suspect wired up and online the way we discussed. I know wiring the dog sounds crazy, but think of it as providing us some needed redundancy. To be clear, Deshaun and O. J. will provide us three GPS-location receiver-transmitter channels; one is the perp's necklace channel, if he falls for the gift, two is the dog channel, and three is on the bike, which will have a frontal-view video channel as well. If this works, then we'll have him, the bike, and the dog on GPS 24-7. After Deshaun and O. J. complete their assignment, we'll know where this guy is every second of the day based on his GPS coordinates, and we'll have audio and video surveillance on him, too. This tells us where he is. The next problem is to know what he is doing. The problem, there is gaining line of sight access to him when he's using his PC, where I'm betting he does his mischief, likely at his home. I want to capture him at his computer in the act invading a website. Abel, tell us what you got."

"Thanks, Charlie. I'm thinking we could employ our latest drone we call Quadtera.[47] Our Quadtera drone has four wing props and has many unique features.

"The Quadtera drone acts as a mother drone in that it has a birthing bay that releases baby drones we call Ovara[48] drones, or an Ovarum[49] drone, from the Greek *ova* for *egg*. The Ovara are little, egg-like drones,[50] small enough, maybe a couple cubic inches or so, to look like an almost real fly on the wall. They are the worker ants, the frontline spies, the pawns of the Quadtera's army. Ovara are camouflaged a number of ways and often customized for each case. Anyway, up to three Ovara can be stored and 'birthed,' or launched, from the Quadtera's birthing bay.

"The mother drone, the Quadtera drone, is a partly human-operator-guided, partly onboard-AI-computer-guided and -programmed, Bluetooth-enabled drone that's programmable in that target-GPS coordinates, route information, target instructions, and more are entered by the human operator but can be AI-altered in-route. It fetches its starting and real-time route coordinates from its onboard computer. Ovara drones are remarkable in that they are Bluetooth linked to their mother, Quadtera, drone and each has a unique ID that shares the same extension with the mother drone. Quadtera acts as the more robust master drone and hovers or docks in range of its children Ovara drones. Quadtera can, through a Bluetooth read, recognize the Ovara that it birthed or are associated with it. It recognizes its children, in other words. We once watched in amazement a Quadtera mother drone autonomously adopt and accept for recharging a lost Ovara that wasn't 'hers.' A string of code was found in the Quadtera birthing record memory that added that rogue Ovara's ID to its birthing record," Abel says. "We still don't know how it overrode the 'you're not mine' auto-immune rejection subroutines for alien Ovara."

"What did he just say? I thought he said something about a mother drone adopting a baby drone? Is that what I heard? Are drones having sex? Somebody?" Ethyn asks, bewildered thinking he's heard everything before.

"I'll explain, Ethyn. Each Ovarum, when in the landed, folded, nonflying position, is coated with an array of micro suction cups, similar to what many insects and frogs have on their feet and toes, so that when it lands or is dropped or placed, and the wings housing the propellers are closed, it will stick to a wall, a helmet, a window, a fender, back of a PC lid, you name it. Some of the functions each Ovarum can perform are acting as a Wi-Fi hot spot, an audio and video recorder, a visual or Wi-Fi keystroke logger, and many others.

"Another feature of the Quadtera-Ovarum relationship is in-flight recharging, the equivalent of in-flight refueling. The recharging isn't the exchange of liquid fuel but the wireless recharging of the Ovara's battery. When an Ovarum senses it's reached a low-battery state, it searches for the nearest Mother Quadtera drone, flies within charging range, enters the birthing bay, and, when recharged, returns to its mission. Each Quadtera and Ovarum has a fiber-optic, 360-degree-articulated camera eye that mimics most of the functions of the living Diptera eye and can detect obstacles along its course. The en route obstacle encounter data are used for automatic, or operator-controlled, escape-and-avoidance flight maneuvers. All obstacles are remembered for future use. Ovarum image data—all encrypted, of course—are fed to Quadtera's onboard computer and can be streamed in real time to the operator at Team Nemesis headquarters.

"Oh, and one more thing. Every Ovarum is 3-D printed. Right now, we still have to print it in sections and hand assemble those, but we're down to just four sections needing human assembly. And get this—the 3-D printer software that completely defines each Ovarum drone and is used to make a particular Ovarum is stored on a male, read-only, wireless memory chip on that Ovarum drone. Think of that memory chip as storing the complete DNA for that Ovarum drone, making it a hermaphroditic creature.

"To reproduce a clone of an Ovarum drone, the Ovarum drone hovers next to a birthing equipped Quadtera drone and wirelessly sends its digital DNA to the Quadtera drone. In that way the Ovarum's memory is read. To its memory is added the interactive memory of the mother drone as in the parent educating the child. From there, the Quadtera can transmit the plans to the nearest 3-D printer to print a clone of the Ovarum drone. Not only is that Ovarum reproduced exactly as it is structurally, the process also reproduces the Ovarum's memory—that is, the entire history of its travels, incidents, accidents, travel obstacles, images, everything. This means the infant Ovarum starts its life with the same historical experiences and memories as its parent. Essentially, we've endowed each newborn Ovarum with preprogrammed memory and behavior that in some ways allows the equivalent of imprinting that occurs regularly in nature. Each Ovarum knows its own family!

"Most, if not all drones, emit noise—some very loud, others quieter. The quietest ones employ insulation and antivibration techniques, but even these may not be good for stealth applications where you want the drone to arrive and land silently. What we've done, in addition to conventional antivibration and insulation techniques, is employ our proprietary near-field, or near-drone, noise-cancellation technology. That drone has a reflecting microphone, like a Dish TV antenna, that samples the drone's noise emission in a three-foot radius from the drone—that is, the system samples the noise as it's heard at a distance of up to three feet from the moving drone. Actually, the sampling distance is almost infinite but diminishes by the square of the distance from the antenna and is just limited by the physics of the flight environment. Then the recorded sound is sent to an onboard inverting amplifier that inverts and then amplifies the signal and sends it to an onboard speaker array. The net effect is to cancel the sound of the drone in the air-space volume where it operates. It works like the noise-canceling headphones, except this works in the surrounding air, not between the ears.

"We have another drone I need to tell you about," Abel says. "It's the mother of all our drones; it's a fighter drone, and we named it Eagle 1. Eagle 1 is mainly a human-flight-controlled drone that's a high-speed, lethal weapon. First, it can fly up to 160 miles per hour, faster than most automobiles and motorcycles will likely travel. It has our proprietary JetAssist capability. JetAssist uses our onboard, ultralight, miniature, CO2-pressurized, soft carbon fiber, self-deflating, carbon-composites canisters. These enable Eagle 1 to accelerate from a current speed to twice that speed for up to ten seconds. This is useful for emergent acceleration needs and high-speed turns that could occur in an active chase. It has 360-degree vision, headless flight, and can 'see' day or night. It carries two lethal lasers that can burn a hole in a tire in a second or take an out an eye in a hundred milliseconds through a helmet visor. It can release up to three GPS-locater, transmitter-equipped Ovara to attach to a speeding car or motorcycle so as to never lose the vehicle being chased even when out of visual sight. One other feature is that when used in conjunction with two smaller, synchronized satellite drones flying nearby, it can project holograms into the space between the three drones. It can even do this even at high speeds while chasing an object.

"All these functions are controlled at the Eagle 1 Monitor Console 3 here at SeeZAll. Charlie, I want to train you on the Eagle 1 to be its commander. I can think of several scenarios where we have this guy on the run and need to chase and stop him. The Eagle 1 would be the obvious asset of choice for this operation," Abel says.

"Unbelievable, Abel. I think once I get my hands on Eagle 1, I'll never want to let go. Thank you for all that," White says. "So, here's a plan. We acquire the hacker's GPS coordinates from the nano-GPS transmitters O. J. and Deshaun will place on him and his bike and feed those to a Quadtera onboard computer. This would include, if we're lucky, real-time GPS coordinates from the motorcycle, from the hacker himself, via the Harley necklace, and from the dog. We also send those to our HQ monitors," White says.

"Charlie, tell us again, why do we need to link up the dog?" Joie asks.

"It's a matter of redundancy, Joie. In a highly sophisticated operation like this, we can't expect everything to work as planned. If we get the dog's transmitter to work, which, by the way, is the easiest one to place, we get confirmation that our transmitter works and will know if the range and power calculations and settings are correct. In addition, if we get both the dog and the hacker's transmitter to work, then we'll have two separate coordinate transmissions to verify location information. By that, I mean if we get both transmissions and the coordinates are the same or close, that tells us the two are together. If the dog is out and running around and the suspect's in the house, then we get more location information. Also, if we have plans to make a house call on the hacker, we might want to do that when the dog is elsewhere.

"So, to continue our plan," White says. "We fly a Quadtera with three Ovara on board to a destination at the suspect's home. We'll need to know in advance where our target destination in the home will be. That will be where the computer he uses is located if we want to catch him in the act of hacking. Preferably, that will be an outside location—say, a lanai or maybe an inside room with an open window so we can fly an Ovarum drone inside. We do this when he is out of the house. We hover the Quadtera close enough to where a good launching spot is, then launch an Ovarum. The Ovarum will land and stick to a spot near his PC—say, a corner of the lanai or the room he's in. Once landed, we want to do a number of things. We will run the Ovarum's onboard keystroke logger app that will record every keystroke he makes. We'll need to learn if he uses a wireless keyboard or hardwired to decide what method of key-logging we'll use. Maybe our inside person can help us with that. From that, we can reconstruct where he navigates on the internet, maybe even read and locate his diary, and find out who else, if anybody, he's communicating with. At this point, I'll stop and take comments."

"I plan to have Maribeth wear a wire so we'll know if anything goes wrong. Deshaun, O. J., can you do that?" Heather asks.

"Wired jewelry[51] is our specialty, Mrs. White," Deshaun says. "For a hundred bucks or so, I can buy a pendant necklace with a GPS signal right off the shelf. I can set geographic limits so I get an automatic alert when it's outside a GPS area I specify and have it send me text message alerts. This is the same basic circuitry in all the bugs, or wires, we placed. And we can add some special sauce to it, like putting in a solid-state laser in a brooch that operates in the UV spectrum. The beam is invisible to the human eye and similar in function to the checkout scanner at the grocery store, that spinning red light that reads the bar codes, only this one's not visible. We'd use it to read data from the Ovara stuck around his apartment.

"The brooch could have stationary crystals that look like jewelry but are grown as lenses. They would scan and search for the ID 'bar codes' we'll place on the surfaces of the Ovara. When Maribeth moves around, the crystals will move with her and, in effect, scan the environment. When it finds a recognizable ID code in range, it uses its Bluetooth-enabled reader to read the memory of the device and stores it in its own memory, then clears the device's memory to make room for more data. The Quadtera and egg-drone memories act as a buffer until they're read by the brooch. Then we 'read' her brooch here when we debrief her and analyze the data."

"Let's be clear what we're doing here," White says. "If the bugs work, we'll know where he is every second of the day. If the drones work, we'll have audio and visual on him, as well, and, if we're lucky, the Quadtera egg running the keystroke logger will log his all his computer keystrokes, which could lead us to his diary and his hacking. Having Maribeth on-site and wired, could be the clincher we need to get our hands on that diary and crack this wide open."

58

"Abel, a smart doctor," White explains, "doesn't plan for every illness a patient might get or even plan for every complication a patient might have. Instead, doctors plan for the *most common* and *treatable* diseases and complications before thinking of the unlikely and untreatable ones. There's a saying for that in medicine that if you hear hoofbeats, think horses, not zebras. Our team, therefore, should not think of every contingency Righteous can bring us but should plan for the most likely ones we can expect and prepare best for those. What worries me the most is if he hops on his Harley and flees," White says.

"Absolutely, Charlie. This is why the Eagle 1 drone is our best weapon if he chooses to flee on his bike," Abel says.

"So, here are the scenarios," White says. "We operate Team Nemesis as a surveillance team monitoring Righteous every second of the day and night. We dispatch Maribeth to become closer with him and help us learn where his alleged diary is while generally keeping her eye on him. We don't know if his PC has everything we need to know or not. Once we're assured we have the record of his dirty work, then we can arrest him," White says.

"Unless he takes off, like you said, Charlie. But don't you worry, I'm going to show you how to stay right with him. Have you ever flown a plane?" Abel asks.

"Yes, but for a very short period. I got some basics under my belt training with an ob-gyn buddy of mine up north several years ago."

"Good. That'll make it easier to train you on how to use our Eagle 1 drone simulator. As our leader, and the one with the most personal investment, you'll be at the controls of Console 3, the Eagle 1 Command Center and, no kidding around, will have laser beams and holograms at your disposal. And that's not even the half of it. Sound like fun?" Abel says.

"Sure does. I can't wait to get started."

"All right, let's move over to Console 3 and get you started. You'll be in total control in no time, and I'll be right there with you, second seat on your right, if you need me. I'm just going to teach you some tricks, then you'll be all set for prime time."

"Charlie, I'm surprised at how quickly you grasped the basic flight skills you need to fly Eagle 1. You can take off and land like a pro and can literally fly circles around things without losing orientation. You're now officially an intermediate-level drone pilot. Well done!" Abel says. "Now, let's say you're chasing the creep on his bike, and you're right alongside him. You need to stop him one way or another. You might harass him enough to get him to pull over and stop, then if he starts to run, use Eagle 1's red Taser—yes, Taser—to take him down until one of our trained Team Nemesis guys or the feds get there, cuff him, and arrest him.

"Here's another one of the most basic flying tricks, known as the roll[52] or barrel roll. This is when Eagle 1 does a full 360-degree rotation along its roll axis and comes out upright again. The roll axis is the long axis of the drone, just like the spear in a shish kebab. Like many of these tricks, a roll will cause a significant loss of altitude, so make sure you have enough space between you and the ground! Eagle 1 has an automatic roll function built in. To do a barrel roll, give full throttle and nose up until you're high enough, then press the barrel roll button on your console, and it'll do it for you."

"What good is a barrel roll chasing a guy going a hundred miles an hour on a Harley?" White says.

"It may be you need to get him to crash. We'd rather he not die so we can interrogate him and let justice have its way with him. The barrel roll could be enough distraction to get him to crash. Here on the Eagle 1 simulator, I can insert a motorcycle going any speed you want and have you practice keeping up and doing rolls around at the driver. Next are flips, which are really rolls along different axes. For left and right flips, you use the roll axis. For front and backflips, you use the pitch axis. You can also do something known as a cross-axis flip, where you push the stick diagonally to give both full pitch and roll. This will flip Eagle 1 diagonally.

"You can easily do more advanced versions of this trick by making more than one flip consecutively, but keep aware of how much extra altitude you need to do this right. A higher control rate may also be useful so that Eagle 1 flips faster and loses less height. Apart from relatively simple flip tricks, you can also step up your game with some more advanced flight techniques. One of the best-looking flight maneuvers is the banked turn. The drone doesn't stay level while turning using only yaw, but banks laterally. Not only does this look cool, it also makes for a much faster turn. You'll want to try these maneuvers nose-in, with the front of Eagle 1 facing toward you when not in headless mode. This is a great way to hone your orientation skills."

"Sounds like fun, but this isn't about having fun; it's about stopping this guy, dead or alive. What do you got for that?" White says.

"Okay. What we've got for that is our laser bullet. You control its energy, or power, light-wavelength spectrum, and target. It has an onboard ToF LiDAR system. *LiDAR* stands for *light detection and ranging* and uses pulsed lasers to gauge the distance to remote objects. So, if you set the target on the bike driver's helmet visor and press Fire, it will shoot a laser beam at the visor on the helmet at just enough energy to cause a glare or even melt it. That should stop him cold."

"Suppose he's not wearing a helmet?"

"He's out of luck. Blinded and still crashes."

59

JULY. *Oh, Diary, it's hot. Rochester it ain't, but I prefer the heat to the cold. It's been a while since we spoke. So much to catch up. I went to a coder meetup and met some nice folks. I have to say, I'm getting more social here in Florida, and I don't know why. I met lots of women coders, too. I didn't know there were so many, and I'm starting to like being around them—women, that is. Folks come from all over. I met my new friends Albert and Lydia from Russia, Gerda from Lithuania, and Lillian and Phyllis from around here, Fort Myers, I think. It was fun.*

I'm seeing Maribeth a lot. I have to say I feel good around her, like a void filled. She comes over a lot. Askim loves her, sits on her lap or at her feet. They're with me on the lanai, where I do my stuff. Neither knows what I'm doing. The dog might.

The Whites had me over for dinner recently. I met some of their friends. One is a French TV reporter who I saw on TV reporting my BEGH deeds. Oh, how much I wanted to tell her it was me—you know, "Say, Joie, I just want to tell you it was my work you were reporting on. Any questions I can answer?" Yeah, right. What a wasted opportunity for both of us. What a headline it would have been. TV REPORTER DISCOVERS BEGH HACKER AT A DINNER PARTY. *The other person I met owns a company here. He was supposed to be a tech guy, but his phone got corrupted and he couldn't fix it. Guess what? I did! They seemed like nice folks. I spent most of the time with my new best friend from the office, Maribeth. Well, Diary, I must be somebody else now, because before I knew it, we were in the grotto bare-ass naked having incredible sex. Then we did it again in their guesthouse. A major turning point for me. Can you believe it?!*

Diary, I think I'm changing, starting to be more in touch with feelings I know are there but haven't surfaced in a long time. You know, the ones that live across that big divide. Why are you changing now, you ask? One, the kindness and devotion Dr. White shows to his patients is new to me, and I like it and I want to understand how to give and receive it. Two, Maribeth. She likes me, and I know I desperately want someone to feel that way about me.

I realize I can't live in two worlds. Who really can? I mean, if I'm going to continue to hack and cause mayhem, I have to do it alone and can't drag Maribeth along. If I want to have a serious relationship with her, I have to quit my shenanigans, don't I? Question is, Diary, is it too late to change?

That said, I need to do my final hack—the big one. If I

don't, then I'll think I'm a failure and my brain might implode. I'll take the risk of getting caught. Funny, some part of me wouldn't mind getting caught. In a way, I want the world to know it was me who did these beautiful hacks because you have to be smart to pull them off like that. And I want them to know what drove me to do them, it's that roaring engine sans governor inside my head that drives my engine of loneliness.

Anyway, from my Stargazer loot, I unscrambled many passwords, some of which were to the network at the Everglades Children's Hospital. What a big prize it would be to hack there.

Looking at the map, they're at the western edge of the Everglades. It would take maybe an hour to get down there on my bike. I'd start on Route 41 South, then head east on the Tamiami Trail taking the small back roads. I'll go as far as Eco Pond. In advance, I'll rent an airboat so when I get there I'll tie down my bike on it and head northeast through the swamps of the Everglades toward Florida City. That's maybe a hundred miles. Once there, assuming I avoid the gators, crocodiles, and cottonmouths, I'll dock near a chickee and dump the boat, then take the Harley south on Route 1 to Largo, where I'll stay put a while.

I've got all the stuff I need for this, especially a satellite nav system and proper National Ocean Survey maps. I'll need to forge a Florida boater's license—can't risk doing it the legal way—and, before I go, take the one-day airboat pilot course at Siesta Key.

Why am I doing this, Diary? Because it's the best way for me to disappear. Flash, boom, gone.

In a few days, I'll pay Everglades Children's a visit just like I did with Beaches End. I'll stroll in, log in to their network, put in a software patch that will do something big later on, log out, and leave. Then I'll hop on my bike and get the hell out of town.

Think that's it for now.

Mr. Sleep is callin' my name.

Good night, Diary.

Good night, my sweet Maribeth.

60

Back at Team Nemesis headquarters. "Ladies and gentleman, welcome, and thanks for coming," White says. "This is our first day of full operation, and I see everyone's at their stations. O. J. and Deshaun installed the electronics on Righteous, his dog, and his bike and provided Maribeth a GPS-wired brooch. We've flown and landed all the monitoring drones to their specified destinations and out of sight. Along with a drone-pilot specialist backup at each station, kindly provided by Abel, we have Deshaun at Monitor 1, O. J. at Monitor 2, and me and Heather at Monitor 3, the Eagle 1 drone station. These will be manned 24-7 with relief from Abel's staff as needed. Joie is an observer.

"Monitor 1 shows the location of Righteous, his apartment, his dog, and his bike. You see four icons, each superimposed over the map of the street they're on in the background. The map changes as each GPS-wired object moves but keeps our target centered. If the distance between any one of them exceeds the range for the map, the software splits up the display into two screens. If one signal is static because the subject isn't moving, then the icon is a static image at its location. If a subject is moving—say, the bike—then the bike icon blinks at the rate it's moving and moves in real time with the map changing accordingly. The icon for Righteous is the shadow silhouette image of his head, the dog icon is an image of his dog, and the bike icon an image of his motorcycle. The bike icon will be shown blinking when the Harley's moving and not blinking when parked. When the bike's in motion, the blink rate is proportional to the speed, and the miles-per-hour number, along with the appropriate N, S, E, W symbol, are displayed over the bike and moves with it. The bike icon can be also overlaid on a 3-D image of what the bike sees, just like in Google Maps. For all intents and purposes, when looking at the video console, we're essentially seeing Righteous on his bike and seeing whatever he sees. We also have audio. As you see on Monitor 1, Righteous, the dog, and his bike are home. I should say, to the extent possible, all of our data are shared with the authorities. So, say we are in a chase with Righteous, the authorities can follow using the shared GPS and other data.

"Monitor 2 shows the location of the Quadtera mother drone and Ovara egg drone they are piloting near the icon for his house. Maribeth is wired with the brooch, and we see her location, as well. If we choose, we can switch views and see the images seen by the cameras in the Quadtera and Ovara drones. If we did, from the Ovara, we might see Righteous at his PC typing on the keyboard. We would dock the mother drone nearby. The Ovara egg drone is connected to our 5G LTE channel and will run a video-based keystroke logger when it's near his PC. We'll see more when Righteous is up, the lights are on, and he's using his keyboard.

"Monitor 3 is devoted to the Eagle 1 drone with me as the captain and Abel at the right chair copilot assist. Heather will stroll the three stations and report critical information as needed. You can see in the image a simulation of me firing a laser beam at Righteous fleeing. I have an arsenal of artillery of every conceivable kind, from laser beams to in-your-face holographic images projected in the reverse on his helmet's visor, which will cause him to see the obverse, or real image, as he looks out through his visor.

"We all have our station assignments, and everyone knows their job. We've set up criteria for when to call a general alert that will occur when Righteous is on the move and a crisis alert when an event occurs outside of our predicted behavior paradigm or where harm is imminent. May the Lord bless each and every one of us in this most crucial mission."

"Amen" is the collective, somber reply.

61

AUGUST. *Diary, my dear friend, it's August and I'm hot. I'm also at the end of my proverbial rope. If I had an oak tree here, I'd tie one end of my rope to it and jump off a box. The Royal Palm outside my lanai won't work. I'm not feeling too well. I've been one step left of center for days, maybe weeks, more actually. I realize I've made a mess of my life and others' lives, too. There's no joy in Mudville for me these days, and I'm just out of steam. How bad off am I? I'm thinking I'd take back all the bad my hacks have caused if I could, that's how bad. I was born with a dark cloud over my head, and it has followed me my entire life. I really think it's time for me to go and leave these earthly chores to others.*

You'd think I'd go quietly, you know, without doing any more harm, but something inside keeps nagging at me. Diary, you may remember me telling you about my tormented mind, my bad side over here, my good side over there, and never the twain shall meet. I thank good old Rudyard Kipling for that catchy phrase, but he was talking about east and west, not the six inches of warped gray matter between my ears.

I know I have growing feelings for Maribeth, but I can't figure out how to come to terms with them. It's sad because I know, I really know, that the rift in my crazy head separating my feelings of affection for her and my ability to act on them is slowly but surely narrowing. I can finally see across that divide, and it's very nice. Maybe I love her? I say that, but maybe I don't really know what feelings of love are? I don't know how she feels about me, and I don't know if it matters at this point. Let's say I care enough about her to not drag her where I'm going next, which ain't going to be a pretty place. Am I going to leave you, too, Diary? No, you're coming with me, of course.

For a spell, I thought she was faking her interest in me, but I caught myself in that little paranoia. To impress her, I showed her how I could bring up her bank account, and maybe that was a mistake. She started asking questions about it, and then I thought she was coming very close to asking me about hacking. She didn't. Probably just more "latent paranoia," as my late, great, whacko, weenyphile, eyebrow-pickin' psychiatrist Rob Norther would say. You know, Diary, I'd be hopping mad if she were faking it or spying on me. Hurt, too.

I told Maribeth I was going away Sunday. No, I didn't tell her where. This was not so pleasant, to say the least. She wants to go with me. I told her that wasn't possible. She asked why not. I couldn't tell her why not. I'm packing up my backpack with what I'll need for the rest of my life and taking a ride on my bike to Everglades Children's. I'll leave Askim with Maribeth; it's not fair to the pooch to have him suffer what I think is coming my way. I'll tell her thanks, and I'll miss her. I really think I will.

I'm torn as to what my parting gift to this world will be. This is not the time to be Mr. Nice Guy. I've done enough damage so far to not change colors now. I'm too angry at my parents for the major mismatch of a marriage they made and then bringing me into their mess. I'm bitter at every kid I see whose life, I'm pretty certain, is better than mine. What was so awful bad growing up? No kid's life is perfect, you say? Wrong. How about you and me, Diary, go back to a typical night of my adulterated adolescent existence. Get it? Adult-er-rated.

It's midnight, and I should be sleeping because I have an early appointment with my psychiatrist to find out why I have an abundance of facial tics, constantly pick on a rag, still clutch a stuffed bear named Bongo, and am failing at school. All he needs to do is come over here and he'll get it. Maybe I'm ten, maybe thirteen, don't matter much. But I'm not asleep. I'm sitting in my pajamas halfway up the stairs that lead from the front door to the second floor of my house. I can see the front door. I'm shivering and shaking in mortal fear and disbelief of the marital combat scene unfolding before me. Bongo and the rag are with me. I cover Bongo's eyes. The tics are intense, and no facial muscle is excluded from performing this evening. My dear father is banging and pushing on the door, turning the knob, peering through the door's small window. He sees me. I see him. He's trying everything to come inside and escape the thirty-degree temperature, this after his all-day-and-night gambling spree, causing him to miss everything, including the dinner my mother prepared for him. "Nora, open the door, goddamn it. Let me in!" he yells loudly enough to wake up the neighbors who live either side of our row house and who I'll have to face tomorrow. The smell of the good wife's earlier cooked liver and onions permeates the house and likely passes through the front door, which only infuriates my father more. The door is locked and barricaded with the back of a kitchen chair that my mother, with my help at her request, wedged under the doorknob. Sorry, Dad. Welcome home, Dad. How was the card game, Dad? You missed the PTA meeting, Dad. And that's just tonight. But not a total loss, as this gives me a great idea for my parting shot at the hospital. Lock doors!

So, I now think a goodbye will be to lock down the doors at Everglades Children's Hospital. It'll be fun to do and watch. I know some black hat dudes recently locked guests out of their Austrian hotel rooms by hacking the resort's room-key computer system.[53] They made the resort pay a ransom to unlock the doors, which the resort did; however, the hackers left a backdoor software patch, allowing them the option to come back and repeat the ransomware hack at any time. I'm not doin' that, 'cause I'm not comin' back. The hospital's door lock system works the same way only there a staff ID card is needed to unlock the doors, and they're not password protected! Why bother? What nut would crack a hospital's door lock system? Yes, Diary, what nut, indeed.

My plan for ECH is to scare them big-time. I'll try to see no one's harmed, but no guarantees. So what if patients are locked in surgery or the ER doors won't open? I just want to make some mischief. So, why am I doing this? Because it will create the biggest bang-for-my-goodbye-buck scare I can think of.

I put code in the hospital's network so, when I start the hack, it will display my Russian Cossack hat image on all the nurses' station monitors, but this time I want to be in lights, Times Square–style. I'll add, "Harken's Comin'." The hospital will stop dead in its tracks. Then, when I get there, it'll change to say, "Harken's Here." That will get their attention big-time. Everyone will be looking for me. I'll have it timed so it'll appear as soon as I enter the building, but I can control it from my phone, too. I expect a lot of commotion. They probably have plans to evacuate the hospital as soon as they get a whiff of me. Security will likely confront me. This is the tricky part. They might try to stop me or kill me, except I'll be holding the key to everything I'm doing, so they know only I can stop the oncoming madness. I need to remember to convey that point.

Once there, I'll start the routine for locking down the doors. I'll do one or two doors at a time and on different floors. First the ER for a bit, then the surgical suite for a tad. Then the pharmacy, and so on. I can't wait to hear the panic on the overhead page: "Security to ER," "Security to Surgery," "Hospital Code Yellow." Major chaos with people running every which way. Yahoo!

Now, you, my dear Diary. Besides the notebook that you are, and which your Florida jacket covers very smartly—it really does become you—I will store you in a thumb drive I keep in a Tic Tac box in my Harley tank bag. These will come with me. Oh, I'm also putting in the thumb drive the history of everything I ever did bad and everything I'm going to do at ECH and the instructions for reversing it all. This program will stop everything I coded for ECH that already started and prevent anything else from happening. It will also print out a complete summary of all my shenanigans from day one and will include my bid adieu.

Why do this? Because it will likely only be found and used when I'm gone. If so, then maybe my parting won't be entirely for naught. I'm thinking, too, that if that's how it goes down, Maribeth won't think so harshly of me. Maybe that's too much wishful thinking. And, if it's never found, so be it. You know, Diary, I'm hoping this will be my last act of harm, that someone will find a way to take me from this earthly torment and that upon my exit from here, peace of mind will await me when I awake.

Diary, did you know I always dream myself to sleep? They're always sweet dreams of me. I dream all the good things I'd like to do but never do. I dream I'm the good person I'd like to be but am not. I really mean it. In my dreams, I have great pity for poor folks, old folks, sick folks, the one's I see out there who're needy and who I'd love to help if only I were someone else. Why only in my dreams? I don't know or understand *that. Yes, Diary, I said, "I'd love to help." Like the old man I see regularly in my dreams who's always standing in a torrential rain, soaking wet, no umbrella. I drive up to him in a car and say, "Hop on in, ole timer. I'll take you wherever you need. Just around the corner, you say?"*

"Mighty nice of ya, young fella. You're real swell, I can tell you are. I know people. No doubt about it."

"You want to thank me? Oh, no. No thanks needed. That's just what I do. My name? My name's Harry, Harry Right. R-I-G-H-T, like in do the right thing. Just call me Harry. Right here, you say? A tip? Oh, no, no tip needed. Oh, here's a twenty-dollar bill for ya. Best you buy a nice, new umbrella. They have ones now that are extra big and light, and the wind can't turn them inside out, either. How about that? Marvels they are. Have a good day, and stay dry out there. Call you Sol, you say? Nice to meet you, Sol. You have a nice day, too, Sol."

"Will do, Harry, will do."

Righteous, now content, dwells within an inner place of peace made of his own solitude, gently snugs his head into the pocket he forms in his pillow, smiles, and dreams himself off to sleep again, no matter the pillow is soaked with the tears of his loneliness and longing.

"That's who I really am, in case anyone's listening," he says, just in case anyone is.

62

"Maribeth, thanks for coming in to Team Nemesis headquarters again to bring us up to date," White says.

"Hello, everyone. Good to see all of you again. It's been difficult, to say the least. I hope I'm helping," Maribeth says.

"Let's have a seat over here. You're doing just fine," White says.

"He's said he's leaving tomorrow, Dr. White."

"That's crucial information. Do you know where?"

"No, not a clue. I wanted to go with him, but he said no. He asked me if I'd take Askim, and he said he likely wasn't coming back. I've developed genuine feelings for him, Dr. White. Everyone knows I was attracted to him from the very first day I saw him in your office, and he felt the same. But those feelings have grown. We started seeing each other more and more. It was very difficult for him at first. I know he has issues with relationships, but I don't know why. We laugh a lot, and you know what he told me? He said he doesn't remember the last time he laughed with someone. He said nothing was funny to him before. I asked him why, but he wouldn't say. He retreats into a shell. That's when I thought I could help him not be so sad, and I think I was doing that a little. Dr. White, do you think there is something wrong with him, mentally I mean? What I'm saying is he seems normal until you want him to draw close, then it's like a wall comes down and shuts him out. Is that a disorder or something, where you can't form relationships? Like his just taking off now and leaving. I don't get it. Is it me?"

"I'm afraid you are right on, Maribeth. You'd make an excellent medical diagnostician. No question he is disturbed, and what is driving his malicious behavior may all be cries for help. He's past our ability to help him, except to stop him as soon as possible," White says.

"When Mrs. White first told me about how Harry was believed to be the person who did all those terrible hacking things, I couldn't believe it. He seemed so nice in the office and when we'd go for rides on his Harley and at your house for dinner. What Mrs. White told me didn't change how I felt about him, but it did make me doubt whether I could trust my instincts. You know, being a judge of character. What Mrs. White told me about him just didn't seem to fit with what I thought I knew about him. She explained that a doctor thought he might be vulnerable to forming a relationship, but it was a long shot. I was the only person she believed could get close to him to help find out if he was the hacker. I agreed, more to prove he wasn't the hacker. I do understand he's accused of doing very evil things, but in a way, I'm glad it's over, as it's getting ever harder to deceive him.

"I've been to his apartment a lot, as I'm sure you know from the brooch, and have been with him when he's on his computer. He has only one computer as far as I can tell. He works on it only on the lanai. It's beautiful there. I'm usually in a chaise sitting next to him, just reading. The lanai's screened but not in good shape, so there are lots of things flying around. Anyway, he does have relationship issues, as I said. He's hot and cold. He's not violent toward me or Askim, but he can get moody and very quiet."

"What about the Harley necklace? We're getting perfect transmission from it," White says.

"Oh, he's always wearing it, even goes to bed with it on. He loves it. He told me it was a gift from a local Harley group. He thinks he's one of them. Oh, this is interesting. He asked me what bank I use, and I told him. He went on my bank's website and brought up my account. I couldn't believe it. He asked me if I wanted him to change my $4,900 to $49,000. I said no. Doing that didn't seem to bother him at all. He said he knows it's wrong but wanted to impress me. Right then, I knew who he really was. At first, I thought I'd pursue it, probe a little, bring up the hospital hack. But something inside said, 'Don't go there.' I was afraid if I went down that road and got anywhere near hacking, he'd become immediately suspicious. It sounds like he knows right from wrong, but he has impulses to do these things. Is he missing something in his head that other people have that tells other people not to do things that are wrong? I mean, if he's breaking into my bank, he certainly can be breaking into a hospital."

"That information is so vital, Maribeth. Is your bank website log-on Maribethinlove@allmail.com and your password MBETH!1400?" White asks.

"How do you know that? You hacked my bank account, too?"

"No, we hacked your hacker. We have a keystroke logger running 24-7 in one of the drones at his place, so we know every keystroke he makes on his computer. We were watching him when you were there. Let's get back to his leaving, something I hoped I'd never hear. Though it sounds like he's leaving for good, it could also mean he's just leaving town or going to scout another hospital. You know what happened right after he visited Beaches End General Hospital. This could be the worst-case scenario of them all and cause harm beyond our imaginations. He could strike any hour and from anywhere. We know his pleasure from hacking comes mainly from witnessing the misery he creates and the taking of things from his victims. And by that, I mean taking their lives, health, or sense of security. If we only knew where he's going to strike next.

"I'd like you to tell him that you'll take the dog. When you get back there, put in these special earbuds with built-in microphones tuned to your voice. Keep your phone with you at all times. I'll give you a code that will cause the phone to play music unless you cough three times. It's wired to know your cough, part of our speech recognition software. If you do this, it will switch into an instant audio-message mode. Someone here at Team Nemesis headquarters can communicate with you during an emergency through the earbuds. We'll communicate with you that way for now. I'll have our manned consoles go on full alert starting immediately. The second he heads out, we'll know it and be with him every step of the way. And one more thing, Maribeth. Do you have any idea if he's bugged his apartment to watch you? Have you spotted any cameras anywhere, including those on the front of his PC, TV monitor, things like that?"

"I haven't seen any."

"I'd like you to behave as if you're being monitored by him, both audio and video. Don't do anything that, if seen or heard, would drive him to get upset. For example, after he leaves, don't rummage through drawers or books or do anything that might look like you're looking for something. I'll see if Abel can do a radio-frequency scan of his apartment for any Wi-Fi signals being sent out.

That kind of thing. Okay, that's it for now. Any questions, Maribeth?"

"No, Dr. White. This is all so sad in so many ways. The destruction he likely caused is unforgiveable. The pain, the suffering, the worry. It's overwhelming. I'm thinking, if you could measure the pain all of that destruction and also measure the pain that must have been inflicted upon him growing up, I'm thinking they must be equal. He's at war, Dr. White. At war with himself, the good and the bad that lives within him. What we are witnessing is the collateral damage of a childhood gone wildly wrong. If parents only knew what they did to their children."

63

"*Attention! Attention!*" The overhead PA system blares White's command throughout TN headquarters. "I just issued the order to activate South Florida All Hospitals Coordinated Breach Response. We are calling this, thankfully, by the shorter name, Code White-X, which means imminent breach warning (IBW). Code White is usually reserved within most hospitals for response to a violent individual or other nonspecific violent or terror inclusive event. We've extended its meaning in our region to include a physical or network breach upon a hospital by an individual—overtly or covertly, violent or destructive. After Code White-X is announced, all relevant first responders at each facility will activate and implement prepared instructions on what to do to prevent a breach from happening. At the moment, it is a general warning, as we do not know where or when the next strike will occur; it's just that we have good reason to believe it's imminent. That's it for now, will keep all updated as we learn more. Will someone get me Dr. Louis Mayer, chief of pediatrics at Everglades Children's, stat?" White barks.

"I have his office on the line. He's not in, Dr. White. They say he's at his weekly conference with Dr. Greenside; they said you know what that means. They say he'll return in about four hours. Do you want to leave him a message for when he's done?"

"No, this is urgent. Please page him, pronto. Or if his phone's off, have a cart go out from the pro shop to have him call me on my cell ASAP."

"Did I say he was playing golf?"

"Actually, yes."

"Charlie, you son of a bitch, you paged me in the middle of my backswing. This had better be good," Mayer says.

"It's good, all right, goddamn 'really bad' good."

"What the hell does that mean?"

"It means it's time."

"Time for what?"

"You may remember at the last meeting of our South Florida All Hospitals Coordinated Breach Response team we finalized the details of each hospital's response when a breach is suspected to be imminent. Well, it appears to be imminent. Hold a second, Louie. I'm at our Team Nemesis headquarters, and one of my team's pointing out that we have him now on his Harley going south on Route 41, possibly heading your way. We have him completely surveilled and will know if and when he gets to Everglades and see what he's doing there. He's likely to stroll in, maybe show his PA credentials, and say he works for me and is there to check on a patient. Who knows? He may have a stethoscope hanging out of his pants pocket or around his neck. That seems to be part of his MO, too. Here's what you need to know ..."

"Dr. White, an urgent call for you on Secure Phone 1."

"Louie, I'm getting an urgent call. Will get back to you."

64

"Dr. White? Maribeth here."

"Are you crying, Maribeth?"

"Yes. Harry just left for good. He asked me to watch Askim and said he really cared for me. I asked him to stay. I said I loved him and pleaded for him not to go. You know, he remembered our birthdays are soon and gave me a gift. He can be so sweet and clever."

"Yes, he is sweet." *And he's clever, all right. I'd never open the gift; it'll probably explode,* White thinks. "Does he have any idea you've been spying on him or working with us behind the scenes?"

"Not that I know of, Dr. White."

"What did he take with him?"

"It looked like he was going camping. His bike was loaded with all kinds of stuff piled on the back, covered with a tarp, and bungeed down."

"Did he leave anything of value to us? A computer, books, maps, notes, trash, cell phone, anything?"

"No. He scoured the place, scrubbed it clean. There

are a few books on technical things. Looks like he never lived here."

"Can you see our drones anywhere?"

"Well, I'm not sure. There are lots of little, brown round things stuck on the walls and corners of the lanai where he always works. Also, lots of spiderwebs; they give me the creeps."

"The brown things are mud dauber nests, a kind of wasp. We camouflaged some of our Ovara drones to look like their nests. Look around and find the biggest one; it'll look a little different from the others. Use your brooch to latch onto it, and that will start the keylogger download. A green light will turn on when you do. Give it a go. And hurry."

"Okay, I think I got it," Maribeth says.

"Great. You did. O. J. just got the transmission. Maribeth, I want you to go home and stay there. Take the dog with you. Leave his collar on, as he's transmitting perfectly. Keep the brooch on you at all times. We'll stay in touch. Thanks for your help. You've been brave and integral in all this."

"Dr. White, please, don't hurt him. Please."

"Will do our best."

65

"Louie, sorry for the wait. He's possibly on his way to you. I don't know. We have him completely monitored," White says. "I'm afraid he probably knows everything about your facility. He very well may have hacked your network already and has his plan in place. Are you ready to implement the Code White-X we put in place for you?"

"Yes, Charlie. I'll announce that we're going Code White-X for a possible imminent breach. All security and uniformed and plainclothes responders will be mobilized and activated. All surveillance cameras have been tested and determined to be operational, all doors will be double monitored by security, all bags and backpacks will be checked. Security has special RFID door-lock overrides and we've taped-open all door latches. We made sure all backup power is operational, and our best IT guys are watching our network for a breach. We changed the network log-on so that an employee must answer a new question that's uniquely related to that employee. If your guy shows up, we'll be on him. We've also got a good number of security folks dressed like doctors, nurses, flower ladies, landscapers, and the like. Even got an undercover guy with a rifle on a gurney with a fake IV running and a security gal packin' heat dressed as a nurse by his side. And most importantly, everyone knows they must remain calm and act routine, business as usual. We have the picture you sent over, so we know what he looks like. We also have our channels of communication set up, so we're good to go."

66

"Eagle 1 monitor here. Team Nemesis, can you read me?" White says, talking through his headset to all the other members of Team Nemesis stationed nearby at their monitors. "Let me bring us all up to date. Our team's all here, and all systems are working. The GPS-location device on Righteous is working, and we're following him. O. J. and Deshaun downloaded the Ovarum drone keylogging data through Maribeth's brooch and are analyzing it for Righteous's diary and, hopefully, his hacking history. This is a tedious effort that could reveal every hack he ever made, which, if successful, would allow us to go full speed ahead to arrest him. I'm at Monitor 3 flying Eagle 1 drone and shadowing Righteous as he travels on his bike. I've got him imaged perfectly and am receiving all transmissions.

"I've got Righteous going south down Route 41. If he stays on that, it will take him south and east across the Everglades, almost due east to Miami. If he turns east onto Interstate Route 75, he'll be going across the

Everglades and will come out north of Miami, around Fort Lauderdale. There are only two hospitals on that route. One is a private hospital, All Physicians Hospital, maybe one hundred beds, at most. The other, Everglades Children's, sits on the westernmost edge of the Everglades about where the Tamiami Trail intersects the old San Marco Road. This is on the edge of the Everglades swamp. There's no going forward very far by car from there, save some one-lane roads. East of there is swampland full of poisonous snakes, alligators, crocodiles, even black bear and panther in the more forested areas. Okay, now he's turning east on Route 41. He just went off 41 but is still heading east in the general direction of the Everglades hospital. He's hard to see, as he's mostly staying under dense palms and giant oaks. If it weren't for the GPS sender on his necklace and bike, and my infrared camera, I'd have lost him. O. J., Deshaun, what have you got from the Ovara downloads?"

"O. J. here. Dr. White, we got a lot, but we aren't finished. You'd be proud of this. We needed the password to crack his PC. We saw it on a screen image from an Ovarum docked nearby. Can you believe he had the 'show password' option set? Most important, our keystroke logging shows he spent a lot of time researching the targets of his breaches before he did them. He logged on to Beaches End General Hospital over a hundred times before he made it go dark. He's been on Stargazer's network about the same amount. Most recently he's focused on Everglades Children's Hospital, exploring everywhere on their network. It's really worrisome that he lingered around their neonatal services, the adolescent outpatient psych services, and the power plant. He also dwelled on the security-systems software, particularly the programmable door locks. Looks like this could be Beaches End déjà vu all over again. Pretty scary, to say the least. We'd better stop him before he hurts somebody."

"I will let Everglades Hospital know where he is. What about a diary or a detailed record of hacks?"

"Okay, Dr. White," O. J. says. "Got something there. No question he's been keeping a diary. He keeps calling it 'Diary' with a capital D and talks to it like a person. I got his keystrokes on it, but they just don't make sense. He's encrypted it from the front end. Not everything is like that, though. He's put a lot of stuff in those funny QR codes, and I used Snagit[54] to snag some of those. We're working on that now."

"Thanks, O. J.. All right, everyone, he's definitely got Everglades Children's in his sights. Right now, he's largely keeping covered by foliage, but by using Eagle 1 drone's infrared imaging, I'm able to follow him closely. I'm getting calls from the feds asking me for his coordinates, but he's now on single-lane roads or some that are more like dirt paths. His Harley can go there, but the cops are out of luck in their squad cars. They've got ATVs and some airboats with divers on the way. We don't know if he is escaping now through the Everglades or if he is going to pay Everglades Children's a visit first. I can't do anything until he declares himself. If I stop him now, I may save the hospital a problem, but then we're left without the key to what he's done. There could be a thousand patients out there with a thousand docs wondering if the labs they're looking at are real or not. Also, if we're unsuccessful with decoding his keystrokes, we may need his help to decipher it and confess to what he's done. Will he cooperate? Doubtful. Unless Maribeth can somehow plead with him. Stranger things have happened.

"Okay, he's about a mile from ECH. I'm going to let Dr. Mayer know and tell him to be ready. The cops have his GPS coordinates. If Righteous parks his bike and just meanders in, we'll watch him very carefully. If he wanders up to a nurses' station and logs in, we'll be at a tipping point. We have our IT guys watching his log-on and will block any hacking, hopefully, without him knowing it. At that point, he might know something's fishy and get scared and possibly flee."

"Deshaun here. Boss, we've got good news and bad news. He's been keeping at least two documents—one is his diary, the other a record of his hacks, plans, and the like. We found his diary in a Word document in a file on his PC's hard drive. The history of his hacks is a little different. We see from our keystroke-logger data the part of his hard drive where the hacks are stored and where the QR codes were created. We probably need another thirty minutes or so to get it done."

"Charlie here. I'm hovering over him but out of sight and sound. Don't think we have that kind of time. Eagle 1 cameras show him pulling up to the hospital and parking his bike just outside the main entrance. Now he's entering the facility. He just walked past the two guards who, as instructed, barely gave him a glance. Righteous doesn't seem to be bothered or alarmed in any way. I'm going to land Eagle 1 on the hospital's garage rooftop where I can see his parked Harley, then switch to cameras inside.

"He just sat down in front of a nurses' station and is starting to log in. Christ! He stopped. He seems distressed. Now he's looking around to see if he's being watched. The agent on the gurney just sat up and the rifle at his side fell off the gurney. Righteous heard it drop. Now he sees it. They look at each other. Righteous just bolted from the terminal! He's running out of the hospital. Now they're chasing him. That's not protocol. They're not supposed to be chasing him. That's my job. I'm thinking it may be time for me to take this bastard down!"

67

"Eagle 1 here. He's speeding due east on 41 and just turned onto Sunnygrove Avenue. Sunnygrove looks like a single-lane road that dead-ends at the edge of the Everglades swamp. Either he's very stupid or very smart. All he can do is go back or ride right into the swamp."

"Boss, Deshaun here. We're almost done. We found a file that had the record of all his hacks and diary, but he cut and pasted them onto a peripheral memory, and we can only see the trail of that. That memory could be a hard drive, the cloud, or even a small flash memory, or thumb drive. He then deleted all that, then deleted his trash file. Unless we can get our hands on his PC hard drive and read the deleted segments, or that peripheral memory, we're cooked. It doesn't look good."

"Eagle 1 here. I landed on the roof of a building near where Righteous parked his bike at the water's edge on a wooden pier. There are three or four airboats docked there parallel to the pier, and a guy is on the pier. Looks like a place they sell airboat rides to tourists. One's filling up with a family with kids now. Now they're pushing the Harley onto one of the airboats. They tied the bike down, then threw a tarp over the bike. Righteous is handing the guy some cash. Now Righteous is showing the guy some documents. They're shaking hands. The guy stepped off the airboat. Righteous is setting up some kind of device, and there he goes. Goddamn, he took off into the swamp and just disappeared into some stands of cottontail reeds."

"Boss, O. J. and Deshaun here. We scrubbed all the downloads. We're still looking."

"Charlie here. Okay, guys. Good job. He's out of the reeds now heading toward Mahogany Hammock. I think he sees or hears the drone; he keeps looking up. His damn fan and blowback are keeping me from getting closer. O. J., Deshaun, I need to know as soon as you believe you have everything we need. Then I can try to stop him without hurting him. Crap, he's gone into the reeds again."

"Boss, O. J. and Deshaun here. We see the malicious code he was going to patch, or did patch, into ECH's network, and it's a doozy. He's messing with lights, door locks, display monitors. We only found it because he made a big mistake on his computer. His intent was to clear the memory where it's stored. Trouble is, he forgot to turn off the autosave backup feature, so we have a copy. We still don't have his diary and the history of all his hacks. Sorry, boss."

"Charlie here. He seems to be stuck in the cottontails just west of Pearl Bay. He could swim to the chickee, but then it's all over for him, as he'd have nowhere to go. He stirred up a mess of snakes and gators when he plowed into reeds, so swimming to the chickee wouldn't be smart."

"Boss, O. J. and Deshaun here. We're done. There's no memory left to scrub. Sorry, boss. We did our best."

"Charlie here. He's out again and at high speed. I see two airboats flagged FBI coming at him from the far side so as to cut him off. I think it's time to stop him. I'm going to jet-assist Eagle 1 ahead of him and do a roll and flip and come right back at him head-on. I turned on the audio blast and am instructing him to stop and go back to the chickee and wait for the authorities to pick him up. They are on their way. The feds and I are blasting, '*Harken Righteous, FBI! Stop immediately!*' He's not stopping. I have no choice but to fire a laser at his helmet, hoping to confuse him enough to slow him down or stop him altogether. Here we go. Fire! Bingo, right on the visor. Stopped him cold. He doesn't know where he is. Now he's off again, but he's doing circles. Fire again! Bingo, hit him in the visor again. He just ran into a thicket of reeds. Oh, Christ, he hit a rotted tree stump and capsized. I think the airboat was top-heavy from his Harley, and the whole thing rolled over. The bike's underwater. I see him flailing around, grabbing at the reeds. The authorities are racing toward him on the airboats. Maybe twenty or thirty yards away. Oh no! A couple of massive alligators just belly-flopped into the thicket where he tried to find refuge. There's a lot of thrashing. A gator has him in a death roll. Oh, Lord, there's a lot of red. I've never seen anything like it. More gators are coming. They're all over him. The waters are starting to calm. Now they're still. He's gone. I'm sure of it. Team, he's gone. Harken Righteous is no more."

68

"Maribeth, Dr. White here. Can you come over to Team Nemesis Headquarters now?"

"What is it, Dr. White? Is Harry okay?" Maribeth asks, believing something is dreadfully wrong.

"I'll explain when you get here."

"Dr. White, Maribeth's here, clutching a gift-wrapped package the size of a deck of cards that won't allow her to pass our metal detector. She says it's a gift, and she won't unwrap it until she gets a call from the person who gave it to her."

"It's never been opened?"

"Looks that way. What do you want us to do?" Sterling Jones at security says.

"Did it pass explosive and other hazardous checks?"

"Yes, sir. It must be covered in lead, as the x-ray shows just a blur. It's about an inch square, that's all."

"Abel, are you okay letting her through? I think the gift holds sentimental value."

"Let her through," Abel says.

Maribeth, White, and Heather meet in a small conference room and sit down.

"Maribeth, we have some bad news," Heather says.

Maribeth is clutching the gift as if it is Harry himself.

"I don't like the sound of that," Maribeth says. "What happened?"

"Maribeth, Harry went to Everglades Children's Hospital," White says. "We have enough evidence to believe, without a doubt, that he was there to commit grievous harm to the hospital and the patients there. I can give you the details later. He became suspicious that he was being watched and might be captured, then bolted before he was able to start his hacking. We followed him to the edge of the Everglades. It became clear to us that he arranged to flee across the Everglades swamp in an airboat. We saw him load his Harley onto the airboat and take off. If allowed, he could have made his way to any number of docking areas and disappeared forever. In his effort to avoid arrest, his airboat capsized. What happened next isn't pleasant. He was attacked by a congregation of alligators, and that was the last we saw of him. I'm afraid Harry's gone."

White squeezes Maribeth's free hand, her other clutching the gift now soaked with her tears.

"I'm waiting for his call to open my gift, and then he'll

open his."

"Why don't you open it now, Maribeth, with us here with you?" Heather says.

"I'm waiting for him to call me."

"Maribeth, he's not going to call."

"I suppose there's no other choice now. I do want to see his gift." Maribeth takes off the gift wrapping.

"There's a box and a letter."

"Read the letter first," Heather says.

"My dear Maribeth, I don't know where I'll be when you read this. It was my wish and dream to be holding you in my arms as you read it, but I feel that will not be the case. My life has been one of constant torment, a daily struggle between the good and evil parts of me. Only in my dreams did the evil in me sleep and the good in me wake up. The part of me you loved was the good part that you somehow managed to find. You, Maribeth, are pure, and only goodness lives within you. I cannot take back the evil I did. I can only confess to everyone all my deeds, apologize, and help the authorities bring closure to the harm that I did. I do that for you. I wish I could apologize to all my victims. I don't ask for forgiveness, only understanding. Goodbye, my Maribeth. May your sweet and gentle soul find nothing but happiness and love for as long as you live. Love, Harry."

The three sit in silence for a while, taking it all in. Maribeth is sobbing uncontrollably. Heather, her arm around Maribeth, consoles her.

"Oh, Dr. White, Heather, this is just so awful. He was such a tortured soul that I only hope he's in a place of greater peace. I'm so glad he confessed to his misdeeds. I'm thinking he was relieved to do that."

"Well, as far as we know, he didn't confess to anything. Did he tell you where he kept his diary and the record of his hacks?" White says.

"No, he didn't."

"We may now never know the extent of the damage he's done. I'd hoped, as he parted ways, he'd have had a shred of decency and put an end to the trail of misery that followed his every step. Wishful thinking, I guess," White says.

"Perhaps you should open the box," Heather says.

Maribeth opens the box with shaky hands.

"Oh, look, it's a heart pendant. How sweet! I think he really did love me."

"It's gorgeous, Maribeth," Heather says. "May I see it?"

Maribeth hands over the ornate pendant.

"Oh, Maribeth, it's gold and silver and loaded with Swarovski crystals. This tells me he must have had great affection for you."

"I'll admit, it was very sweet of him. May I see it, Maribeth?" White says, looking at it closely. "I think it's much more than just a heart pendant." He pulls the pendant apart, revealing a USB plug.

"Oh, Dr. White, you broke it!" Maribeth says.

"No, Maribeth, look, it's a flash drive. I'm betting it's the memory drive with the diary and the record of all his misdeeds we've all been looking for!"

THE END

EPILOGUE

The heart-shaped thumb drive Harry gave Maribeth revealed the identities of every person he'd ever hacked, every hospital he'd invaded, and everything he'd maliciously changed. It also included his diary, every image, and every QR code, which provided much of the detail used to write this book.

All patient records were restored to normal and all signs of intrusion erased.

Harken Righteous's corpse, what remained of it, was returned to his family and buried in a private ceremony in Rochester, New York.

The federal goverment, by way of presidential executive decree and congressional action, created new legislation for securing medical devices to help prevent this type of hacking from ever happening again.

Team Nemesis, including Dr. White, Heather, Abel, Larry, O. J., Deshaun, Joie, Maribeth, and Cassandra, were each awarded the National Medal for extraordinary service to country for their roles in bringing the Righteous nightmare to an end. The mayor of Beaches End awarded each the key to the city. They were congratulated by the president of the United States in an official White House ceremony and later offered jobs with the FBI and CIA with the mission to reproduce a Tean Nemesis capability at Crystal City, Virginia, near the Pentagon at the newly formed Cyber Threat Intelligence Integration Center (CTIIC). They were all considered national heroes. Joie Jergé produced a CNN Special called *Digital Threats to Our Modern Life*, which was watched by more than twenty million people worldwide. She received the Pulitzer Prize in investigative journalism for her work.

Not to be outdone, Netflix produced a documentary and then Amazon Prime, a series for TV. Tom Cruise played Dr. White, Leonardo DiCaprio played Harken Righteous.

AFTERWORD

Over the course of little more than four months, Harken Righteous created more than a medical hell for the residents of Beaches End, the small Florida town he invaded like a plague.

When Righteous infected the medical world there, he affected more than the medical lives of the patients and doctors he targeted. His actions caused a veil of pervasive doubt to fall over everything the residents of Beaches End previously took for granted. Citizens began to question every aspect of their digital lives. Everything was, at once, doubted, then checked, then double-checked, before being believed, if believed at all. Invoices of every kind, bank statements, credit card statements, online checking account balances, IRA balances—all documents and the systems that generated them previously taken for granted were now questioned, shaking the foundations of their daily life. Anything and everything online or in print or on a monitor was placed in doubt.

Righteous's actions replaced truth and fact with uncertainty and disbelief, undermining the basic assumptions by which most daily life were previously conducted. Doubt replaced acceptance, trust in anything became impossible, and life was conducted as if nothing were true or real. Skepticism ruled. Parents became incapable telling their children the meaning of truth or what constituted a lie.

For all the bad he did, Righteous, unintentionally, may have done some good. He laid bare the new and yet to be fully understood and accepted fact of our modern digital life that what we see on a monitor, or printed out, is ephemeral, and just the graphic representation at a moment in time of the ones and zeros in a hackable and changeable register in a server somewhere on earth, and perhaps beyond. Even though what we see before our eyes is there, what we see there is not necessarily the correct reflection of what it is intended to represent. If Righteous caused us to doubt more what we see and trust less than we do, then, perhaps, he did us some good. He was telling us how our digital daily life is relative, mutable, fungible, rather than absolute.

If showing society its vulnerabilities by conducting evil experiments is a positive thing, then Harken Righteous deserves some credit. But it is not.

There are better ways to awaken and teach a culture the self-destructive consequences of so-called technological advances. Righteous's approach was only one way, and a reprehensible one at best. It is just one of many corollaries of techno-destruction where civilized life is savaged by the same technology intended to advance it.

That a team of citizens could form to discover and stop the creator of so much chaos in one town is testimony to the resilience and resourcefulness of our American way of life. The remaining question, however, is whether such energy can ever be found again to eliminate the newer threats that are now coming our way and at any time?

DR. WHITE'S TOP HEALTH-CARE HACKS OF 2018

1. Phishing hacks breach 20,000 Catawba Valley patient records by Jessica Davis, October 25, 2018. *"North Carolina-based Catawba Valley Medical Center is notifying 20,000 patients that their personal data was breached after three successful phishing attacks."*

2. CMS responds to data breach affecting 75,000 in federal ACA portal by Susan Morse, October 22, 2018. *"CMS responds to data breach affecting 75,000 in federal ACA portal."*

3. Minnesota DHS breach 21,000 patient records by Jessica Davis, October 12, 2018. *"The files of an estimated 75,000 individuals were accessed in a breach of Healthcare.gov for Affordable Care Act enrollment, according to the Centers for Medicare and Medicaid Services."*

4. Update: Misconfigured database breaches MedCall Advisors, by Jessica Davis. October 10, 2018. *"For the second time in one month, a researcher discovered North Carolina-based MedCall Healthcare Advisors has been leaking protected, personal data through a misconfigured Amazon S3 storage bucket."*

5. Employee error exposed Blue Cross patient data for 3 months, by Jessica Davis, September 21, 2018. *"An employee uploaded a file containing member information to a public-facing website in April, but officials did not discover the error until July. The breached information included names, dates of birth, diagnosis codes, provider details and information used for claim processing purposes."*

6. 417,000 Augusta University Health patient records breached nearly one year ago, by Jessica Davis, August 17, 2018. *"According to the notice, hackers targeted the university health system with phishing e-mails Sept. 10–11, 2017."*

7. Canadian pharmacist fined for routinely accessing health records of acquaintances, by Lynne Minion, August 13, 2018. *"A pharmacist in Canada has been fined and suspended from practice for six months for spying on the electronic health records of 46 people she knew, including her child's girlfriend."*

8. 1.4M records breached in UnityPoint Health phishing attack, by Jessica Davis, July 31, 2018. *"This is the second breach for the health system this year, and the* *biggest health data breach of 2018 in the U.S. According to the notice, the health system's business e-mail system was hit by a series of targeted phishing e-mails that looked like they were sent from an executive within UnityPoint. An employee fell victim to the e-mails, which gave hackers access to internal e-mail accounts from March 14 until April 3."*

9. Ransomware, malware attack breaches 45,000 patient records, by Jessica Davis, July 26, 2018. *"An investigation into a ransomware attack found hackers peppered Missouri-based Blue Springs Family Care with a variety of malware. The investigation couldn't rule out access of theft. The impacted data included patient names, Social Security numbers, account numbers, driver's licenses, disability codes, medical diagnoses, addresses and dates of birth. Combined, this type of data could be used by hackers for both identity and medical fraud."*

10. Long Island provider exposes data of 42,000 patients in misconfigured database, by Jessica Davis, March 26, 2018. *"Long Island-based Cohen, Bergman, Klepper, Romano MDs misconfigured its online database, exposing the personally identifiable information of about 42,000 patients. Misconfigured databases are a continued issue for the healthcare industry. The exposed data doesn't require a hacker to inflict the damage. Many cybercriminals actively scan for these types of misconfigurations so there's a clear risk of both exposure and the data being used for medical fraud. The database contained a wide range of patient* *data including names, Social Security numbers, dates of birth, insurance information, phone numbers, addresses and other personal data. It also contained more than 3 million clinical notes from patient visits."*

11. Allscripts hit by ransomware, knocking some services offline, by Jessica Davis, January 19, 2018. *"Users took to Twitter to complain about the cloud EHR being down, with some unable to access patient information all day. Allscripts by the numbers: 45,000 physician practices, 180,000 physicians, 19,000 post-acute agencies, 2,500 hospitals, 100,000 electronic prescribing physicians, 40,000 in-home clinicians, 7.2 million patients."*

ENDNOTES

1 Not to be confused with sensory processing disorder.

2 "Study Shows Hackers Could Modify Medical Test Results in US," Verdict Medical Devices, August 30,2018, https://www.medicaldevice-network.com/news/ study-shows-us-medical-record-systems-vulnerable-hacking/.

3 "Cossacks," *Wikipedia*, https://en.wikipedia.org/wiki/Cossacks.

4 "Professional Practice FAQs," Florida Academy of Physician Assistants, https://www.fapaonline.org/page/faqprofpractice.

5 Erin McLaughlin, "Florida Teen Charged with Impersonating Physician's Assistant," ABC News, September 3, 2011, https:// abcnews.go.com/US/teen-posed-physician-assistant-fl-hospital/ story?id=14443046.

6 Tom Lehrer, from his song "Smut."

7 Kim Zetter, "It's Insanely Easy to Hack Hospital Equipment," *Wired Magazine*, April 25, 2014, https://www.wired.com/2014/04/ hospital-equipment-vulnerable/.

8 Paul Roberts, "Code Blue: Audit Reveals Desperate State Of Medical Device Security," Veracode, May 5, 2014, https://www.veracode.com/blog/2014/05/ code-blue-audit-reveals-desperate-state-of-medical-device-security.

9 Kevin Mitnick, *Ghost in the Wires* (New York: Back Bay, 2012).

10 "Social Engineering (Security)," *Wikipedia*, https://en.wikipedia.org/wiki/Social_engineering_(security).

11 Eric Griffith, "How to Create an Anonymous Email Account," *PC Magazine*, December 3, 2017, https://www.pcmag.com/article2/0,2817,2476288,00.asp.

12 Institute of Medicine, "Hospitals and Acute Care Facilities," chap. 7 in *Crisis Standards of Care: A Systems Framework for Catastrophic Disaster Response* (Washington, DC: National Academies Press), https://www.ncbi.nlm.nih.gov/books/NBK201068/.

13 There are many commercially available phone control apps. Caution: Websites may contain viruses that can corrupt and damage the device installing it. Do not install any! https://www.google.com/search?q=how+to+turn+on+iphonemike+remotely&ie=utf-8&oe=utf-8.

14 https://null-byte.wonderhowto.com/how-to/hack-like-pro-remotely-record-listen-microphone-anyones-computer-0143966/.

15 Spying with phones: https://www.flexispy.com/en/features/bug-their-phone-secretly-spycall.htm.

16 "Catch Me If You Can (book)," *Wikipedia*, https://en.wikipedia.org/wiki/Catch_Me_If_You_Can_(book).

17 Frank W. Abagnale, *Catch Me If You Can* (New York: Broadway Books, 1980).

18 Kent C. Berridge and Morten L Kringelbach, "Pleasure Systems in the Brain," *Neuron* 86 no. 3 (2015): 646–64, https://www.ncbi.nlm.nih.gov/pmc/articles/PMC4425246/.

19 "Vacutainer," *Wikipedia*, https://en.wikipedia.org/wiki/Vacutainer.

20 Dennis J. Ernst, George A. Fritsma, and David L. McGlasson, "Labeling Tubes Before Collection Threatens Patient Safety," *Annals of Blood* 3, no. 2 (2018), http://aob.amegroups.com/article/view/4318/5055.

21 "Medical Errors Are No. 3 Cause Of U.S. Deaths,Researchers Say," NPR, May 3, 2016, http://www.npr.org/sections/health-shots/2016/05/03/476636183/death-certificates-undercount-toll-of-medical-errors.

22 Dennis J. Ernst, George A. Fritsma, and David L. McGlasson, "Labeling Tubes Before Collection Threatens Patient Safety," *Annals of Blood* 3, no. 2 (2018), http://aob.amegroups.com/article/view/4318/5055.

23 "Acute Hemolytic Transfusion Reaction," *Wikipedia*, https://en.wikipedia.org/wiki/Acute_hemolytic_transfusion_reaction.

24 "Trauma Center Levels Explained," *American Trauma Society*, https://www.amtrauma.org/page/traumalevels.

25 Florence D. Hudson, "Biomedical Device Security: New Challenges and Opportunities," NCHICA, https://nchica.org/wp-content/uploads/2015/06/Bruemmer-Hudson-Wirth.pdf.

26 "Florida Cracker Architecture," *Wikipedia*, https://en.wikipedia.org/wiki/Florida_cracker_architecture.

27 https://healthitsecurity.com/news/siemens-flags-cybersecurity-vulnerabilities-in-rapid-blood-gas-analyzers.

28 Denver Nicks, "Obamacare Website Was Hacked in July," *Time*, September 4, 2014, http://time.com/3270936/obamacare-website-was-hacked-in-july/.

29 Jeff Seldin, "Concern Fitness Tracking App Exposed US Military Bases Just the Start," Voice of America, January 30, 2018, https://www.voanews.com/a/strava-heat-map-sparks-concerns-of-military-security/4230808.html.

30 "Reporting Computer, Internet-Related, or Intellectual Property Crime," US Department of Justice, https://www.justice.gov/criminal-ccips/reporting-computer-internet-related-or-intellectual-property-crime.

31 Yolanda, "How Many Times Are You Caught on Camera Per Day?," Reolink, October 19, 2018, https://reolink.com/how-many-times-you-caught-on-camera-per-day/.

32 Susan Scutti,"Hacking Into Hospital Computers Reveals Vulnerable Medical Records And Blood Supplies," *Medical Daily*, April 28, 2014, http://www.medicaldaily.com/hacking-hospital-computers-reveals-vulnerable-medical-records-and-blood-supplies-279246.

33 "The Biggest Healthcare Data Breaches of 2018 (So Far)," *Healthcare IT News*, https://www.healthcareitnews.com/projects/biggest-healthcare-data-breaches-2018-so-far.

34 "Mass Murder," *Wikipedia*, https://en.wikipedia.org/wiki/Mass_murder.

35 "Weapons of Mass Destruction," *Wikipedia*, https://en.m.wikipedia.org/wiki/Weapon_of_mass_destruction.

36 "The Biggest Healthcare Data Breaches of 2018 (So Far)," *Healthcare IT News*, https://www.healthcareitnews.com/projects/biggest-healthcare-data-breaches-2018-so-far.

37 "Insider Threats as the Main Security Threat in 2017," *Tripwire*, April 11, 2017, https://www.tripwire.com/state-of-security/security-data-protection/insider-threats-main-security-threat-2017/.

38 http://docs.media.bitpipe.com/io_10x/io_102267/item_465972/Insider-Threat-Report-2015.pdf.

39 "Everglades Regional Medical Center," Abandoned Florida, https://www.abandonedfl.com/everglades-regional-medical-center/.

40 Brian Eastwood, "How Boston Children's Hospital Hit Back at Anonymous," *CIO*, September 15, 2014, https://www.cio.com/article/2682872/healthcare/how-boston-childrens-hospital-hit-back-at-anonymous.html.

41 "Amazon Rekognition," Amazon, https://aws.amazon.com/rekognition/.

42 "NMVTIS and ITS Benefits to Law Enforcement," National
Motor Vehicle Title Information, https://www.vehiclehistory.gov/
nmvtis_law_enforcement.html.

43 Tyler Durden, "National Facial Recognition Database to Use
Loyalty Rewards to Identify American Shoppers," ZeroHedge,
November 14, 2018, https://www.zerohedge.com/news/2018-11-
14/national-facial-recognition-database-use-loyalty-rewards-identi-
fy-american-shoppers.

44 "Summary of the HIPAA Privacy Rule," US Department of
Health and Human Services, https://www.hhs.gov/hipaa/for-profes-
sionals/privacy/laws-regulations/index.html.

45 David Shamah, "World's Smallest GPS chip Makes Wearables
More Wearable," *Times of Israel*, September 5, 2014,
https://www.timesofisrael.com/
worlds-smallest-gps-chip-makes-wearables-more-wearable/.

46 "Small GPS Tracker Pendant," SecurityBees, https://www.se-
curitybees.com/products/small-gps-tracker-pendant; "Streetwise
Cross Necklace Bodyworn Spy Camera 480p DVR," Home Security
Superstore, https://www.thehomesecuritysuperstore.com/home-
spy-equipment-spy-cameras-covert-spy-cameras-cross-pendant-
hidden-spy-camera-hc-cross-dvr-p=5127.

47 Quadtera is a trademark of MD-CAREWARE LLC, Louis Siegel,
2018, All Rights Reserved.

48 Ovara and Ovarum are Trademarks of MD-CAREWARE, LLC,
Louis Siegel, 2018, All Rights Reserved.

49 Ovarum is a Trademark of MD-CAREWARE, LLC, Louis Siegel,
2018, All Rights Reserved.

50 "Amazon.com: Egg Drone," Amazon.
Amazon, https://www.amazon.com/s?k=egg+drone.

51 "Small GPS Tracker Pendant," SecurityBees.

52 "Quadcopter Trick Flying Basics," Rotor Copters, http://www.rotorcopters.com/quadcopter-trick-flying/.

53 Dan Bilefsky, "Hackers Use New Tactic at Austrian Hotel: Locking the Doors," *New York Times*, January 30, 2017, https://www.nytimes.com/2017/01/30/world/europe/hotel-austria-bitcoin-ransom.html.

54 "The Leader in Screen Capture Software," TechSmith, https://www.techsmith.com/screen-capture.html.

NOTE ON QR CODES

QR codes are read by installing and opening a QR code reader app on a smartphone and hovering the app's code-read area over the QR code image. The text message encoded in the QR code will appear on your device.

BIO

Louis Siegel earned his BS in electrical engineering from the Johns Hopkins University, Whiting School of Engineering, and an MD with Distinction in Research from the University of Rochester School of Medicine and Dentistry. He practiced internal medicine in Rochester, New York,.

He co-founded Seecor Inc. to manufacture and market medical devices he invented. One, the Cardio-Probe, a device he invented to prevent heart block in children during open-heart surgery, was sold all over the world, with one of the earliest users being Dr. Christian Barnard of South Africa, the first cardiac surgeon to perform a heart transplant.

Another device was the StatPACE, a transesophageal cardiac pacemaker used to restore abnormal heart rhythms to normal in infants and children.

His knowledge of computer design and computer applications goes back to the mid-1960s, programming the LINC computer developed at MIT for laboratory research. From that experience, he coauthored chapter 16, "The Laboratory Computer in Psychophysiology," in the text Methods in Psychophysiology (B. Weiss and L.

Siegel, edited by C. C. Brown, Baltimore: Williams and Wilkins Press, 1967).

Dr. Siegel has published many papers in the fields of biomedical engineering, medicine, surgery, and the behavioral sciences in such journals as the IEEE Transactions on Biomedical Engineering, the Annals of Thoracic Surgery, and the Journal of Behavior, among others.

He is a past chairman of the Rochester, New York, chapter of the IEEE Group on Engineering in Medicine and Biology.

In November 2014, he published his first book, Exam Room Confidential: The Wellborne Files, a medical exposé mystery novel exposing the dark side of medical practice.

Photo Attribution
Photo of Dr. Siegel by Billy Elkins,
June 2014, encompasscreative.net

Louis Siegel, M.D.
255 N. Washington St., Apt. 350
Rockville, MD 20850
lsiegel1234@gmail.com
(585) 703-6585

54272328R00199

Made in the
USA
Lexington, KY